HIGHLANDER'S BRIDE

Called by a Highlander Book Seven

MARIAH STONE

Stone
Publishing

GET A FREE MARIAH STONE BOOK!

Join Mariah's mailing list to be the first to know of new releases, free books, special prices, and other author giveaways.

freehistoricalromancebooks.com

ALSO BY MARIAH STONE

MARIAH'S TIME TRAVEL ROMANCE SERIES

- CALLED BY A HIGHLANDER
- CALLED BY A VIKING
- CALLED BY A PIRATE
- FATED

MARIAH'S REGENCY ROMANCE SERIES

- DUKES AND SECRETS

VIEW ALL OF MARIAH'S BOOKS IN READING ORDER

Scan the QR code for the complete list of Mariah's ebooks, paperbacks, and audiobooks in reading order.

When you awaken in the morning's hush
   I am the swift uplifting rush
   Of quiet birds in circled flight.
   I am the soft stars that shine at night.
   Do not stand at my grave and cry,
   I am not there; I did not die.

—*Mary Elizabeth Frye*

PROLOGUE

The Borderlands, 1306

She would finally be his wife.

Raghnall's heart slammed in anticipation as he patted the ring in his pocket. His horse trotted down the foot-worn road to Mòrag's farm. Clumps of dandelions and foxtail flanked the path, and sunbaked, open pastures could be seen through the scruffy brush and trees.

The whirring of crickets and grasshoppers, the chirping of birds, and the wind rustling came together into a happy melody, as though they all knew he would finally propose to marry the woman he'd loved. He began to hum along, enjoying the scents of flowers among the weeds, dust, and sheep manure...and something else.

His humming died.

He could smell the smoke even though he didn't see the house. His stomach dropped as he spurred his mare, his sword flapping against his back as the horse galloped up the hill.

She's just firing up the oven, he told himself, *just using wet firewood...*

He couldn't hear anything beyond the drum of his horse's hooves. As bushes and trees flashed past him, and the scent of smoke grew stronger, he knew he was lying to himself.

Mòrag knew how to fire up an oven. She'd been doing it since she was twelve years old. And, as a widow, she'd been living without a man's help for six years. No one cut her firewood, no one fired her oven, and no one brought her game for a stew.

And then he saw it, behind the hill, among fluffy clouds—the dark-gray wall of smoke rising into the windless blue sky like a tower.

His whole body went numb. He didn't feel his feet lifting and his heels digging into the sides of his mare. "Come on, lass!"

His horse neighed, and the kickback of air told him she'd darted forward. Finally, as they crested the hill, he saw what he'd already known.

Mòrag's farmhouse was on fire. As was her barn, her shed, and the field of barley.

And then, in the small courtyard formed by the surrounding farm buildings, he saw a female figure lying on the ground and a smaller figure holding her.

Nae, nae! Please, Jesu, nae...

Raghnall didn't realize he was whispering as he spurred his horse forward furiously, galloping down into the valley.

This couldn't be her. This couldn't be Mòrag, and her son, Seoc, not today...

Not ever...

Not when Raghnall was finally ready to wed the woman he loved.

Because if it was her, it would destroy him.

Closer and closer he rode, and the rip in his heart grew wider. He coughed from the black smoke and the ashes in the air. He strained to see, though he was afraid to know for sure.

Only as he rode through the broken, hanging gate that led into the farm could he clearly see the long red hair spread on the black ground.

"Mòrag!" he yelled.

The boy raised his red-haired head, face ashen, lips trembling, just a six-year-old lad holding his mother, who was covered in blood. Raghnall rode into the farm and jumped off the horse, barely letting it stop. He staggered as he landed, not caring if he broke a leg.

"Mòrag..." he whispered as he dropped to his knees by her side.

His hands shook as he took her hand in his, eyeing the gash in her side from where blood was oozing. The skirts of her simple, dark-red dress were lifted up past her knees, and there were fresh finger marks on the exposed, creamy skin of her legs...

Legs he'd never touched, no matter how much he'd wanted to, no matter how many times she'd suggested she would like him to have her, even out of wedlock.

Helpless rage shook him, and he felt his chin tremble as his teeth clenched to the point that his jaw hurt.

"Mòrag," he whispered, meeting her golden-brown gaze clouded by pain. "Hold on, love. We'll stop the blood and I'll take ye to Carlisle..."

"Raghnall..." she croaked out. "'Tis too late."

The blood oozed quickly, aye, and she looked pale, her lips bluish purple... He'd seen enough deadly wounds on the battlefields to know that she had lost too much blood. Her wound— they must have nicked the kidney... There was no way she'd survive that. His whole body went cold and numb.

"I came to propose to ye," Raghnall said, hooking his hands under her arms and dragging her gently up so that her head lay on his knees.

A weak smile touched her lips. "Ye did?"

"Aye," he whispered, stroking her hair, painfully ignoring the bruise that was blooming on her cheekbone under her weathered, sun-kissed skin. "I love ye, Mòrag. I love ye, Seoc." He glanced at the lad, who blinked, and his hand relaxed around the small dagger that lay on the ground by his side. Wee, six-year-old warrior...

Raghnall went into the leather pouch on his belt and retrieved the ring. It was silver, with simple, interwoven Celtic knots.

Fighting tears, he swallowed a knot that scratched his throat like a knife. "I have loved ye from the moment I peered from between those bushes and saw ye commanding yer harvest workers like a queen." He brushed his knuckles against her skin, and her eyelashes fluttered.

She chuckled softly. "And yet I'd thought 'twas my bowl of gruel that made ye lodge with us."

He exhaled softly. "'Twas just an excuse. A young widow like ye, a good farm, a lad and no one to protect ye... I couldna stay away... I couldna have left these golden-amber eyes of yers."

He'd stayed with them for a few sennights, watched the harvest laborers, protected the farm from occasional reivers and small bands of robbers. They'd talked. They'd kissed. He'd whispered sweet words of love and seduction into her ear while he'd brought her pleasure with his hands... For months, they'd been like this. He'd taught Seoc sword fighting and archery. He'd become familiar with the ins and outs of the farm. He'd practically been her husband, without the church ceremony.

And so, she'd suggested it.

And he'd wanted to. The words had itched his tongue several times—*Marry me*.

But every time, fear had gripped him in its icy claws as the memories of his father chasing him away from his family, from his clan like a rabid dog, had invaded his mind. His father had taught him that loving people meant that he'd lose them. That he'd be alone sooner or later, anyway.

And so when Mòrag had suggested they get married, he'd left. Like a coward. But a few sennights away from her and Seoc were an agony, and he didn't want to ever be away from her again. He loved her more than he feared heartache.

"Dinna speak to Ma like that," Seoc growled and stabbed the ground with his knife. "Nae about her eyes, nae about her anything. Daidh and his band came back. Had ye nae have let them go, or had ye been here..."

The lad's fierce words pierced right through Raghnall, tearing his heart into shreds. Raghnall had had a long history with Daidh, who was a Borderland reiver together with his men. Reivers raided farms, villages, and homesteads along the border between England and Scotland. Long ago, Raghnall had been one of them, and Daidh had never forgiven him for leaving. Raghnall should have killed the man when he had had the chance; he shouldn't have let a dangerous man like that walk away.

"Ye're right, lad," he croaked. "'Tis my fault. All of it. Mòrag, had I marrit ye a while ago, like ye had asked me to, I'd have been here. I'd have protected ye..."

She squeezed his hand weakly. "But ye're here now."

Wind blew smoke into his face, burning his eyes and making him blink. "I am." He brought his forehead to hers, inhaling the scent of her—something flowery, and feminine and hers alone— spoiled by the scent of death, of blood and smoke.

But he'd make it right. He'd do anything to atone for his guilt. "Will ye marry me, lass?"

"I kent ye'd ask one day." She gave a weak laugh. "Aye. Of course I'll marry ye, my fearless Highlander."

Fearless? He had a soul darker than the depths of hell. The life of the woman he loved would be on his hands, thanks to his fear.

She blinked slowly. "Will ye take care of Seoc?"

Seoc...the lad with hair the color of flames and eyes as hard as gemstones. He reminded Raghnall of himself as a lad. Stubborn. A rebel.

A loner.

But the lad was about to be an orphan. He needed someone to protect him, to take care of him.

"Aye. Of course I'll take care of Seoc."

She met his gaze, her eyes pale and weak. "Thank ye." She looked to her side, at her son, and, stretching her hand to him, smiled at him. With bloodshot eyes, but with no tears, Seoc grabbed her hand like a sinking man grabbed a rope. "Be well, Seoc. Listen to Raghnall. He'll be yer stepda now..."

"Ma?"

But she didn't reply, and her chest didn't move again.

Fire was raging around them, wood was cracking, and heat radiated from the inferno of the burning buildings. Ashes and sparks flew in the air, scalding Raghnall where they landed on his face.

But he didn't care. He stared at the dead body of the woman he loved, of his betrothed, with a darkness warping, raging, sucking everything around his heart.

He wanted to be dead, too. From regret. Had it not been for his misgivings, she'd be alive.

Had he not been a coward, he'd have protected her.

Someone tugged him at the sleeve and he looked up. Seoc was standing by his side, his shoulders sunken, cheeks crimson from the heat or from emotion.

Raghnall looked at the wall of fire surrounding them from three sides. "We must go. Come on."

He picked up Mòrag's body and walked. Ashes and sparks rained on him and on the lad walking by his side. Distantly, Raghnall thought this might be the apocalypse. Perhaps not the whole world had ended, but his certainly had.

He'd never allow himself to love again. He couldn't let another woman die because of him.

And he'd do anything to protect Seoc and ensure the best life for the lad.

Even if it meant going back to Eilean Donan, to the Mackenzie lands—the home and family his father had driven him from eleven years ago—and demanding his birthright.

CHAPTER 1

Eilean Donan, September 2021

This would be the place where she'd die.

Bryanna's stomach twisted at the sight of the Eilean Donan castle, which looked almost black against the granite sky. There it was again, in her mind, the image that had haunted her ever since she was sixteen.

Her limp body in the arms of a tall, broad-shouldered man dressed in a homespun tunic that reached the middle of his thighs, a sword on his hips, long, muscular legs in something like breeches, long, dark hair waving in the wind as he carried her. But as many times as she dreamed of him, she couldn't see his face.

"'Xcuse me, do you mind?" an angry voice said, and a large man brushed past her, pushing her with his shoulder.

She staggered from the impact, bumped into her sister, and grabbed her sleeve. Around them, people spoke Chinese, Russian, Italian, and French, the mixture of voices a lulling noise. The museum had reduced their hours because of recent disappear-

MARIAH STONE

ances within the castle, and undaunted tourists were trying to squeeze in during the open hours.

Including Bryanna Fitzpatrick and her family.

"Hey!" Pamela Fitzpatrick cried after the man. "That was rude, sir!" She turned to Bryanna and put her hand on her shoulder. "Are you all right, honey?"

Mom's sweet face was flushed in outrage. Cold wind blew the scent of the loch into Bryanna's face and threw a lock of her mom's strawberry-blond hair into her eyes. Bryanna's own honey-colored mane was dancing all around her in the wind, and Mom tucked her hair behind her ear. She reminded Bryanna of a mother hen. Being a nurse, she always cared for people, especially her diabetic daughter.

Bryanna flashed a smile she didn't feel. "I'm fine, Mom."

"You look pale suddenly." Mom pushed her gently towards the stone fence along the bridge. "Here, let's measure your glucose. Get your kit out."

Kris, Bryanna's older sister, turned to them. "Do you need help?"

She was another strawberry blonde, taller and prettier than Bryanna.

Also healthier. And she lived in her own apartment, had a better-paying job, and a boyfriend. Yes, Bryanna loved teaching music to kids, but her insulin alone cost her half of her monthly paycheck.

"I'm fine," said Bryanna, but opened her purse nonetheless. It would be easier not to argue with Mom. "Just taking in the beauty, that's all."

She wished she could tell her mom and Kris about her visions. About the Highlander with long, raven hair, battle wounds, and a bloodied medieval tunic. About other visions that had come true, things like how she'd get diabetes at the age of sixteen, which was her first vision ever. Her dad having a heart attack and dying. Dreaming of the music teacher in her old

8

school deciding to move to another state and leaving a job opening that wouldn't be advertised anywhere.

But she never told anyone. They'd think she was crazy at best.

At worst, they'd tell her going to Eilean Donan was a bad idea after all and drag her away. And she wouldn't be able to forgive herself if that happened. Visiting Scotland had been Mom's dream. She and Dad had been here for their honeymoon, and today was the five-year anniversary of Dad's death.

They all missed him, and it had been especially hard on Mom. So no, Bryanna couldn't ruin it for her. She had to go through with this, visions or no visions.

Besides, what if this vision had been wrong? After all, where would she encounter a Highlander in a medieval costume and a bloodied sword?

"Come on," Mom said, helping her to place the new lancet into the kit and insert the new testing strip. Bryanna pricked her ring finger at the side where it hurt less and pressed out a drop of blood, then wiped it away with a clean tissue to avoid alcohol dilution. Then she squeezed more of her blood onto the strip. The electronic screen flashed 135 mg/dL.

Mom tsk-tsked and rummaged in the pocket of her red jacket. "A little high for my liking. Do you want your insulin shot?"

Bryanna put everything back into her purse. She knew her mom worried, but she was tired of being fussed over. "Thanks, Mom. But I'm fine. No need for insulin."

Mom sighed and pinched her lips in that way she did when she was worried, but Kris put her arm through Bryanna's. "You have your insulin pens, right?"

Bryanna clapped a hand on her over-the-shoulder purse. "Always."

Just in case, she had taken three with her. Of course, she wouldn't need that many just for a museum visit, but she had learned it was always better to be overprepared.

9

As the three of them joined the crowd of people trailing down the bridge, Bryanna wished she could just stop and let the beauty of the Highlands take her breath away.

Greenish-brown mountains surrounded them, the seaweed floated on the dirty blue surface of the loch like flecks of rust, and even the blue sky seemed to be muted here. She'd never been abroad before—heck, she'd never been out of Illinois—so just breathing this foreign scent of loch and sea, and grass and algae, should excite her to the core.

Instead, with every step that she took towards the castle, dread weighed in the pit of her stomach. The gorgeous gray-brown walls didn't seem like they contained adventure. It felt like a death sentence waited for her behind them.

The crowd passed through the gate and entered a dark court-yard that was surrounded by buildings and walls from all sides, and she had an odd sense that she was at the bottom of a deep well. Inside the main keep, the narrow corridor in front of her blurred and swam.

Her glucose level must be rising still, she thought, willing the sudden nausea to go away. She was so tired. She needed to do another test, but she didn't want to worry her mom again...

Eyes bright with emotion, Mom was cooing as they turned left and followed the crowd into the Billeting Room. "Aw, it looks just like on our honeymoon!" and "Look, look, your dad really admired that sword..." and then, squeezing Bryanna's hand, "He would have loved to be here with us."

Had Bryanna believed her dream that night five years ago, had she told him to go to the doctor and check his blood pressure, he might still be alive.

But she had dismissed that dream. She was afraid to tell anyone about her premonitions, especially since not every dream came true. She was already a burden to her parents with her diabetes and the medical expenses—how could she make them worry about her mental health, too?

Her dizziness pulsed within her head, making her mind blurry, sluggish, filled with custard...

Custard... No. She wanted a big glass of water.

Great, now she was thirsty, too. Definitely the signs of hyperglycemia. But how could it hit her so unexpectedly when she was fine just a few minutes ago, on the bridge? The Billeting Room was packed with people, and, leaving Mom and Kris, Bryanna staggered towards the nearest wall so that she could hold on to something. Maybe she should ask one of the museum workers for help. But just as she was about to raise her hand to get the attention of a woman, someone else called her and she went in the other direction.

As Bryanna plastered herself against the rough surface between two paintings, the headache kicked in. She needed to do a test, which, most likely, would show that her glucose was way too high, and then she'd need her insulin. She needed to find a bathroom or something.

She couldn't see Mom and Kris above all those heads. She'd just text them from the bathroom. Slowly, she made her way through the crowd of people back into the hall. There was a door at the end of it, perhaps to the restroom.

Thankfully, there were fewer people in the hall. Her vision blurry, she saw some sort of a sign on the door, and, assuming it was the restroom—it didn't even matter if it was ladies or gents at this point—she opened the door and descended the narrow stone stairs illuminated by a dull yellow bulb. Her palm on the wall, she carefully stepped down the stairs. The air here was much more humid, which made her even more thirsty.

As she reached the bottom of the stairs, she saw a large underground space and, even though it was hard to see in the poor light, she thought there were several doors.

"One of those must be the restroom," she muttered as she walked down the hall towards one of the doors.

As she opened the door, coldness seeped into her, and the scent of something grassy and lavender-like. Probably air freshener, she thought as she stepped inside. But as the door closed behind her with a thump, she saw no stalls or sinks. The same dull electrical light illuminated an arched ceiling, packed-dirt floor, rough walls, and a pile of crumbled rocks to her right.

She blinked and shook her head. She was clearly in the wrong room.

She turned to walk out and gasped in surprise.

A woman stood between her and the door, dressed in a green medieval dress with a hood and a cloak. It was hard to see her face, but Bryanna thought she was smiling.

"Excuse me," said Bryanna. "Can you let me pass through?"

"Ye're right where ye're supposed to be, dearie."

The voice was Scottish, melodic, and full of enthusiasm.

"No, I'm just looking for the restroom..."

"Come, sweet." The woman clasped Bryanna's hand and led her towards the pile of rocks. "Just sit down. Ye'll be all right. I'm here."

Her hand was cold and as smooth as polished stone, and it soothed Bryanna. The woman was right. She could do her test here, after all.

She helped Bryanna to sit on one of the flat rocks on the pile. Bryanna realized there were some sort of carvings on the rock, though she couldn't concentrate enough to distinguish what... But she did notice a handprint...odd. In the stone? She itched to put her hand there and see if it would fit.

"If ye do that, ye'll travel in time," said the woman.

Bryanna chuckled and looked up at her. "What?"

"I'm Sìneag, a faerie. Ye dinna have much time, sweet. Yer sickness is making ye weak, I see, so I'll explain quick. Ye'll travel in time and ye'll meet Raghnall Mackenzie, the love of yer life. He may also be yer destruction. The rest is up to ye."

Bryanna blinked and shook her head. The woman's words were echoey, and even though she heard them, she struggled to place their meaning...something about travel and love and destruction...

"I need to measure my glucose," she said as she opened her purse, but she lost track of her thoughts again as her eyes fell on the carvings and on the hand. Something about that print made her really, really want to put her hand against it...

She reached to the print with her right hand.

The carvings began glowing as though neon colors had been painted over them.

"Cool." Bryanna chuckled. "Reminds me of a prom two years ago in the school where I work."

She looked up, but the woman in the green cloak was gone. "Hello?" Bryanna called.

But no answer came. She returned her gaze to the rock. She would just touch it...just to see if her hand would fit...

Raghnall Mackenzie...she thought as her hand came closer and closer.

And as it did, the air around her hand became cooler, and she felt a draft brush against her skin. And then the force with which her hand was advancing towards the print became unstoppable. Her hand practically slammed against where the rock would have been. She gasped as it went through empty air, and she was falling and falling.

Falling through darkness, tumbling, until she finally fell into sleep.

CHAPTER 2

Eilean Donan, September 1310

Raghnall undid the bull-leather money purse and looked at its contents again. Three silver merks were the last of his savings, worth two months of a knight's wages. He didn't have much left, but if today went well, he wouldn't need coins for a while because his estate would finally belong to him. He tied the straps of the money purse together, leather smooth against his fingers, and wrapped them around its mouth to make sure nothing could fall out. Then he handed it to Iòna, one of the Mackenzies' best warriors, who eyed him solemnly.

"This should do, Iòna," Raghnall said. "Just bring the lad to me safely."

Iòna took the purse. "Of course I will. But are ye certain ye dinna wish me to tell Angus about yer son? I'm sure the laird will wish to ken about the nephew he never kent he had."

Wind brought the scent of lake water and seaweed from Loch Duich, which lay behind the Dornie houses with their thatched roofs. Every single curve of the mountains that rose along the shores of the loch was familiar and dear. Dogs barked, and sheep bleated on the pastures in the distance. Raghnall's jaw worked. He hated lying to his clansman, especially to Iòna, who'd been like another brother to him. They all had grown up together, trained on swords and in archery, hunted and fished and pranked village lasses.

But Raghnall knew Iòna wouldn't have gone to the Borderlands for a strange lad, not when the Ross clan could attack them again at any moment. Not when his clan needed him.

"I'll tell Angus myself." Raghnall glanced behind Iòna at the small square in front of Dornie church. His family would come to the wedding soon. As would his bride. "But dinna ye fash about him. There should be enough coin to buy passage with the MacDonald ship, and to bring ye both back. And this..." He went into his belt purse, ignoring a tremor in his fingers as they clasped around a small circle. When he retrieved the simple silver ring that Mòrag never got to wear because of him, his chest clenched painfully as though crushed between two boulders. "This ring belonged to his mother...Mòrag. Show this to him and he'll ken ye came from me. He'll trust ye."

Iòna nodded, his pale blond eyebrows drawn together, and took the ring from his hand. Raghnall inhaled deeply to release the pain that felt like a stake pierced right through the middle of his chest. As Iòna hid the ring in his own belt purse, Raghnall swallowed a hard knot in his throat. He could almost feel the sting of fire burning his eyes, smell the smoke of the farm where he'd been so happy, where he'd thought he'd spend the rest of his life.

He clapped Iòna on the shoulder. "Just bring him to me safely," he repeated. "The MacDonald clan are friends and their ship will take ye as close to Carlisle as they can. I told ye how to find Seoc's uncle's farm."

"Aye." Iòna clapped Raghnall's shoulder as well and climbed onto his horse. The man wore the *leine croich*, the heavily quilted Highland tunic, and a long cloak. The sword in his sheath had seen enough battles, and the scars on Iòna's weathered face would tell anyone to stay away. Really, Raghnall couldn't have wished for a better chaperone for Seoc.

And yet, worry nagged him. Was he right not to go himself?

He needed to marry today, to satisfy Angus's ultimatum. To prove Raghnall had changed his rebellious ways and was ready to settle down. Then Angus would give Raghnall back Tigh na Abhainn, the small estate to the west that their now-deceased father had taken from Raghnall when he had chased him away and cast him out of the clan fifteen years ago.

And he needed the estate to take care of Seoc, to give him the best life possible. He could not give him back the life he had on the farm. The life he would still have had Raghnall not been a coward. Had he married Mòrag earlier. Had he been there to protect her. But he could give Seoc a better place in the world.

"Dinna delay on the way," Raghnall said.

"I wilna. I ken the clan will need me. I dinna go with a light heart, to leave ye all waiting for the Ross clan to strike again."

Bringing a child into what was essentially a war between clans was dangerous, but Raghnall didn't know if he'd survive the upcoming attack. If he wanted to ensure Seoc's future, he had to act now. Chances were, Seoc would arrive when the conflict was resolved. And if the lad did arrive in the middle of the war, Raghnall would make sure Seoc was safely inside the castle. Besides, clan Ross was interested in the Mackenzie lands, not in hurting children.

"Godspeed." Raghnall clapped on the horse's side, and Iòna let the horse walk. When he disappeared behind one of thatched houses, Raghnall shook his head once, willing the dark thoughts of worry and angst to go away.

Now he had to focus on the next task.

The wedding.

Where was Èibhlin?

He glanced at the small wooden chest with beautiful carvings of ladies walking in a flower garden. The chest contained his bride's wedding dress. Èibhlin was a lass from one of Angus's tenants, a young woman with more mischief in her eyes than an unmarrit lass should ken. Raghnall had offered her his hand in marriage, knowing a lass like that would be the right wife for him.

Even though he had heard rumors she had a lad in another village that she fancied.

No chance of falling in love with her. Bonnie, aye, but nae substance to her. Wind in her head, and he wouldn't be surprised to find she wasn't a virgin on their marital bed and later that she'd cheat on him.

All he needed from her was her "aye" and for Angus to witness that. He'd provide for her in his estate, and, most importantly, he'd provide for Seoc. And any other children Èibhlin would give him.

Èibhlin had demanded a bonnie dress. Catrìona, Raghnall's younger sister, together with Mairead, Raghnall's oldest brother Laomann's wife, had just finished the dress last night, so Raghnall hadn't had a chance to give it to her before the wedding.

The dress was expensive, with gold and silver threads and made of silk that was produced in the Kingdom of Naples and very hard to come by in the Highlands. It had cost him every penny that he had accumulated through his service to the Crown and through serving as a hired sword in the Borderlands.

But even as his family started gathering in the square, his bride had still not appeared.

They arrived from Eilean Donan Castle, which was on the island in the loch behind the village, towering over the surrounding landscape like another mountain.

Angus and Rogene, his new wife of about two moons, already pregnant, arrived first. Angus was as tall and dark-haired as Raghnall, only his hair was ear-length, whereas Raghnall hadn't had his hair cut in years.

Rogene's younger brother, David—an odd lad, if anyone asked Raghnall—followed on their heels. He spoke strangely, wore his hair so short it looked as though he'd just had lice, and even at his age of eighteen, he'd never been trained to fight on a sword or shoot a bow.

The lad had a lost, anguished look in his brown eyes, as though he'd been trapped here and didn't know how to get out. But Raghnall liked him. There was fierceness within the lad and a core of steel. Even with barely any combat training, David didn't lack courage and had gone with Angus's troops to protect the lands against clan Ross but four sennights ago.

Just like Catrìona's husband of less than two sennights, James Murray, a Sassenach who'd arrived at the castle searching for Rogene and David and had stayed to help protect the clan from a murderer set on killing Laomann. Thankfully, James had discovered the murderer, and in the meanwhile, managed to steal Catrìona's heart and steer her away from becoming a nun.

Raghnall hadn't trusted the man in the beginning. He'd seen enough Sassenachs to know they couldn't be trusted. He'd fought for King Robert the Bruce against the English Crown for four years now and killed enough English to have assumed a Sassenach in the Highlands was the enemy. But James had proven himself a trusted friend.

Like with Rogene and David, there was something strange about James. Though their accents were different, there was a similar oddness about their choice of words and their mannerisms. Aye, they were all not from here...but sometimes he had a sense they had more secrets than he knew.

Who was he to judge people with secrets? He had enough darkness in his past, and he had never told anyone about Seoc and Mòrag, except Iòna...and even then, it wasn't the whole truth.

He hadn't even told Angus, who was not just his brother but his best friend.

Laomann followed with Mairead, who bounced their ten-moon-old baby boy attached to her in a sling. Ualan grinned as he saw Raghnall and gave him a delighted squeal.

Raghnall didn't want to admit it, but seeing his family come to his wedding warmed something in his chest. Aye, he'd been cast out from them for fifteen years, but they hadn't chosen to chase him away. They were glad he wanted to be part of the clan again.

And he'd give his life for every one of them, whether they wanted him as clansman or not.

Catrìona, who'd gained a healthy amount of weight and sheen ever since she'd stopped fasting a few sennights ago, brushed something away from his tunic.

"Ye look very handsome today, brother," she said, beaming at him. Being marrit suited her. Raghnall could see the new shine of happiness in her blue eyes, the rosy color in her cheeks.

"Where is yer bride?" asked Angus, looking around.

Father Nicholas, the village priest, came out of the simple stone church. "Ah, everyone is here," he said as he looked at them with a kind smile. "Shall we begin?"

"It seems we're missing the bride," said James, his English accent melodic.

"Oh." Father Nicholas glanced around the small crowd.

"She's coming." Raghnall's jaw tensed. "She's coming."

Angus's heavy gaze fell on him. Raghnall swore the man could see through him. "Where does this Èibhlin come from, anyway?"

"She's a local lass," Raghnall said through gritted teeth. "Ye'll be happy, brother. A wife, just like ye ordered."

"Dinna ye bite, brother." Angus picked a stone off the ground with the edge of his shoe and kicked it. "Ye ken 'tis for yer own good. A wife will ground ye."

Raghnall scoffed. "Ye ken nothing."

David came to stand next to Raghnall. The lad, unlike any other time Raghnall had seen him, wore a rich tunic—almost indigo, with intricate, Celtic interwoven patterns around the neck. His hair was longer and wilder now, and he even sported a short beard, which was the most facial hair Raghnall had seen on him. It made him look older than his years, as did the sadness and the guilt of a man who'd had to kill.

An experience Raghnall had known for years. Death, it seemed, followed Raghnall like a loyal dog.

"Want me to go and look for her?" David asked Raghnall in his usual odd manner of missing words in a sentence and still being able to convey his meaning.

"Thanks, lad." Raghnall looked around his family. "I ken she'll come." He wasn't usually one to ask for favors, but he swallowed his pride, for Seoc, and met Angus's dark eyes. "Please, just wait a wee bit."

"Of course, brother," Angus said and hugged Rogene, who gave Raghnall a reassuring smile. "We will wait as long as it takes."

Raghnall's chest squeezed at the sight of love and tenderness between his older brother and his wife. The love they shared was unmistakable. Raghnall had known this was it for his brother as soon as he saw how Angus looked at Rogene.

Watching them now, Raghnall thought of Mòrag and how part of him wished he had someone like Angus had Rogene.

But he had resolved four years ago, holding the dying woman he loved in his arms, to never love again.

Because loving meant losing, sooner or later.

They all chatted a bit, though everyone's eyes darted to the streets and houses around them. The news of the wedding of the youngest Mackenzie son, who'd returned, had spread quickly over the past few days, and a good crowd was gathered around them. Would a female figure appear from behind one of the thatched-roof houses or squeeze between the villagers?

But Èibhlin's small figure didn't step out from behind the crowd, and no one came to tell him any news. The shorter the shadows grew, the heavier Raghnall's heart weighed.

She may have tricked him. Changed her mind or decided to save herself and run.

When the sun was up high, indicating it was midday, Angus

sighed heavily and came to Raghnall. He bit his lower lip mournfully. "I am sorry, brother. We waited half a day…"

"She'll come," Raghnall said, although even he could hear the doubt in his own voice.

"Ye'll find another bride," Laomann said as he clapped Raghnall on the shoulder.

"'Tis good ye didna tie yerself to a woman who canna keep her word," Angus added. "We're going back to the castle. Ye'll find a better woman."

As his family gave him benevolent smiles and nods and turned to go to the pier and board the boats to the castle, Raghnall stood, helplessly clenching and unclenching his fists.

No, this couldn't be it. Seoc was on his way. Raghnall needed the estate. He needed the lands to provide for the lad he considered his son…

But as he stood in front of the church in the middle of the empty square, he knew that yet again destiny had had her say and taken hope out of his hands like a bully took candied fruit from a child.

CHAPTER 3

"LASS..." Someone shook her shoulder.

Bryanna opened her eyes. Above her was a dark stone ceiling and, illuminated by real flames, two faces were leaning over her. One was an older man in his fifties, deep creases of wrinkles on his face. The other was a young, dark-haired man with chin-length hair. Both stared at her as though she were a ghost.

She sat up. Where was she? And who were these two? It smelled faintly like smoke and wet dust, clay and damp earth. She felt heavy but rested, as though she had just woken up from a good, long sleep.

Then she remembered. Right. She'd needed to test her glucose and probably use her insulin pen, and she'd been searching for a bathroom to do that. Then she'd met an odd woman, Sineag, who'd said she was a faerie and talked about time travel. Then she'd passed out.

But she didn't feel dizzy or weak anymore. Her headache was gone, and she wasn't thirsty or nauseated. What a relief...only, why?

These men wore medieval clothes—dirty, worn tunics, belts on their waists. The older man's gray beard was long and ungroomed. There was one more man in the dark space around them, standing by the farther wall on some sort of a short, wooden scaffolding, frozen with a hand trowel and a rough rock in his hand. Now that she thought about it, he was rebuilding one of the walls; the mortar looked wet and there was a bucket next to him. A large, flat stone with carvings and a handprint stood nearby.

"Are ye all right, lass?" asked the older man.

"I think so, yes," she said, feeling surprisingly fresh and awake. Where had the sluggishness and the blurred vision of hyperglycemia disappeared to?

"Where did ye come from, lass?" said the younger one, eyeing her like she was a dangerous animal.

All this was odd. Her feeling so good... These men who looked like extras in an epic fantasy movie...

Ah! She must be having one of her dreams. Like that dream with the Highlander—although she couldn't see his face, and she could see the faces of these guys perfectly well, they did wear the same clothes. So maybe this wasn't one of her psychic dreams.

Maybe this was one where she created whole worlds and had adventures—she had those dreams sometimes, too.

Her favorite type.

She beamed. She could relax. In these dreams, she had no diabetes, no medical bills to worry about, and no mother and sister who watched her every step. She didn't have to be a tiny little music teacher who told her students to chase their dreams but never chased hers, who was afraid to leave town without checking that she had her pens with her.

In this dream, she could be someone else.

Even better.

She could be her true self.

Bubbles of excitement prickled her stomach. Freedom! For the duration of this dream, she'd be free. She'd live.

"Kind sir, don't worry about me," she said, still smiling. She patted her purse. "And my apologies for having scared you."

She giggled. She even spoke a different language...Gaelic! How fun. That hadn't happened before.

She rose to her feet, delighted at the onrush of energy in her body. "I have to go. There's a whole world I need to discover outside before I wake up."

They frowned at her, looking confused. The older man mumbled something about the actions of deranged Highland faeries, but she ignored him and hurried to the door, marveling at the lightness of her step.

Behind the door, a large space with crates, chests, and medieval weapons and armor was illuminated by several torches. She realized she hadn't felt this delightful squeezing somewhere deep in her stomach since before she'd known she had diabetes. As she climbed the narrow stone stairs, the same ones she had taken when she had been awake, she remembered the last time she'd had this exquisite anticipation of wonder.

Her junior prom, when her dad had been alive.

Her first date ever, Jacob, came to pick her up and gave her a bouquet—first time in her life. And her dad had looked at her with tears in his eyes and kissed her on her hair, which was straightened to perfection, and whispered that she could come back home half an hour later than they'd initially agreed.

As she opened the heavy arched door, the ache of nostalgia mixed with the sunlight-like warmth in her stomach. She missed her dad so much.

She looked around what appeared to be a storage room with more crates, barrels, and sacks. It was a square room, and certainly not anything like the Eilean Donan she had stepped into when she had been awake.

Fascinating that her mind could create all this; everything looked so real. As she moved towards a tall, arched door, she could even smell hay and grain.

Outside, the sight of the massive castle around her robbed breath from her lungs. There were several timber, thatched-roof buildings and a looming wall that surrounded the perimeter. They definitely weren't in the same Eilean Donan she had visited with her mom and sister. Feeling like Alice in Wonderland, she thought to herself, *Curiouser and curiouser...*

There weren't many people here and, like the three men in the underground, all of them were dressed in medieval clothes. Warriors with bows on their backs stood on the walls. A man was cutting firewood on a stump, swinging the ax rhythmically against the wood. Even the smell was different—manure, and lake, and woodsmoke. A horse neighed somewhere, and Bryanna bit her lip in anticipation.

As she walked towards the gate down the slight slope at the top of which a tower stood, she wondered if this dream would allow her to finally fulfill one of her greatest wishes—to ride a horse.

She'd always begged her parents to let her do horseback riding, and just after she'd started a beginner course, she'd found out she had type one diabetes. That had been the end of that. Her mom had practically forbidden her from doing anything remotely dangerous. Diabetics could have all kinds of complications if there was an accident, and Mom wanted to avoid any danger.

As her simple white walking shoes sank into the drying mud of the courtyard, she realized that her life could be divided into before diabetes and after.

Right now, she was like the Bryanna "before."

Free. Dreaming of riding horses and pursuing a career as a singer with a band.

As opposed to her "after," a music teacher living in her mom's home with more expenses to sustain her health than she was earning.

She approached the inner wall, went through the gates, and walked through a similar inner bailey, with more thatched buildings, a small garden, as well as cows and chickens and a few pigs wandering around. People were busy here, too, feeding animals, cutting wood, carrying heaps of hay and firewood, and baskets. The gate in the middle of the outer wall was open, and although a few of the guards standing on the walls glanced at her with suspicion, they let her pass.

She was dressed so differently from everyone else. Her blue jeans stood out especially. She hadn't seen a woman in the castle yet, but she imagined in this medieval world they probably didn't wear jeans. Her dark-red cardigan was probably also not the best for blending in among people who mostly wore variations of beige, natural browns, and dark greens.

But this was just a dream, she reminded herself, and she couldn't wait to explore the outer world.

When she came out of the gates, the sight took her breath away. She'd just seen it in real life—the loch, gray and leaden, the brown-green hills surrounding the loch, the rust-colored seaweed, the mossy rocks, the flowers.

And yet, the village across the loch was different from the Dornie she'd seen before. There was clearly a small church, and the houses were timber with thatched roofs—just like the buildings inside the castle walls. And there was a small harbor with several piers and lots of boats—fishing boats, she guessed, based on the nets. Several of them floated in the middle of the loch.

On this shore, there was a quay also, and she saw a large barge being prepared to depart. If she wanted to leave and explore the world outside, she should hurry.

"Wait!" she cried as she ran down the jetty. The man who was untying the rope glanced up at her with a frown. "Can you take me with you?"

He nodded, thoughtfully looking her over.

She climbed onto the barge and after some awkward questions about where she'd come from and if she'd lost her proper clothes, the man concentrated on navigating the barge, and Bryanna lifted her chin, letting the soft breeze kiss her cheeks.

Freedom.

The man docked and Bryanna stepped out. Giving him the biggest smile and a thank-you, she proceeded into the village. The scent of fresh and stale fish was stronger here, in the small harbor, but Bryanna didn't pinch her nose. She wanted to drink everything in, and the stinky harbor was part of it.

It was probably around midday, and work in the village was in full swing. People carried buckets of water in their hands, full sacks of what looked like corn on their backs, pushed one-wheeled carts with firewood in front of them. They talked, cleaned horse and cow sheds, weaved baskets. Surprised glances followed her just like in the castle. A boy of five or six pointed at her and yelled, "Ma, why is the lass dressed like a lad?"

Bryanna beamed. "I was just trying to pass as a man, but you got me there!"

The boy chuckled, pleased with her praise but still puzzled. He held on to his mother's skirt, and she pressed him closer to her. There were many women here, unlike in the castle, and they were all, indeed, dressed very differently from Bryanna. Long, simple dresses of wool and linen. Most of their heads were covered with veils, and a lot of them wore aprons, dirty from work in the kitchens, or with animals.

As she walked, she noticed the pungent scent of brewed beer and the mouthwatering aroma of baked bread, mixed with the odor of manure and animals. Indeed, mooing and the bleating of sheep and goats came from here and there. Geese honked, and chickens squawked. A dog barked at her as she walked by, but still wagged its tail. She waved to the dog and kept walking.

Soon, she found herself at a small and mostly empty square by the church where a few people stood talking to each other. As she walked towards the church—a rectangular stone building with a bell tower—she saw a man sitting on a chest, watching her.

A chill rushed through her, making her stop for a split second. Even though he was sitting, he was clearly tall, with long legs half bent, and his elbows pressing into his knees. Broad, muscular shoulders stretched the fabric of his rich red tunic, which stood out against the earthy tones she'd seen in this world so far. He wore something like dark breeches and pointy medieval shoes.

His hair was almost black and long, tied behind his head. A short, dark, groomed beard covered the lower half of his face, and his broad black eyebrows furrowed above his eyes.

God almighty, the eyes... Talk about piercing—they drilled into her soul. If there was a devil, he must have eyes like that—black and searching and scorching, deep darkness playing in their depths.

As his gaze slowly went up and down her body and his frown deepened, some sort of fire started in her veins. She kept moving towards him, as if pulled by the force of his gaze.

As though he'd been waiting for her, he stood up from the wooden chest, stealing any breath she had left.

God, men like him couldn't exist. Couldn't be real. They did belong in dreams and came from the imagination. She'd created the most beautiful man she'd ever seen. Even taller than she'd thought—towering over her like a castle—and all muscle and lean, male body, he emanated strength, power, and danger. It was in the way he was holding his arms, the half-clenched fists, the scars on his face.

As she stood before him, unable to take her eyes away from his perfect features, she swallowed a dry ball in her throat. If she could pick an actor to play him, it would be Aidan Turner. His eyes were set a bit deeper, with long black eyelashes framing the slightly slanted, Celtic eyes. His nose was a bit crooked—broken, and probably not just once. Full lips were visible in his dark beard. High cheekbones protruded from under the sun-kissed skin that told her he was not a stranger to the outdoors.

The man clearly had zero body fat. Like the warriors she'd seen in the castle, he had a sword on his belt, but had no other weapons that she could see.

"Who are ye, lass?" he asked, studying her with clear interest.

God, that voice! Low and rich, like a great Scotch whisky sipped by the fire in winter, it spilled through her veins in a hot rush. Clearing her throat to chase away the complete stupor he'd put her into, she searched for words. "Um..."

CHAPTER 4

THE WOMAN WAS SO BEAUTIFUL, his breath caught. Honey-colored hair, long and straight, eyes the brightest green he'd ever seen, like fresh grass still covered by the last snow of winter. And the way she was dressed...strange. Only once had he seen clothes like she wore—on David Wakeley, when the lad had followed his sister, Rogene, as she'd stopped Angus and Euphemia of Ross's wedding right here in front of the church two moons ago.

But he'd rarely seen a woman dressed in a man's clothes. Not a noblewoman, anyway. He'd known women from robber and reiver camps who dressed like that.

But she...she wasn't a woman from a robber camp. If anything, she was noble. And the way she carried herself, there was something about her...

Like she didn't have a care in the world, wasn't concerned about anyone's opinion of her. Like she was herself, and it was the happiest place to be.

If the sun became a person, it would be her. Because the piece of ice that his heart had been ever since Mòrag died began to melt in her presence. Looking at her, bright-eyed, red-lipped, and freckled, he became warm.

She swallowed and cleared her throat. "No one," she said.

Her voice was melodic and beautiful, and even though she spoke Gaelic, she had an accent. But it was so soft, he couldn't understand where she came from. She didn't sound like David or Rogene, or James, who had a strong English accent. Nae, hers was a combination of those two, perhaps, and again, different. Being skilled at music and singing, Raghnall could easy pick up on people's accents and intonations, and learning languages came easy to him. "Just visiting this beautiful place. Enjoying being here."

Enjoying... Aye, that was the word that was key about her. Enjoying. Joy. It was as though she radiated that, and infected him, too. Despite himself, he found the corners of his mouth rise.

"Aye, I can see that."

She looked him up and down. "And you? Are you waiting for someone?"

Waiting for someone... Ah, damnation, he was. She made him forget what was supposed to happen today. Like an idiot, he was still waiting for Èibhlin, even though he'd already gone to her house and found out that she wasn't there and no one knew her whereabouts. He'd sent a few men to search for her and was waiting for her by the church in case she still showed up.

"I was and they didna come. But, perhaps, 'twas ye I was meant to meet here."

She frowned and then her lips spread in a smile that was so beautiful he wanted to howl at the moon. "Me? Why?"

"Because I have to get marrit today. And my intended didna come."

She opened her mouth in surprise. "So you just want to marry a strange woman?"

"Ye wouldna be more strange than my bride."

She bit her lower lip, as through attempting to contain a huge grin. "I mean, I don't even know your name!"

"Raghnall Mackenzie," he said. "What do they call ye?"

"Bryanna Fitzpatrick."

Bryanna Giolla Phádraig... Her clan name was in Irish Gaelic. Was she Irish? He supposed it didn't much matter where she came from. She was here now.

"Good. What do ye say, Lady Bryanna? I am in need of a bride. Today. Do ye have a husband?"

"No, but I don't even know you!"

He'd just opened his mouth to reply when she interrupted him and mumbled to herself, "Well, I suppose it doesn't matter, none of this is real, anyway... Just an adventure..." She met his eyes and grinned. "Yes, I'll marry you."

He chuckled and shook his head. "But this marriage will be real," he said. "I need a real wife, but once I get my estate back, and my brother is satisfied and agrees that I'm changed and ready to settle, ye'll be free to live wherever ye want."

She nodded. "Sure. All sounds great. Don't you want to know more about me?"

Suddenly, he did want to know more. He wanted to know everything. "Aye... I suppose ye're a noblewoman? Is yer clan from Ireland?"

She looked around. "Well, I'm actually a quarter Scottish, half Irish, and a quarter German. My Fitzpatrick ancestors were from Ireland—so I guess that's my clan?"

"And what are ye doing here?"

She waved her hand. "I told you, just visiting."

"What about yer father? Wouldna he want to know who ye're marrying?"

Suddenly, the lightness in her eyes disappeared and they filled with pain. "My father would have loved to know, if he were alive." She shook her head and met his eyes. "Shall we do this thing, or what? You need the estate, right?"

Did it really matter who he was marrying? He didn't know this woman, but neither did he know Èibhlin. And he wanted more of that warmth, more of that joy and that sense of freedom she radiated.

But... He really didn't know anything about her. What if she was lying? What if she was a charlatan? Who agreed to marry a man they just met?

What if she was sent by Euphemia?

But he needed a woman. Seoc would soon be on his way.

"Look, lass," he said, scraping the ground with the edge of his shoe, "I think I was in a hurry, after all. Perhaps 'tis best we get to ken each other a wee bit and set the wedding day in a few days...a sennight or so? To meet yer family?"

"I'll be gone by then," she said with a sad smile. "But if you don't need my help, it's fine. I'm okay either way."

"But how can ye say yes to marrying a perfect stranger? Usually marriages are arranged years before, and ye—"

She shrugged. "Everything is an adventure, Raghnall Mackenzie, isn't it?" Then her face fell and she went silent, staring at him like he was the worst news she'd ever gotten.

"Lass?" he said.

She shook her head and the dreadful expression was gone. "I heard about you," she said.

He sighed. Based on her expression, this was bad. "Aye, I see that ye did."

"No." She smiled. "What I heard was good, it just means..." She shook her head again. "Never mind. Everything's fine. Look, I'm on an adventure and I want to enjoy my time. And if it means marrying a jaw-droppingly gorgeous Highlander, then so be it."

He eyed her, his lips spreading in a grin again. She was odd, and different, and...like a gulp of fresh air. "No one ever called me that before."

She arched her eyebrow. "Well, their loss. Look, I'm not sure how long this adventure will last, so I don't have tomorrow or a week from now. It has to be today. It has to be now."

She was right. It had to be now. And if she was a spy, or a madwoman, or the Queen of England in disguise, he'd deal with that later.

"Aye, lass," he said. "Adventure, ye say? I ken what an adventure is. Only, with me, ye may be in for more than ye've bargained for. Come." He took her hand in his, and the touch sent a burst of warm tingling through his veins, like he'd just plunged his hand into a bucket of starlight. "I have a dress for ye."

He leaned down and picked up the chest he'd been sitting on, then tugged her into the church and found Father Nicholas. While the lass was changing in Father Nicholas's quarters, Raghnall explained that he'd found his bride. He also sent a village boy to the castle to fetch Angus and the rest of the family for the wedding, and to tell them to continue preparing the wedding feast.

Then he waited outside for what felt like another eternity. But surprisingly quickly, his family appeared at the square before the church, looking around.

"Where is she?" Angus barked. "What kind of bride is almost a day late?"

The kind of bride that Raghnall had just met. But before Raghnall could say that, the church door opened, and she walked out, and everything around Raghnall stopped existing. Angus, Rogene, Laomann...all of them.

Because seeing her in this dress made all the trouble of making the dress, and waiting for a bride who'd disappeared, worth it.

From an odd woman in a man's clothing, she'd turned into the most beautiful lady he'd ever seen. The rich blue silk of the dress streamed like water down to Lady Bryanna's thin waist and feminine hips. The silver and gold patterns of flowers and leaves on her bodice sparkled like morning dew on a spiderweb. The long sleeves covered her arms and fell almost to the ground, their insides lined with golden silk. The skirt of the dress fell from her round hips to the earth, and as she walked towards him, it moved around her long legs. He'd seen them earlier, being hugged by her breeches, and yet this movement of the silky fabric made his imagination run wild.

Made him want to put his hand under her skirt, run his palm up her leg, and feel how smooth her skin was.

She stood before him, her eyes locked with his as though she didn't see anyone else, either. Raghnall itched to take her hands in his.

This wasn't real, he told himself. Well, the marriage would be legal.

As he took her hands in his, he told himself he wouldn't fall for her. He wouldn't truly consider her his wife in his heart. That was the only condition upon which he'd marry her. He wouldn't tell it to her, but he couldn't love her. No matter how bright her green eyes were, sparkling like the surface of the loch in the sun.

No matter how soft and warm and right her hands felt in his.

No matter that no one had made his blood boil like she had just now—not since Mòrag.

Maybe not ever.

He'd give her everything that a wife would want from a husband.

Except for his heart.

CHAPTER 5

THEY MADE their way back to the castle in the early afternoon, and Bryanna wondered how long she'd be dreaming this strange, beautiful dream.

Walking by her new husband's side, she marveled at the great hall of the main keep. She was pretty sure she'd never seen the heraldry of clan Mackenzie, the burning mountain on the tapestries that hung all over the rough stone walls.

As newlyweds, Bryanna and Raghnall sat at the great table by the fireplace with Angus and his wife, Rogene. The long tables were full of food—dishes of baked ducks in crispy coating and chickens and even a boar. People ate bread, sweet pastries with a custard-like filling, roasted ducks, chicken and geese stuffed with plums, apples, and pears. Servants poured wine and something like beer from clay and glass pitchers into the guests' cups.

Talking with her new husband, Bryanna'd learned that Angus was Raghnall's older brother, but he was the chief of clan, not their eldest brother, Laomann, who sat at the other end of the table with his wife, Mairead. Raghnall had explained to her that Laomann used to be the laird but was weakened by several murder attempts on the part of Euphemia of Ross. He had given his position to Angus because he felt his brother would be able to protect the clan better against the powerful enemy.

Angus offered a saltcellar to the people at his table one by one—that must be a sign of wealth or status. How interesting.

Raghnall's younger sister, Catrìona, a lovely young woman, was freshly married to an Englishman, James, who was so clearly in love with her, his eyes burned when he looked at her. They seemed completely wrapped up in a cocoon of honeymoon, with their hands touching, brushing against each other, some part of their body needing to touch the other person. But sometimes the Englishman threw piercing glances at Bryanna, as though trying to resolve some sort of a puzzle.

The hall was full of people but probably not many noblemen, based on how they were dressed. It seemed the whole village was here.

She looked down at a trencher in front of her—no plates and no forks. Everyone had a cutting knife that she'd seen them retrieve from their belt, and they used it to eat. As she watched Raghnall devour a duck leg covered with a golden crust probably made from breadcrumbs and something buttery and delicious, her mouth watered. She had dreamed of eating food, devouring it, often. The dangerous food she could eat but had to be careful about—chocolate and cakes and chips... But the taste in her dream was never satisfying, and she was never full, not like in real life.

She picked up her knife and carefully traced along its sharp edge with her finger, then she pressed lightly on the edge with her thumb.

"Ouch," she whispered as the blade bit into her skin and a tiny dot of blood formed.

That was strangely vivid. Actually, it felt super real. A chill ran down her spine.

Angus got to his feet and raised a glass. He was so tall and large, muscular like a bodybuilder, and Rogene looked tiny next to him. There was something of a bear about him—he looked cuddly and kind enough, but the danger was right there, and she had the sense that he wouldn't hesitate to do anything to protect his family. She immediately felt trust for this man. He reminded her of Dad.

When the hall went quiet, Angus looked at Raghnall. "I didna think I'd see this day," Angus said with his cup raised. "The day when my youngest brother would find a wife. When he'd return home." He met Bryanna's eyes. "I wish ye luck, Lady Bryanna of clan Giolla Phádraig. Raghnall isna the easiest man. But ye wilna find one more loyal. A man who'd lay down his life to protect those he loves."

Everyone raised their cups at that and drank, and the hall filled with cheers and exclamations. The noise resumed, but Bryanna didn't touch her cup because the only person who hadn't drunk to that was Raghnall.

Instead of the graceful, charming wolf she'd seen by the church, he was a cornered animal. He stared into empty space, somewhere Bryanna couldn't see. His dark, bloodshot eyes were open wide, horror and heartache on his face like a mask. The knuckles of the fist that held the cutting knife were as white as snow.

Well, that didn't look like a wonderful dream, either.

It didn't look like a dream at all.

"Raghnall, are you okay?" she whispered and touched his arm. He jerked it back, as though she'd just poked it with a burning stick.

He shifted away from her, his upper lip curling in a predatory snarl. "Dinna speak to me yer strange words and dinna look at me with those innocent, kind eyes."

Hurt stabbed her in the chest like a blade. "But I only—"

He came closer to her, shifted like a snake, graceful and efficient. His black eyes held her in captivity, and it wasn't joy or admiration that shone in them this time.

It was threat. That darkness, somewhere deep in his soul,

was staring straight at her, and for the first time since meeting him, she didn't feel happy, adventurous, or joyful.

Icy dread paralyzed her.

"I should have been clear before," he said in a low voice. "By marrying me, ye dinna get love. Ye dinna get happiness. Angus doesna ken what he's talking about. I canna protect ye, I'm nae a god or a saint. I may well be yer demise, lass. What do ye think about that?"

She opened her mouth, but no words came.

Her demise...

This felt less and less like a dream with every second. Then where the hell was she?

"Kiss!" a woman cried—Rogene, Bryanna realized.

"Kiss?" followed Angus's booming voice.

"Yeah!" shouted David, Rogene's younger brother, drunk and slurpy, his accent strong now. If she didn't know better, she'd think he sounded like an American. "Kiss her, ye lucky sonuvabitch..."

"David!" came Catrìona's outraged call.

Raghnall's gaze fell on Bryanna's lips, and a different sort of darkness filled his eyes. The chill in her bones was suddenly chased away by a scorching heat wave that rushed through her body.

"A kiss?" murmured Raghnall. "A husband kisses his wife, aye, lass?"

He took her hand, his warm, rough skin scraping against hers, and stood, pulling her up. A kiss...the thought of his lips on hers turned her legs into melted chocolate.

It's a dream, she kept repeating inside her head. *It's a dream. You can kiss him. You can do anything you want with him.*

And she wanted to do...everything.

He pulled her to him and wrapped his arms around her, clasping her in his steely prison. God, he was hot...hot and hard-muscled underneath that dark crimson tunic.

But all awareness evaporated from her head when he leaned down and his lips met hers.

They were like falling into a cloud...a warm, soft, light cloud, where just those kisses existed. His scent was in her nostrils, something musky and earthy and mysterious. Like burning a fire in the middle of the night in the woods, under a sky of stardust spilled all over endless indigo.

She surrendered completely, forgetting everyone and everything around them, as the warmth of desire spread through her veins. As though he'd felt it, too, he deepened the kiss, pressing his lips into hers, urging his tongue inside her mouth. And she opened up, letting him in, drinking him like exquisite wine.

His tongue brushed against her, gliding, teasing, tickling. He set a fire somewhere deep within her; the apex of her thighs began tingling and burning. She wanted more of this—his hot, hard body, his tongue, gliding and teasing and playing—all over her skin. She wanted to dissolve around him, to become one, to lick and glide against him, to...

"What the fuck is this?"

The male voice came from somewhere nearby. She ignored it at first, brushing it off like an annoying fly, but Raghnall froze and pulled away. She clenched Raghnall's sleeves to her, willing him to continue this heaven, never wanting it to stop, but he stared at something behind her. She looked back over her shoulder.

David held her bright-purple purse, glaring at it like he was trying to make it spontaneously combust.

"Are ye all right, lad?" asked Raghnall, letting her go.

David didn't look all right. His eyes were glossy and blood-shot, his disheveled hair was strangely short, looking like a modern-day haircut that hadn't been trimmed for a long time. He was standing but swaying a little at the same time.

He was clearly drunk and pointed at her purse with his finger. "That"—he stabbed the air—"does not look medieval."

Raghnall frowned at Bryanna's violet, faux-leather fringed purse. "Medieval? What the hell are ye talking about, lad?"

But David ignored him. "Rogene, is this your purse?" he yelled in perfect American English.

Bryanna frowned. Yes, things were often odd in her dreams: her speaking Gaelic, people switching to American English in the middle of a medieval feast.

But things that were odd were accumulating. It didn't feel like a dream. It all looked too real, too logical, and everything around her had too much substance. And then that feeling she had gotten when Raghnall had looked at her like she'd burned him...

That coldness... That rejection...

She'd thought it was emotional. But actually, it was physical.

The dizziness returned. The weakness in her legs that she'd thought was from the shock of Raghnall's cold reaction to her was still there. Things were swimming in front of her, and it wasn't the light-headedness from a kiss anymore.

It was the light-headedness of a diabetic with too much glucose in her blood. All those custard pastries she ate, and the battered duck, and the ale she drank...

Rogene stood up and came to them, frowning. As though acutely attuned to Rogene and David, James came, too, followed by Catrìona and Angus. Everyone gathered around Bryanna, Raghnall, and the purse.

"Is this your purse?" David repeated in English, his consonants slurred.

"Mate, speak Gaelic if you don't want to attract attention," said James, still in English.

"No." Rogene frowned at the purse and then met Bryanna's gaze, wide-eyed. "It's yours, isn't it?"

"Speak Gaelic!" demanded Raghnall. "What is going on?"

The rest of them, except for Bryanna and Raghnall, exchanged concerned looks, and then David chuckled, his mouth crooked. Ignoring Raghnall's demand, he continued in English. "You came through the rock, didn't you?"

She nodded, feeling like the floor was slipping from under her feet.

Rogene was looking between her and Raghnall. "You know what it means, don't you?"

She remembered Sìneag, the woman in a green medieval dress down in the underground room. *Ye'll travel in time and ye'll meet Raghnall Mackenzie, the love of yer life.*

Travel in time...

She looked around at them all, her head spinning. She held on to something—someone... Raghnall, his arm firm and steady.

"Are ye all right, lass?" came his voice.

No, she refused to believe this.

"It means I'm only dreaming," she said to Rogene as firmly as she could. "None of this is real."

James sighed and exchanged a look with David and Rogene. "Then you better wake up, sweetheart. You're in the year 1310."

CHAPTER 6

EVERYTHING WAS like a nightmarish déjà vu. Bryanna's hand was brushing against the rough stone wall as she hurried down the slippery, narrow stairs into the underground. Her head spun, and the damned long skirts of the otherwise absolutely stunning and comfortable dress were tangling around her legs, threatening her to make her stumble and fall.

"Lady Bryanna!" came Raghnall's voice behind her. "Wait! Where are ye going?" And then his steps were behind her, closer. "What did they say?"

Her purse, which she'd just grabbed from David, knocked against her side with every step.

"This is not real!" she yelled back. "This is all just a dream!"

It was like a mantra she needed to keep repeating to stay sane, like a spell she was trying to cast. As she reached the underground space, she ran towards the door she'd emerged from—despite her dizziness, despite her high blood sugar, knowing all too well that she shouldn't, that she was just making it worse.

"Wait!" he called, hurrying after her. "What isna real? What's a dream? Do ye think I'm yer dream? Is that why ye marrit me?"

She ignored him. If she'd really traveled in time, if she really was cut off from an insulin supply and modern medicine, doctors, and hospitals, the thought meant one thing.

Death.

No, no. That familiar dread crawled up her spine yet again, paralyzing her with fear like a poison. There was the door, and she stopped abruptly to open it, breathing heavily, sucking in the stuffy, humid underground air.

But before she could pull the door handle to herself, a loud crash, bangs, and yells of pain came from behind the door. Her stomach dropped to her feet.

No! No!

She opened the door, and small clouds of dust rushed out of the semidarkness. "What—" Raghnall was right behind her, his hand on her shoulder protectively. "Stay back." He stepped before her, shielding her with his strong arm.

He looked inside, and as the dust began settling, Bryanna coughed. She could see what had happened there...

A disaster.

The wall and part of the ceiling must have crumbled—and buried the exact place Bryanna needed.

The rock with the carvings and the handprint.

The rock that had, supposedly, brought Bryanna through time.

But the older man lying on the ground with a trickle of blood flowing down his forehead looked suspiciously real. The air smelled like dust and wet earth and...did she get a whiff of lavender and grass?

She noticed the younger man who'd talked to her was on the ground as well, sitting up and taking his head into his hands. The third man rose to his hands and knees and crawled towards the old man with the wound on his head.

Raghnall rushed to him, too, while Bryanna stood and gaped at all this like a fool. Her head swam, and normally she'd sit down and do her blood strip test, but there was nothing to sit on.

And nothing normal about what was going on around her.

"I'm all right," said the wounded man, sitting up with the help of Raghnall.

"What happened here, Amhladh?" Raghnall asked, looking around. Two of the torches cast light that jumped around the walls.

"I dinna ken," said the old man. "We were working, and then all of a sudden, there was a loud crash and the rocks crumbled. Our scaffolds broke from the weight of the stones. We could have been buried underneath all that rubble."

With a coldness spreading through her middle, Bryanna mumbled, "Almost like someone wanted it to crumble and bury that rock underneath."

"What?" Raghnall looked up at her. "What rock?"

"The faerie rock," said Amhladh, looking somberly at the pile of rubble. "I heard stories as a lad."

"Oh, aye?" said Raghnall, his expression suddenly curious.

"Nothing particular. A faerie helped a druid carve those symbols on the rock. They say whoever puts his or her hand in the handprint would go to another time."

Silence fell in the underground room as all four men looked at her.

Involuntarily, she took a step back. With shaking hands, she clutched her purse. When she opened it, relief washed through her. Three insulin pens lay on the bottom, just like she remembered.

If she wasn't dreaming, which seemed more and more true with every second, and if she had indeed traveled in time, she needed to get to that rock and go back to her time where there was insulin.

Without it, she'd die. It was as simple as that.

"Did you smell lavender?" she asked. "Before the crash."

The younger man scratched his head. "Come to think of it, aye, I did. I thought mayhap my wife put a branch or two in my tool basket and I hadna noticed. But aye, lavender, and then grass."

Just like what she had smelled when Sineag had appeared.

"Lady Bryanna..." growled Raghnall. "Ye're confusing me. Why is lavender even important?"

Wake up, she commanded herself. *Wake up!* If this was a dream, she had to wake up. Because if she really had traveled back in time, the huge pile of rubble hadn't just buried her only way back.

It had pretty much buried her, too.

"I need this to be cleared," she whispered, not recognizing her own voice.

Raghnall rose, the concern and annoyance on his face replaced by pure worry. "Lass, ye're shaking." He walked to her and grasped her upper arms, steadying her. His firm, warm touch calmed her. His black eyes were searching hers. "Ye're so pale... Ye need to see my sister, she's a healer."

"Please," she whispered. "Please, get this rubble cleared. I'll help. I'll remove those rocks myself if I have to..."

"Lass," said the old man, standing up. "We have to repair the wall, anyway. There are a few cracks and we must secure the castle before the attack. 'Tis why we've been working here."

A knot hardened in her stomach. "What attack?"

Raghnall sighed. "We're at war with clan Ross. We ken they're coming—they've been trying this whole summer. My brother was supposed to marry Euphemia of Ross, but he fell in love with Rogene and chose her. We also owe them tribute that we've yet been unable to pay. Euphemia...she wants her revenge. That's why she sent a murderer to kill Laomann and the whole clan. She failed, thanks to James. But we know she won't stop. So we're bracing ourselves."

A war between clans... Now she was in the middle of a clan feud?

The image of her, dead, being carried by a medieval warrior from Eilean Donan flashed through her mind.

46

This would be the place she'd die...

She had to get out of here.

"How long will it take?" she asked.

The old man scratched his head. "At least a sennight, I reckon."

A week...

She watched the rubble with dread growing in the pit of her stomach. She should be fine insulin-wise, if she was careful with her diet. Her insulin pens were good for about twenty-eight days without being refrigerated.

But she had to use them sparingly, and only if there was no other choice.

"Come on, everyone," said Raghnall, his voice surprisingly soft. She didn't expect a man like him, a rugged warrior, to speak like he was soothing a hurt child. "Amhladh, 'tis best if Catrìona looks at yer head, and Lady Bryanna, she better take a look at ye, too."

He gently led her out of the room and into more darkness. "And once ye're well," he whispered to her, his voice low, "ye're going to tell me the whole truth about who ye are and why ye need that rock so much."

CHAPTER 7

JUST BEFORE BRYANNA could enter the great hall, Raghnall gently took her by the elbow and pulled her to him.

"Nae yet, lass."

Amhladh and the lads went into the great hall to get checked by Catriona and tell Angus what happened. But Raghnall wanted to be alone with his wife.

His wife...

The woman looking at him with those big, translucent eyes with an odd mixture of apprehension and hope. Where had the radiant joy and liveliness gone? She looked unwell, which concerned him greatly. Her pale skin looked carved out of ivory, practically glowing in the semidarkness of the landing. She could be a vision from a dream, not a woman of flesh and blood.

A dream...she was talking about things not being real, and then why did she hurry downstairs into the underground, to that rock? She was hiding something. Her elusive answers back at the church, her stating she'd be gone tomorrow... James, Rogene, David—they all spoke English with her, so they were in on this, too, his whole family. And he wasn't going to be the outsider yet again.

"Tell me what's going on," he said. "Who are ye, really? Why do ye need to get to that rock?"

She frowned her elegant eyebrows in a pained, thoughtful expression. Then, as though having made an internal decision, her face straightened, and she freed her arm from his grasp. "This sounds like an interrogation."

He blinked. "Ye're my wife, lass, I will interrogate ye as I please."

She gaped at him. "Are you serious?"

"Aye. I dinna often make mistakes, but I may have made one by marrying ye. I should have insisted to ken ye better first, and I was a fool believing yer story about being of clan Fitzpatrick."

"I am Bryanna Fitzpatrick. And same goes for me. I should have never offered you my help. I don't want you as my husband, I don't want you as my *anyone!*"

His jaw muscles worked. Even though he'd known her for only a few hours, hearing that she didn't want him stung. A wee bee she was, small and sweet, but she could sting, too.

"So what about it, then?" She crossed her arms over her chest and glared at him. "If you think it was a mistake to marry me, and I certainly don't want to be married to you, can we annul the marriage or something?"

He heard a low growl escape his throat. She was right, that would be the best thing to do. He didn't want a wife.

But he needed one.

He had to take care of Seoc. He had to honor the memory of the woman whose life was on his conscience. And now Angus seemed to agree with him, for the first time in years. He couldn't lose this woman.

Raghnall glanced back at the open doorway into the great hall. "No annulment."

Bryanna frowned. "But—"

"For better or for worse, ye're my wife, lass. 'Tis done."

Her mouth fell open in clear indignation. "Just like that? But what about my say in this?"

Oh nae. She was going to stir a storm, wasn't she?

"Ye had yer say by the church when the priest asked if ye'd take me, and yer answer was yes."

"I didn't know I was really marrying you!"

"So what were ye thinking, 'tis all some kind of a jest?"

She inhaled sharply, her lower lip twitching as she looked like she was searching for words, and he came one step closer to her, deliberately menacing and towering over her. "Do I look like I'm a man who likes to jest, Lady Bryanna of clan Fitzpatrick?"

He knew it worked—her eyes darkened and widened in a flash of panic. But then, she covered the rest of the small space between them like a little warrior woman and stabbed her index finger into his chest. "I don't care. I do not want to be married to you and I'm going to your brother to tell him so. He's the boss here, right? The laird? So if you don't want to annul this marriage, I'm sure he'll know how."

Oh, the minx.

While she turned on her heel, about to march to the great hall, Raghnall's mind raced.

If she went there now, and if she told Angus she'd married Raghnall by mistake, Angus would never force her to stay married against her will. And an annulment was very much possible since they hadn't consummated the marriage yet. Normally, Raghnall would also let her go—he would never force a woman to do anything.

But if she got the marriage annulled, Raghnall wouldn't get Tigh na Abhainn, and Seoc wouldn't have the home he deserved. Raghnall would break his word to Mòrag. And that word was the only thing that kept him living, kept him on the side of the light.

Because the other side of him—the darkness, the easiness with which he went to battle and met death, the indifference to what would happen to him—would take over.

And he'd never be able to go back to a normal life because he'd never be able to forgive himself.

So he had to stop her. And he had to act fast. He'd explain all of this to her later, when she was a safe distance from Eilean Donan and unable to tell Angus anything.

By then, he'd get to know her better and find out the truth. Perhaps he'd change her mind about him, too.

Perhaps she wouldn't want to leave him, after all.

So before she could take another step, Raghnall blocked her way, bent his knees, and threw her over his shoulder. She gave out a surprised, furious squeal, and battered her fists against his back as she tried to free herself.

Raghnall stepped into the great hall and yelled, "Wifey and I are off to Tigh na Abhainn!"

Everyone looked up at him, and a surprised, pleased grin spread on Angus's face. Rogene's eyebrows crawled up to her hairline, and James frowned as he stared at them doubtfully. David, Raghnall noted, was snoring on a bench by the wall.

"No! Let me go!" Bryanna yelled.

Raghnall clapped her on her arse, which stuck up in the air above his shoulder. "'Tis just a wee game we newlyweds play. Ye ken how 'tis. She's excited."

With that, he nodded to Angus, who nodded back to him, squeezing Rogene's hand. She whispered something hotly into Angus's ear, throwing a concerned look at Raghnall. But Raghnall wouldn't wait to see if Rogene had an objection.

He had to leave before his bride ruined everything.

So under Bryanna's enraged yells, he hurried down the stairs, making his way towards the gate, as his wife's bright-violet purse banged his back with every step.

CHAPTER 8

"HOW COULD YOU HAVE DONE THAT?" Bryanna growled through her clenched teeth.

They'd been on the road for what felt like an eternity. They were riding through the hilly woods at the edges of the Highland mountains. The air was different here than around Eilean Donan —rich with the herbal scent of greenery, pines, moss, and flowers. It was quiet as the nature around them was getting ready for the night. Orange sunlight shone through leaves that rustled peacefully in the wind. Occasional flies and bees buzzed by, and birds called to each other.

If she hadn't been treated like a sack of potatoes and kidnapped by a Highlander with steel in place of muscles, she might even be enjoying herself, especially given that her sugar level had probably stabilized—she'd stopped shaking and feeling woozy.

Her back was pressed against his hard chest, her ass situated neatly between his thighs, and she felt something long and hard.

She was pretty sure it wasn't a wooden stick.

He held the reins on either side of her, and it was clear there wouldn't be any escape. She'd been contemplating the whole way how she could slip out of his grasp, and she had tried elbowing him in the stomach. But she was still weak from her high sugar levels, and he'd just grunted and chuckled, congratulating her on her attempt but warning her that he'd tie her hands if she tried it again.

"Sorry, lass," he said, surprising her with the softness in his voice again. "I'm nae in the habit of kidnapping women. But as much I'm nae enjoying being marrit to ye, I dinna have a choice."

"There's always a choice," she mumbled. "Your damned clan are all a band of kidnappers, aren't you? I screamed my throat out as you carried me out of the castle, and no one lifted a finger to stop a man carrying a woman clearly against her will."

He shifted behind her. "'Tis called loyalty, lass. And again, I am sorry for causing ye distress. I promise as long as ye stay in the estate and dinna try to escape, I wilna do such a thing again. And, of course, ye have my full protection."

She shook her head. "Wow. How noble of you. But I can't promise to stay put, Raghnall, I have to get back to Eilean Donan."

But as she said that, doubt crept into her mind... Did she really have to return immediately? If it would take days until the pile was cleared, and that vision she'd had of herself, dead and being carried by a Highlander at Eilean Donan... Actually, being away from the castle for a while probably wasn't a bad idea, especially since she still had her insulin pens.

Besides...minus the kidnapping and her anger with Raghnall, she was actually kind of excited. In just one day, she'd experienced the most adventure she'd ever had in her life. Part of her had always craved adventures, had always wanted to live a full life —a normal life.

A life where she could ride a horse, where she could do anything and be anyone.

Where she could be herself.

Exactly how she'd felt in front of the church in Dornie, marrying this man.

"Because of that rock?" said Raghnall. "Why do ye need to get to it?"

Could she tell him the truth? The truth she didn't understand fully herself. The truth that sounded insane.

Just like her psychic abilities would sound insane.

Yeah. There was a lot about her he didn't know...a lot no one knew. Would it be so bad if she told him the truth and dealt with his reaction later?

Gosh, it had been so much easier when she'd thought she was dreaming.

"Because what Amhladh said is true."

Behind her, his chest stopped moving. "What, that old story about the faerie rock and going to a different time?"

His voice was tense, taut like a guitar string. Did he believe her or not?

Her fists clenched around the horse's coarse mane. "Yes."

"Lass, do ye want to tell me ye're a stranger from another time?" His voice was cold and hard, like the sword on his belt— which she suddenly became very much aware of.

She wanted an adventure, right? Here she was, right in the middle of it.

She might not even die of diabetic shock. This man behind her might kill her before she had a chance.

But there was no backing up now. She had made her bed, all she had to do was lie in it. And she may have avoided dangers to her health because of her parents, but she wasn't a coward. "Yes. I am from another time."

Silence hung between them. After a while, as the horse continued walking forward and Raghnall still said and did nothing, Bryanna turned to look over her shoulder at him.

To find him staring straight at her, his black eyes wide but his gaze hard.

At least he wasn't laughing at her or ridiculing her. "That's why I need to get back there," she pressed. "I need to return home."

He winced and shook his head. "Lass, dinna take me for a fool."

"Trust me, Raghnall Mackenzie, I think many things of you, but a fool isn't one of them."

"Do ye expect me to believe faeries exist and there's magic and ye really are from another time—which time would that be exactly?"

She turned away from him and stared at the road in front of them. "The future. I came here from the year 2021."

The forest ended and opened up to a ravine, and the view took her breath away. The gray mountains of the Highlands were splotched with deep, brownish-green moss and vegetation. The silvery sky was endless, and rows and rows of mountains spread out to the horizon in all directions.

"Look how beautiful it is..." she whispered.

"I am," he said, but when she met his gaze again, he wasn't looking at the nature around them.

He was looking at her.

Their eyes locked, and she was gone, evaporated like a puddle under the Texas sun. She felt as weightless as air, drifting, soaring up and up.

Hold me, she thought, *or I'll be gone, dissolved in this breathtaking Scottish beauty, molten from the heat of your body and woven into the matter of this odd time. Hold me, or I'll disappear into nothingness between epochs and dreams.*

As though he'd heard her, he pulled the reins of the horse, bringing it to a halt. He jumped off the horse and stretched his arms to her. As if charmed, she fell into his arms, his hands sliding along her sides and up to her armpits, steadying her. When she stood on the ground, he didn't let go of her. The skin where his hands touched her body was burning, warm and tingly, as though charged with electricity.

He held her in his gaze for a while, and when his eyes dropped to her mouth, that feeling of evaporating came back, and she stopped breathing, waiting for him to lower his head and kiss her.

But he didn't.

Instead, he let her go and stepped back. "Ye wilna run from here," he said. "We're almost at Tigh na Abhainn, and ye wilna find yer way back to Eilean Donan by yerself. There's nowhere to run, lass, and nowhere to hide. Ye're mine before God and before men."

Ye're mine...

The words shot straight to her groin in a hot surge of desire.

"And as my wife, ye will tell me the truth."

He didn't believe her, after all. Should she be disappointed or elated? And this commanding tone... After all, he was a medieval man. He probably thought women were only good for raising children and sewing clothes.

"I don't owe you anything. As I told you several times, I don't want to be your wife. I don't want to be your anything."

Devils played in his eyes as an amused half smile spread across his lips. He grabbed her hand, bent her elbow, and put her arm behind her back, pushing her to him and locking her in a steely embrace. "What are ye hiding? Why do ye have to create a story as odd as traveling in time?"

She jerked, trying to free herself, but it was like trying to escape the embrace of a statue. "Let me go!"

"Ye ken, we already had an impostor just over one moon ago. The man appeared to be a friend, even saved my life. And yet, he was an enemy spy who tried to kill my family."

"I'm not a spy."

"Ye ken what I did to him?"

With his other hand, he searched somewhere and then with a quick movement, something cold and sharp bit against her throat.

"I'm guessing you killed him." She straightened her back.

"See, ye're a smart lass. So do ye understand how important

'tis that ye dinna insult me with some nonsense about time travel and faeries."

Good grief, he wasn't even joking. Every trace of warmth and admiration in his eyes was gone, and with a cold shock, she realized they were alone. If he truly believed she was a threat, he could kill her and throw her body off this mountain and tell his family she ran away. No one would ever know what had really happened to her.

He wasn't an honorable man. The darkness within him was real and life-threatening, and she'd be a fool to trust him or let herself have a crush on him.

This man knew death, and probably more intimately than she could ever imagine.

But she wasn't a damsel in distress, either. She may not know sword fighting, she may not even know self-defense, but she knew where every man's weak spot was. She'd show him not to threaten her.

It was an odd angle, but she got all her strength ready and kicked him right between the legs with all her might.

He grunted in pain and lowered the dagger. His grip weakened, and she tried to free her arm, but he was still stronger. Goddamn muscles of steel!

"Let me go! I'm not a threat, I'm not here to kill anyone, I just want to go home."

His face reddened, the muscles on his neck taut with pain. Part of her felt bad for him. He grunted, "Ye wicked minx, why do ye have to kick in the balls?"

"Because I won't let you threaten me. I won't let you stop me from going home. And I won't be your wife for much longer."

CHAPTER 9

WHEN THEY ARRIVED, Raghnall's groin was still aching.

But as the old walls of the tower house came into sight, he forgot the physical pain as memories flooded him. His father, the deceased laird Kenneth Og Mackenzie, had brought the family here in his last attempt to get his rebellious son under control. When fists and threats didn't help, he must have hoped that motivating a fourteen-year-old Raghnall with land and his own house might change something.

Only, land and wealth were never important to Raghnall. The four-story, rough-granite tower house with five household buildings made of timber and with thatched roofs didn't make him want to do anything but laugh in his father's face. How little his father knew him—none of them knew him, actually.

None of them knew that all he'd ever wanted as a child was their approval. For them to say that once in his life he'd done something right, that he'd been a worthy son and a beloved brother.

And not a changeling, a demon-child, switched with a true Mackenzie at birth.

That was where his early impulses to bring chaos, to challenge his father, to do the opposite of what a good lad would, came from.

Because it was better to be beaten than ignored. When he was bad he was important, even though the attention he received was mainly about shutting him up. He caused anger in his parents, not love, like Laomann, Angus, and even the quiet Catrìona.

He stopped counting how many times he'd heard, "One day ye'll be the death of someone!" because he'd started believing it.

The estate wasn't big. It was nestled in a valley at the foot of the mountain range right on the northwestern border of Kintail, on the shore of the River Croe. The mountains loomed above, as tall as giants and still green at this time of year. The estate had plenty of flat land, allowing for enough farming to sustain the lord of Tigh na Abhainn and the fifty or so tenants. Mostly, they had sheep and cows, as crops didn't grow as well on the rocky, harsh land as they would in the Lowlands, but oats and barley grew fine enough, and the sheep could graze anywhere. Raghnall's main business would be to sell raw wool, which was something the lord of this estate had done for generations. And he had good connections to clan MacDonald, the biggest and the richest clan in the west. They were sea merchants and would buy wool from him to resell it abroad.

Raghnall didn't care what he'd have to do. The main thing was, this place would be safe and prosperous enough to provide for Seoc. Perhaps he'd grow to enjoy the life of an estate lord one day and have a family right here, among the steep green slopes and the gurgling mountain river.

The sky darkened, the western horizon golden behind the angry clouds. The air here was different from the loch—the barely noticeable tang of the sea was gone, and it was crisp here, more of the scent of wildflowers and moss and rocks. The house was whitening against the greenery, smoky-gray in the dusk.

Goddamn his father for making him an outcast who became a reiver, which later caused the death of the only human being he'd thought could love him. Raghnall clicked his tongue and let the horse descend the rocky mountain path.

"Are we there?" asked the honey-haired minx who had first rubbed his cock with her delicious arse all through their journey and then kicked him right in the balls, making him blind with pain.

"Aye, we've arrived," he grumbled. "Rejoice."

He felt her still between his arms. Good Lord, her scent was in his nostrils the whole way, tickling his desire, making it hard to concentrate. He tried not to think of her, not to imagine that taste of hers—something citrusy like lemon or orange, the fruit that grew only in the south of Europe. He'd once tasted some when he'd pleasured a rich widow in the Lowlands. And the herbal-lilac scent of Bryanna's skin, would it taste as sweet if he licked her? How would that long, pretty hair feel wrapped around his fist as he made her come over and over and over around his hot, hard cock?

"Why would I rejoice?" she asked.

"Because 'tis where ye will live as my wife. All of this is yers."

She sighed. "This is breathtaking, but as I told you, as far as I'm concerned, I'm not your wife, and I never said I wanted this. You said something about needing this estate, and I wanted to help you."

He grunted and sighed out as the horse followed the path and turned left before a large bush. "What a good Samaritan. So ye're a time traveler from the future who marrit me because ye wanted to help me. A stranger ye just met... Aye, that sounds very believable."

To his surprise, she said nothing to that, and he imagined her bonnie, sulking face as she stared at the road. He wondered what she hid behind that story, and who she truly was.

If she were a spy, he couldn't imagine a worse cover than saying she was a time traveler. A true spy would come up with something like what Tadhg, Euphemia's last spy, had done—he had infiltrated the castle, pretending to be more wounded than he was, and poisoned Laomann and himself. So, what drove his new wife to tell such a strange story?

And what if...against all logic and his beliefs about reality... she told the truth?

Then everything about her would make sense—her clothes, her scent, the odd brightly colored purse she had with her, and even her speech. The accent, the things she told about herself—or didn't...

But he wasn't a fool, and he wasn't a child to believe odd stories of magic and faeries.

He'd find out what she was hiding sooner or later. She had nowhere to run from here.

As they passed by the farms with occasional farmhouses here and there, it was clear everyone had already finished their jobs for the night. The tiny, bare windows of the farmhouses glowed with the weak light of inexpensive tallow candles, and crickets chirped. An owl hooted from somewhere back in the trees, closer to the completely black shapes of the mountains against the indigo sky.

The river gurgled to their left as they proceeded to the white outline of the tower house. Raghnall thought distantly that the estate's name—house on a river—wasn't sophisticated by any means, but it suited the place well.

On the second floor, one of the narrow windows was glowing. Only the servants lived here now, maybe even just one. Without the lord, there was nothing much to manage, not a lot to cook, and no cleaning to be done, so there was probably just the housekeeper and a maid. Raghnall hadn't had a chance to ask Angus.

When the horse approached the tower, Raghnall jumped off. Supporting his wife as she slid down, he noticed yet again how narrow her waist was and how warm she felt through her elegant dress, which, even though beautiful, didn't compare to her natural beauty.

He tied the reins to the hitching post and banged on the

door of the tower house and looked up, waiting to see some movement up in the window. Moments passed, but nothing happened. Was there anyone around? The kitchen building was only six feet away, but judging by the lack of smoke coming out of the chimney, no one was there.

With her mysterious purse tucked under one armpit, Lady Bryanna looked around, rubbing herself from the cold. What he wouldn't give to look inside that purse. All answers to her secrets must be hiding there. He itched to come to her and wrap his cloak around her to keep her warm, but he stopped himself. She shouldn't assume he cared about her, so he didn't move a finger, even though he wanted to.

No one answered the door, so he repeated his banging, the heavy, iron hardware rattling. The door jumped off the frame from his effort.

"'Tis nae locked," he murmured, opening the door into the darkness.

He remembered the house well. Even without any light, he knew the scent of rot and mold that breathed onto him came from the storage space—just like in any keep.

He carefully walked through the darkness towards a weak light that came from up the wooden stairs. "Goddamn, is there nae housekeeper? Come on, lass, give me yer hand. Follow me."

He stretched his hand to her, and her small, warm, silky hand lay in his like it had always belonged there.

As he moved towards the stairs, he cursed himself. What was the point of liking her touch if he'd never be with her? She was a bad liar at worst and a madwoman at best.

When they reached the stairs, faint voices came from up above, and Raghnall took out his dagger just in case. As they climbed, the voices became louder and the light stronger. They reached a small landing with one door, and Raghnall saw the fireplace in the small lord's hall was still lit. The next landing would lead to a guest bedchamber.

As Raghnall and Bryanna kept climbing, he realized the

voices were actually moans and grunts of two people. The sounds were pained—or very much pleasured.

He let go of Bryanna's hand to be able to react faster. "Stay behind me, lass."

"I don't need you to protect me."

"Ye dinna ken what ye're talking about. Shush."

She gave out a slight gasp, but he ignored her and kept climbing. They passed the floor above the main hall where doors led to a clearly unoccupied chamber and climbed another flight of stairs. Finally, he stood before the door to the lord's bedchamber. It was half open, and the light and the stench of a tallow candle came from within.

"Stay back," Raghnall said and turned, expecting to see a worried look in her green eyes. Instead, they were blazing with ferocity and excitement.

There she was, that woman who'd come to him by the church, so full of joy she might as well have radiated light around her.

What was it that stopped her from casting that inner light? He had demons that haunted him...did she, too?

But then the sounds behind the door stopped, and her eyes widened in alarm. Before Raghnall could react, something heavy hit him on the back of his head and pain exploded in his skull with a flash of blinding light. And then everything went dark.

CHAPTER 10

BRYANNA JERKED HER HANDS, which were tied to the back of her chair.

"I'm telling you, he's the lord of the estate, Raghnall Mackenzie, and I'm his wife!"

The shirtless man, staring at her and the unconscious Raghnall, who was tied to another chair by her side, raised one eyebrow.

"Ye think she's telling the truth, Eanar?" asked the young woman, tying the straps of her simple, greenish-brown dress at the back of her neck.

Eanar narrowed his gaze at Bryanna and then at Raghnall, the wrinkling skin around his eyes showing he was older than he'd seemed at first, perhaps in his forties, despite a very impressive, muscular build. With a slightly crooked nose, he looked like an eagle.

"I dinna ken anything about Raghnall Mackenzie. He hasna been part of this clan for years."

Her heart ached for Raghnall, limp and defenseless, his head hanging. Even though she didn't know the whole story, she wasn't a traitor. And if she was Raghnall's wife now, she'd be loyal to her husband.

Better to choose the devil she knew, in any case.

She straightened her back. "He's back now, and he's the rightful lord of Tigh na Abhainn."

"He might be anyone." The man crossed his arms over his chest, his impressive biceps bulging. "An impostor. And so might ye. Why didna Laomann send word?"

Okay, there was a lot she didn't know about the clan's politics, but she knew more than this guy. "Laomann isn't the laird anymore," she said. "Angus is."

Eanar exchanged a look with the young woman. "Angus?"

"Seriously, how often do you guys get any news here?"

His sharp, eagle-like expression was replaced with doubt. "Nae so often, but we'd get news like this right away."

With doubt planted, she decided to go on the offense. "And who would you be?"

"I'm the tacksman."

The tack—who? But she couldn't ask without raising more doubt. It was clear he was someone who was in charge while the lord was absent. Like a vice principal, perhaps.

"I'm Teasag," said the woman.

Bryanna waited for her to explain her role, but she didn't proceed, so Bryanna said, "Right. You realize then that your lord won't be happy at how you treated him and me once he wakes up?"

"Remains to be seen if he's my lord or nae."

A movement from the side made her look at Raghnall. His eyes were open, and he was glaring at Eanar. "My name is Raghnall Mackenzie, and I am yer rightful lord. My father brought me here many years ago as a lad, trying to convince me to become an obedient son, and I only laughed into his face. For that, he beat me so hard, he broke my fingers so that this finger still doesna bend fully when I play the lute. He then chased me away and disinherited me. My brother Angus promised this estate back once I marrit someone. Here she is, my wife. And here I am, yer lord and the lord of these lands. Nae that I owe an explanation to ye."

The young woman touched Eanar's shoulder. "I think he's telling the truth, Eanar..."

Eanar was studying Raghnall with his eagle eyes, still unconvinced.

"I'd be a bad tacksman if I gave away the keys to the estate to every stranger who claims he's my lord."

Bryanna stared at Raghnall with wide eyes. She'd just found out more about him in under one minute than she had the whole day. He was chased away? He played lute? His father beat him as a child?

Her eyes dropped to his tied hands, and she wondered how she'd never noticed that broken finger that had never healed, and how it must have killed him to never be able to use it fully. And how he must love music if he learned to play even still.

Something she knew she'd do, too, in his place. Diabetes felt like a disability to her sometimes. Although she was fine now, having diabetes meant she had lower blood flow to her feet, and therefore she would be under an increased risk for neuropathy and getting her limbs amputated, eye problems, kidney disease, and a number of other complications. That was where her family's concern had come from. That was why she had made an agreement with Mom and Dad early on not to do horseback riding and other sports that would have a higher chance of an injury.

That was why she had felt her whole life as if she lived under a dome, like in that movie, *The Truman Show*.

Music had always been her lifeline. She'd been the lead singer in her school acapella group, had played guitar and piano. She'd hoped to have a real music career—being a singer, writing her own songs, and, hopefully, playing concerts. She'd wanted to live a big life, chase her dreams...

But after she'd gotten her diagnosis, the motto of her life had become play it safe.

It wasn't anything conscious, she supposed. She'd been diagnosed as a teenager, and it was natural that her parents took care of her. However, once she'd become an adult, she'd carried on in the same way. During the first years as a diabetic, she'd learned to put her parents' worries first, and she'd just never stopped.

So she'd become a music teacher and hadn't moved to a big city like she'd always dreamed. Staying home, next to her family, was playing it safe.

But now she was as far away as one could imagine—hundreds of years in the past. And there was no one except for herself to worry about her life and death, even if her mom and sister must be absolutely freaking out by now. So she needed to be strong.

She imagined she was the medieval lady everyone had thought she was and straightened her back. "Eanar, you're making a big mistake treating your lord like he's your enemy. Is that how you want to start your relationship with him?"

The man's eyes glistened in amused appreciation. He nodded. "If he *is* my lord, then nae."

Raghnall's gaze on her felt warm and made her whole body tingle. "Then untie us."

The man nodded in a gesture of compliance and moved behind Raghnall's chair. In a moment, Raghnall was on his feet and staring at Eanar like he wanted to burn him. "Wise," Raghnall said. "I'm coming here to stay and this wilna work if there's nae trust between the lord and his tacksman."

When Eanar said nothing, Raghnall moved behind Bryanna's chair and untied her.

"So," Raghnall said. "'Tis late. I dinna suppose ye have any supper left?"

"Aye," said Teasag. "There's still boiled mutton and yesterday's bread. I'll go and fetch it, Lord."

"My thanks," said Raghnall.

Bryanna stood up, rubbing her wrists, which were aching from the rough rope. She really did need to eat something, but she needed to check her sugar levels even more. And she had to find a quiet place where she'd be alone.

When Teasag disappeared through the dark doorway, Raghnall looked around. "'Tis the lord's bedchamber, aye?"

"Aye."

The room looked like it was well lived in. The bedding of the four-poster bed with a simple blue canopy and curtains gathered at the corners was crumpled, and the plain white sheets looked a little dirty at the foot. The pillows had dark-brown smudges, and Bryanna wondered when they'd last been washed. Some of the six chests that stood along the wall were open, and some clothes spilled from them. Another chest had grooming things—a mirror, which was essentially polished metal, a few combs that looked like they were made of ivory, and some sort of rough scissors.

"Well, there is another chamber," said Raghnall. "My wife and I will sleep there tonight but expect that ye and yer... woman...would get this chamber freed for us on the morrow."

Eanar crossed his arms over his muscular chest. "If ye're the real lord here, aye. Ye may have this bedchamber on the morrow. I'll send a lad to Eilean Donan with the first light to make inquiries."

Raghnall nodded. "We'll find our own way to the bedchamber. I trust ye will take care of my horse?"

Eanar's jaw worked, but he nodded and left the room. Bryanna let out a long breath of relief. The confrontation with Eanar made her feel like she and Raghnall were a team, like she could trust him, even though they had quite a few unresolved questions between them. His dark eyes searched her. "Are ye all right, lass? They didna hurt ye while I was out?"

And even though he didn't trust her and didn't believe her about time travel, he still worried about her. Something in her chest melted. No matter what, circumstances made him the closest person she had in this strange, medieval world.

"Thanks...yes. I just need to use a toilet."

He nodded to a small door. "There's a privy there. I'll wait."

When she opened the door, there was a tiny room—a closet, more like—with a sitting platform and a big hole in the middle of it. A bunch of hay lay near it.

She did her business first, and wiping with hay was...interesting. She cleaned her hands with the antibacterial hand wipes she always had with her.

Then she quickly did her test. It showed 156 mg/dL. Her blood sugar had climbed, but she could still wait with her insulin. Normally, she'd have taken the shot if she was in the twenty-first century, but she needed to save her insulin here.

She put her things back into her purse and walked out of the latrine, feeling lighter and calmer, only to find Raghnall pacing the room. He looked her up and down. "Ye took yer time."

And, again, from someone who showed care and compassion, he'd turned to a cold, temperamental jerk.

She gave him a hard glare and walked out of the room to the dark stairs. "Excuse me for taking my first time in private since this morning."

Pale orange light flickered on the stairs, coming from behind her. Raghnall must have taken the candle that stank like old, putrid animal fat. "One flight down is our bedchamber," he said behind her.

"Our bedchamber?" she asked, climbing down.

"Aye. Our. Ye're my wife."

His wife... Something hot and quick rushed through her. Husbands and wives shared a bed...

"So ye will sleep in my bed. Unless ye want to sleep in the cowshed," he added.

Stepping onto the dark landing, she scoffed. "If anyone is going to sleep in the cowshed, it'll be you, my friend."

He walked around her with the candle in his hand and opened the single door on the floor. The candle illuminated a room the same size as the one upstairs with a double bed. It also had a four-poster canopy, but unlike the bed upstairs, this mattress was bare. It was actually several thin mattresses on top of one another, she saw. A large blanket was folded neatly and lay at the end of the bed. Several pillows without cases were at the head. There was also a gigantic barrel with stairs, which, Bryanna guessed, must serve as a bath.

There were no embroideries, no decorations, and just a single table with two chairs in the middle of the room.

"This will do," Raghnall said, entering the room. He lit several more candles and it started to even look cozy. She looked around dubiously.

"No it won't. I'm not going to sleep with a stranger."

He undid his belt and took several of his leather purses from it. "Suit yourself, lass." He stretched out on the bed, putting his hands behind his head and letting out a long, satisfied grunt. "I'm nae going anywhere. I'm home and ye have no idea what it cost me to get here. I had to marry ye."

She gave an outraged laugh, but he didn't react, watching her with a calm, amused expression from under his long black eyelashes, curious at her next move.

CHAPTER 11

SOMEONE KNOCKED BEHIND BRYANNA, and Teasag entered with two trenchers, one in each hand, and put them on the table. There were some sort of oatcakes, as well as bread and pieces of boiled meat, parsnips, and a bowl of something that looked like gray dishwater with grains floating in it. There were also two clay cups. Behind her, Eanar emerged with a clay jar and put it on the table next to the cups.

"I'll make yer bed, Lord," said Teasag.

"Teasag..." said Eanar in warning.

"What? He's the lord, I can tell," she said, smiling at Raghnall, and something about her flirtatious, submissive tone set outrage burning in the pit of Bryanna's stomach. Was the woman really flirting with her husband? Especially when she was right there, in the same room.

Suddenly, Bryanna really wanted Eanar and Teasag to leave. She shouldn't care who flirted with Raghnall. And she shouldn't fight his battles. He was no one to her. "If you show me where the bedsheets are, I'll do it myself."

She felt everyone's eyes on her. They all froze for a moment. "Ye, Lady?" said Teasag. "But ye're..."

Right, she wasn't supposed to offer to make beds, was she? Her high status and whatnot.

"Just hurry up, Teasag." Raghnall went and sat at the little round table. "My wife and I canna wait to be alone. After all, 'tis our wedding night."

As he stretched out his long, muscular legs, his tunic tightened over the hard muscles of his chest. *Hot damn...* Bryanna's heart skipped a tiny beat. How could this man emanate this aura of power and danger? How could he make the words *wedding night* sound like the dirtiest, most carnal thing he'd ever said?

While Teasag and Eanar set about making the bed, Bryanna took the chair across the table from him. He poured something that smelled like beer into their cups and handed one to her. He cut the meat with the small eating knife and put a piece in his mouth. As he chewed, his eyes glistened in the dim light of the tallow candle, never moving away from hers.

A shiver ran through her from the impact of something she saw there. She didn't remember ever feeling anything like this—a desire to sit on his lap and rub against him like a cat.

And that was exactly the reason she shouldn't. He had too much sex appeal, too much of that macho-something going on. And she was not the only woman who felt it.

The proof was Teasag, who was making the bed and yet throwing glances full of meaning at Raghnall, even with her lover or husband, or whoever Eanar was to her, in the same room.

Bryanna had to eat, so she followed Raghnall's example and cut a piece from the cold boiled meat and the bread and chewed. They weren't particularly delicious. There was no salt, just the intense flavor of the mutton. The bread was coarse and dry, and her jaw ached from chewing it.

But it was food and it would make her feel better, so that was all she needed. When Teasag and Eanar left the room, she didn't feel relieved. On the contrary, the room suddenly shrank to the size of a shoebox. All the air disappeared from the space and the vacuum between them sparked with electricity.

They were alone. The fire in the fireplace crackled and the candles gave soft bursts of flame as fire ate into more of the fat.

He was so strong, she remembered suddenly. So strong he could easily do anything he wanted with her. If he intended this marriage to be consummated, he'd do just that, whether she wanted it or not. She remembered the muscles of steel that had kept her steady on the horse, his powerful arms as he'd lifted her like she weighed nothing. His scent—leather and steel and that earthy, piney whiff of a man—brought a deep longing within her.

He emptied his cup down his throat and took the last bite of bread from his trencher when another knock sounded and Teasag stuck her face in. With a sweet smile, she showed them something through the dark space between the door and the doorframe.

"Ye said something about a lute, Lord..." She cleared her throat and coughed nervously, then stepped in, holding a musical instrument. "There was one back in the storage, but no one kens how to play it around here... Um..." She took a few apprehensive steps towards him. "Mayhap ye'd like this?"

Raghnall's face lost all expression. He straightened in his chair and held both hands out for the lute as if it was a baby.

As if it was a treasure.

He wiped the dust off its surface with his bare hand, slowly, as though he was caressing skin.

"My thanks," he said with a raspy voice. "'Twas the only gift my father had ever given me."

Teasag's cheeks flushed in delight. "Oh! Would ye play something, Lord? Please?"

He cleared his throat, his expression soft, innocent, his eyes wet and glistening. He wasn't a medieval warrior anymore, as deadly as a razor blade in the wrong hands, but a boy who'd just touched a wonder.

"Aye," he said, wiping the rest of the dust off the lute, "I think I will. Only, I need a quill."

He looked up at her, and Teasag's lips spread in a wide grin, showing two long front teeth that made her look like an excited squirrel. "I'll fetch it, Lord."

When she disappeared, he sighed and looked at Bryanna with a crooked half smile. "I dinna really need a quill to play. There are nae such luxuries on the road, and I learned to play it with just my fingers."

The anticipation of what was about to happen tightened her stomach. He didn't want Teasag here while he played, but did he want her?

"I can leave you..." she offered, though without much enthusiasm. "I understand what it's like to want to be alone with your instrument."

As he ran his hands over the strings, he studied her as though he was seeing her for the first time in his life. "Ye do? Do ye play?"

"Yes, but not lute..."

He nodded and began tuning the lute. The sounds were softer than what she was used to from the steel or nylon strings of a guitar, and she wondered what these strings were made of—perhaps animal guts. Finally, when he was satisfied with the tuning, he arranged the fingers of his left hand to create a chord, then ran the fingers of his right hand over the strings, producing a sad, beautiful sound...the beginning of a ballad, perhaps.

And then, one chord after another, a slow, melancholy melody was born from his lute, and Bryanna stilled, mesmerized.

But when he opened his mouth and a deep, rich voice took over, she must have stopped breathing.

Or living altogether.

Because nothing else existed but his voice and his words.

THERE LIVED A MAN IN A KINTAIL HOUSE,
   A man with a hole in his chest.

He searched for a heart to fill the hole,
But all he found was dust.
Ohh, all he found was dust.

WHILE HE PLAYED SOMETHING LIKE A PRE-CHORUS, BRYANNA'S blood tingled as though a draft of unbearable cold had just taken over the room.

HE PUT THERE GOLD AND HE PUT THERE SILVER,
and he put there much, much wine,
But only true love of a bonnie lass
Made him feel alive.
Ohh, made him feel alive.

BRYANNA'S HEART DRUMMED, BEATING PAINFULLY AGAINST HER rib cage. He was singing about himself, she knew. That voice...so much richness, so much emotion... He was the man with no heart. But who was the bonnie lass who made him feel alive? Did he still love her?

BUT THE BONNIE LASS COULDNA KEN
That he'd never be her love.
All he'd brought upon her fate
Was fire, ash, and demise...

HIS VOICE SHOOK AND THE LAST LINE CAME OUT SLOW AND quiet.

"Ohh...fire, ash, and demise."

Bryanna wiped away her tears when he slowly looked up and

met her gaze. Pure agony was thundering in his eyes' dark depths. "I hope ye are from another time and leave soon, lass. Death follows me like a cloak but 'tis others that get hurt. I hope ye wilna be one of them."

CHAPTER 12

THE NEXT DAY...

ACH, NAE!

Standing with her back to Raghnall, Bryanna was petting his horse's mane with one hand while checking the saddle with the other as though she was preparing to ride.

"Ye're nae going anywhere!" Raghnall barked, marching through the courtyard of Tigh na Abhainn towards her.

She turned her head to him, frowning, her honey-colored hair streaming down her straight back. There it was, the delicate, thin curve of her waist under the old dress that Teasag had found for her. The curve of her hip that he'd ached to touch the whole night. She'd been lying right by his side in the same bed, and he'd been staring at her thin silhouette, illuminated by the moonlight that fell on her from the slit window of their bedchamber...and he'd been burning for her.

Burning and trying to restrain himself from reaching out and stroking that feminine curve with the tip of his finger, hearing her moan or sigh in pleasure, then turning her around on her back so that she faced him, and covering her mouth with his...

He'd barely slept all night, but he'd sworn he wouldn't do anything she didn't want him to, and he knew she'd come to him herself.

That was, if she didn't escape before then.

He stopped before her. She met his eyes with the same fierceness he'd seen before. "I'm not trying to escape." She petted the horse. "Just saying hello to this beautiful animal."

"As though I'm going to believe ye."

Her shoulders slumped, just a little. "I don't know how to ride, anyway."

He looked her up and down. "Ye dinna ken how to ride? But noble ladies are usually taught…"

He trailed off, remembering the nonsense she'd told him about being from another time. The nonsense he refused to believe.

"Even better, then." He turned to walk away, but her voice stopped him.

"Can you teach me?"

Normally, he'd say of course nae, he wouldn't teach her. He wouldn't give her a means to escape from him and ruin his plans.

But there was something in her voice. A vulnerability…a hope…a trust… An extended hand that he just couldn't refuse.

And so despite his better judgment, he looked at her and said, "Aye."

The smile that lit up her face was worth it. It was as though the sun had returned to a dark world, and she was shining with joy from within.

"Really?" She swallowed. "Oh, thank you so much, that really means a lot. I've always wanted to, always thought I'd enjoy it, but my parents didn't allow me…"

He slowly walked to her and took the reins of his horse and led it into the small pasture that was behind the house. "They didna? Why?"

She walked beside the horse. "Being overprotective, I

suppose. They always said they were afraid I'd fall and break my neck."

He chuckled. "Aye, 'tis always a possibility. Are those parents of yers from the future, too?"

Her face cooled. "Look, if you don't believe me, then let's just not talk about it. I have nothing more to say to convince you and I don't want to lie."

Raghnall nodded. He had secrets of his own he'd rather not talk about. He'd never told anyone that Mòrag's death was on his hands. That had he not let Daidh the reiver go, Mòrag would still be alive. No one knew but him and Seoc—it was the dark, heavy past that they shared, that united them in a perverse way. What would Bryanna think of him if she found out?

And he, a fool, had pretty much told her with his ballad. That music, the melody, and the words had haunted him for months after the fire. He'd gone to war and fought for the Bruce after it happened. He remembered lying in the grass, covered with his cloak, looking into the endless, starlit sky, surrounded by the warriors just like him, and playing that melody in his head, tears of grief—hot and burning and silent—rolling down his temples. And in the rare moments when he was alone, he'd picked up his small lute, beaten and uneven, and played, humming that melody.

And it made it better.

Drop by drop, it had allowed him to let the poison of heartache pour into the words, into the music...and not to die of guilt.

He'd been thinking of letting a sword pierce him in the next battle, to end his suffering, his undeserving life. Who cared if he lived or died, anyway?

But then he'd thought of Seoc, and of his promise to Mòrag. And he'd kept going.

Once the grief had subsided to the level where he could think more clearly, the plan had emerged in his head.

To go back to Eilean Donan, now that his father was dead. To take his estate back.

And to present Seoc as his son and give the lad the future he deserved.

To fulfill his promise to his dead beloved.

Bryanna and Raghnall reached the pasture, and the sheep looked at them with their strange eyes, bleating worriedly. Raghnall picked a place where the horse would have enough space to walk and gallop. He helped Bryanna get into the saddle, and as always, as he touched her legs to help her up, it was like he brushed against liquid silk that burned him.

She looked beautiful on the horse, her back straight, her cheeks rosy, lips dark and red in a bright smile of delight. Her hair shone and played in the sun, an instrument strummed by the wind.

As he gave her instructions, and she listened to him with curiosity and interest, he couldn't help but let himself relax. Just for now, just for today, he was home. In this moment, when there was just the horse, and him, and the bonnie lass who made the ache in his chest loosen up, there was no past and there was no future.

There was just now.

He didn't know how much time passed, but soon, Bryanna could even let the horse trot. She got it to listen to her well. Raghnall became lost in her smiles and in her laughter and questions. She loved it. He could tell because her joy infected him, leaving him feeling warm, as though touched by the sun.

When they walked the horse back towards the stables, she laughed. "My backside hurts, is that normal?"

His gaze grazed over her, landing on the body part in question. "Yer arse, ye mean, Lady Bryanna?"

"Well, if you put it that way, yes, my arse. Do you remember when you learned riding? Was it the same for you?"

He chuckled as the memory of him and his father flooded

him. "Aye, 'twas, and, surprisingly, 'tis one of the rare good memories I have of my father."

"Oh, really? How old were you?"

"Dinna ken." He let the horse stop before the water trough next to the hitching post and the animal began drinking. "Mayhap six or seven."

"So young?"

Raghnall patted the animal's long mane as it drank, the hair coarse, warm from its body heat. "'Tisna young, lass. 'Tis how 'tis done. He was surprisingly kind and even looked proud of me. Constantly told me how I'm definitely his son because I took up horse riding so quickly—quicker than all his other sons, and I was the youngest of them." Raghnall turned to her and put one hand on the hitching post. "The bastart could do it so well. He could be so misleadingly kind, and the next moment, he'd stab ye in the back by criticizing ye. And if ye didna agree, he'd make sure ye kent there was either his way or the fists. And that ye were nae worth a slug's shite."

Bryanna's hand covered his, and the touch sent a small jolt of awareness through him, something sweet and prickly and delicious. Her beautiful eyes were big and green in the semidarkness of the stables. "I'm so sorry, Raghnall. No one deserves a parent like that."

Raghnall swallowed hard. How could she do that? Get into his heart just with one touch and a few words, making him all warm and melting?

He shouldn't let her. He withdrew his hand from under hers and stepped back. "'Tis all right, lass. The man is dead, thank God, and I'm back in the clan. My past is my own to carry." He looked at the horse, which stopped drinking and raised its head.

"Who was she?" The question came soft, but the impact of hearing it hit him like a hammer.

He froze. "What?"

"Who was she, the woman from your song?"

He looked at her, not sure what to say. She'd caught him so easily, so unexpectedly.

His first reaction was to deny everything, and he opened his mouth to do just that.

But, surprisingly, part of him wanted to tell her. Wanted to open that door into the dark corners of his soul and let her light shine there, chase the darkness away, and warm him. Heal him.

But no. He'd lived this way for years. He couldn't trust her, couldn't let himself get close to her. He'd only hurt her in the end.

He lifted the reins back over the horse's head and put one foot in the stirrup. "Ye had yer fun and rode him, but I still need to visit my tenants and show them I have arrived."

Knowing he'd been dismissive, he mounted the horse. This was for the best, he thought as he put distance between himself and Bryanna. Even if he opened up to her, it wouldn't change his past.

And not even the sun itself could light up his dark soul.

CHAPTER 13

Two days later...

THE SCOTTISH HIGHLANDS ROLLED IN FRONT OF BRYANNA AS far as she could see. God, could anyone ever get used to this view? The endless, leaden sky, the colors of rust, moss, and yellow ochre spilling over mountains dotted with dark patches of pine trees.

And would she have ever seen this beauty back in the twenty-first century? Would she ever have allowed herself to go into the deep wilderness of Scotland with nothing except for a purse with three insulin pens?

Never.

Bonnie, the horse she was mounted on, snorted peacefully and lowered its head to the ground to graze. Raghnall's horse, standing next to hers, did the same, and the soft sound of ripped grass added to the gentle whooshing of the wind in Bryanna's ears.

"Ye've done well, lass," Raghnall said, gazing at the view. "I didna think ye'd be able to go this far."

She chuckled. "Thanks."

His profile was calm, the strong, straight nose, the deep-set, beautiful dark eyes under thick eyebrows. She'd never noticed, but when he smiled with his eyes, the small wrinkles at their corners made him look ten years younger, and his soul ten pounds lighter.

"We can ride down this way." He gestured at a thin path down the slope among the rocks and boulders. "There's the last homestead I havena visited as the new lord. We can have a meal there, on the shore of the river."

Her stomach tightened at the prospect of letting the horse go down the steep path, but she knew she could do it. And she trusted Bonnie. Bryanna clapped on the mare's neck gently. "We ladies stick together. We can do it."

Raghnall nodded and gave her a few tips on how to act, and then he led the way. Bryanna's breath caught as Bonnie's hooves slipped on a rock one time and sent a small shower of rubble down the steep slope, but the mare was able to recuperate and calmly proceeded down the barely visible path. They passed small patches of short grass, heather, wildflowers, and moss-covered rocks. After the steepest part of the path, the decline lessened, and Bonnie could walk easier and faster.

Soon, they were arriving at a simple croft—a stone house with a thatched roof, a cowshed, a barn, and a toolshed. A man, a woman, and three children between the ages of twelve and sixteen were working in a small field, gathering the dried hay with pitchforks and throwing it into heaps. A teenage boy stood atop one heap, picking up the hay thrown at him and tossing it onto the top.

"God bless!" called Raghnall.

The people stopped working and stared at them, frowning.

"Are ye the new lord?" asked the man.

He was in his forties, a graying, shaggy beard sticking out on all sides.

Raghnall stopped his horse and jumped off. "I am. And this is my wife, Lady Bryanna Mackenzie. Ye must be Odhran. 'Tis what Eanar told me."

In the past two days, Eanar had gotten confirmation that Raghnall was the lawful lord of Tigh na Abhainn. Despite how Raghnall disliked the man because of his initial mistrust, he had managed to talk to him and ask about the tenants.

"Aye. I remember ye as a lad. Ye came here with yer father, the old laird."

Raghnall nodded, giving a small smile. "Aye."

"Ye were a wee rascal, were ye nae?"

"My father kept reminding me of that."

"Aye, yer father wasna an easy man."

Bryanna's heart squeezed as she heard that. She knew it was hard for Raghnall, and it broke her heart that his father hadn't treated his son with the love and appreciation that hers had always shown her. They seemed to have had opposite child-hoods. While she had been completely overprotected, he had been abused and neglected.

"Aye, but he's long dead, and I came to get my rightful estate. I wanted to introduce myself and ask how yer farm is doing and if ye need anything."

Appreciation lit up Odhran's gray eyes and he scratched his head. "'Tis certainly something different than I had expected. Thank ye, Lord. We farm oats, as ye see, 'tis a small field and only lets us feed my family and the animals. Our main source of income is, of course, sheep." He gestured at the low rising slopes of the nearby mountain where Bryanna saw gray and brown sheep grazing. "Wool, mostly. We do need the wool scissors sharpened and one fixed..."

As Odhran and Raghnall walked into the barn, Bryanna descended from the horse and smiled at the woman and the kids, who offered her tentative smiles, also.

The woman approached her as the kids resumed throwing the hay. "My name is Eamhair, mistress. Welcome to our modest homestead. May I offer ye a trout? My son caught three this morning and my youngest daughter is just roasting them for the midday meal. Ye came at the right time."

Bryanna smiled. "Thank you, that would be very kind. We have some bread and cheese and boiled eggs we can share with you."

When Raghnall and Odhran returned, both looked satisfied with each other, which made Bryanna smile. She shouldn't care, but she wanted to see Raghnall respected and loved by his people. After years in exile, it would be nice if he was accepted in his homeland again.

They shared the meal inside Odhran and Eamhair's house. There was just one room, which included a hearth and two big beds that, Bryanna suspected, the family shared. Probably, the children slept in one bed and their parents in the other.

The floor was covered in reeds and hay, and there was a weaving loom. The big table they sat at had benches on both sides. There were several chests that stood in the corners of the house, for storage. The open door gave the only source of light, but Bryanna didn't feel claustrophobic. Clearly, these people weren't rich, but there was no doubt they were happy. The warm gazes that Odhran and Eamhair gave each other and the friendly bickering between the children warmed Bryanna's heart.

The trout was amazing—there was nothing like freshly caught fish, she thought.

Raghnall's dark gaze was heavy on her skin, and she stopped and whispered, "What is it?"

He shrugged and put a small piece of fish into his mouth. "I like watching ye eat."

A blush burned her cheeks. "What? Why?"

"'Tis like ye havena eaten fish in yer life."

"Not like this!" She chuckled. "This is amazing," she told the family, and the children exchanged pleased glances. Perhaps a compliment from the lord's wife meant a great deal to them.

Supermarket fish didn't taste half as good. Often it was

farmed fish full of hormones and transported frozen, so it had a strong fishy flavor and lost its natural juiciness.

This trout didn't even need much seasoning. The crisp, fatty goodness had just a touch of woodsmoke and the tender taste of nature. She wouldn't need to worry much after meals like these, with no sugar and salt and only organic ingredients, this was as healthy as it could get.

"Then I'll catch ye trout every day of my life if it makes ye smile like that," Raghnall whispered, and fireflies began buzzing at the bottom of her stomach.

At the end of the meal, Raghnall and Bryanna thanked the family. Raghnall went to the horses, but Bryanna stopped him. "Can we stay here for a bit? Ride some more along the river? We don't have to return now, do we?"

Raghnall looked around. "I suppose so. Ye still want my company, lass?"

Heat crept up to her cheeks again. She didn't have the courage to tell him she didn't think she'd ever get tired of his company. "If you want mine..."

He chuckled. "Of course I want yers."

She climbed onto the saddle, feeling awkward under his attentive gaze. Then they let the horses walk down the shore. It was so beautiful here, just like Tigh na Abhainn, but even wilder. Here, it felt as if they were alone, cushioned by the tall mountains from two sides, and the river at their feet. The fresh scent of the clear water reached her nose as it gurgled quietly.

Heartache stabbed at her chest. "You know, I can just imagine you living here for years and years. Hopefully, your clan war will be finished soon, and you can just relax. Go fishing. Grow vegetables. It's so peaceful and beautiful... A simple life."

Only, he would live it without her. So she should enjoy this while she could.

Raghnall stopped his horse, got down, and helped her down, too. He laid his cloak on the border between the grass and gravelly beach of the river. When they sat down, he circled his knees with his arms and looked at her. "When ye say 'ye' ye mean ye and me both, aye?"

She didn't, of course she didn't. "I wish I did. You know, my life back home is so monotonous. Every day, I do my work, I go home. I might meet a few friends, but even though I'm a grown woman, I feel like I should always let my mom know when I'll be home because she'd worry..."

She wasn't sure how much detail she should tell him, since he didn't even believe she was from the future. Would he understand it if she told him she loved interacting with her students and giving them the gift of music? How she adored when they all could play their instruments and produce a beautiful melody? When they all became one through the music?

Her very soul buzzed with pride and excitement when a normally shy student would open up as they performed. She could relate to that.

That part, she liked.

But she wondered why she supported her students but never herself. Week after week, she watched *The Voice* and wished to apply for the program and maybe get noticed.

But she never did. Instead, she'd chat with her friends about their marriages, their children, and feel like she was living someone else's life.

"You know," she said. "I haven't had this feeling for a long time."

His dark eyes glistened. The wind picked up a strand of his hair that had escaped his long ponytail and brought it to her cheek, tickling her. "What feeling?" he asked.

"Like I'm right where I'm supposed to be."

He blinked, the tension in his face melted away, and he looked younger again. Something darkened in his eyes, and he leaned forward to her.

"Then this is what is supposed to happen."

As if in slow motion, his lips found hers. It was a soft kiss at first, tender. But the moment his scent was in her nose, and the taste of his lips reached her tongue, the gentleness, the tenderness turned into something more. An avalanche of want, a hunger for him that felt like fire in her belly. She deepened the kiss. This place, this man, the peacefulness and adventure, the sense that she had finally arrived, filled her with an ache, and he was the only cure. She wrapped her arms around his neck and felt the iron clasp of his arms around her waist, bringing her closer to him.

Raghnall Mackenzie was like Scotland. Rough and difficult but so gorgeous and warm he was worth risking being lost in the wilderness.

But was he worth dying for?

He pulled away, breathless. His gaze as dark as the depths of a starless night, he said, "Lass, yer kisses are testing my restraint..."

She swallowed and leaned back, biting her lip. "I didn't mean to. I just got caught up in the moment... Let's just go back to Tigh na Abhainn."

He nodded, the damn perfect gentleman, and gave her his hand, helping her to stand. "Aye, let's go, lass. But if ye think that this is over, ye're wrong. We're just getting started."

CHAPTER 14

TWO DAYS LATER...

BRYANNA PULLED ON THE REINS AND LET THE HORSE COME TO a halt before Raghnall. As it had many times during the past few days, her heart did something odd in her chest, that little jump that she'd never felt before with anyone—like she'd just dove off a cliff into the vastness of the sea and was weightless.

Soaring.

She beamed at him, and he cocked his eyebrow in return and didn't smile. But his eyes sparkled, gleaming. That was his way of smiling, she knew, in response to her.

There was still that darkness within him, something related to the woman from that ballad he'd sung to her on the night they arrived here.

And she couldn't get that out of him.

As she jumped off the horse and into his arms, there was that moment again, like always, when he caught her and held her close, towering over her like a mountain. She thought for a moment he might kiss her, and she knew she'd let him. Since their kiss by the river, despite the constant danger of her suddenly developing hyperglycemia, strangely, she'd never felt safer, more alive, and more present than she did with him here in Tigh na Abhainn.

Even though he was sulking and never let her out of his sight. And she loved it. That feeling that she was in the right place at the right time continued, but she realized it wasn't about the place.

It was about the man.

Something about him made her feel calm and optimistic, like everything was finally all right in the world. Even though, realistically, it was the opposite. She was in the wrong time, in the wrong place, and with the wrong man.

She needed to be back in the twenty-first century, somewhere near a hospital, and making sure her mom and her sister knew where she was and that she was fine.

"Enjoyed yer ride?" asked Raghnall, not letting her go. She rubbed his shoulder, steely under the indigo linen tunic, with her thumb and tightened her lips so that they wouldn't spread into the most ridiculous smile.

"I did." She met his eyes and felt as if she swam in their depths, light-headed and warm and fuzzy. "Maybe next time we can go even farther into the mountains? It's so beautiful here, I want to see more of—"

"Lord!" The cry came from far off, and the drum of horse hooves followed it. "Lord!"

When she turned, there was a rider approaching at full speed from the northwestern side of the river. Raghnall let her go and stood between her and the stranger, shielding her. His hand landed on the sword at his belt in a casual way, but his body tensed and there was no doubt in her mind that he'd react fast if he had to.

The horse galloped closer, and it was clear it was exhausted, poor animal, with foam forming at its mouth.

"They're coming!" the rider cried as he approached. "An army, from the northwest!"

Raghnall sputtered an oath under his breath.

Bryanna stepped forward. Raghnall's face was pale. "Who's coming, the Ross clan?"

Raghnall left his hand hanging by his side. "Aye, the Ross clan."

The rider brought the horse to a halt, and the beautiful animal nodded its head repeatedly, breathing heavily, glistening with sweat. "Poor thing, it needs to drink." She could trust herself enough now to take the horse by the bridle and lead it to the trough. "Come, sweetheart, it's okay."

"Aye, I ken I drove the poor beast hard, but it couldna wait. Lord Angus did right to put the net of sentinels up north to give enough time to prepare. A man came with the news this morn. They've camped two days away in Ross."

As Bryanna let the horse drink, she looked back at the man, hanging on to every word, her heart drumming hard in her chest.

Raghnall handed a waterskin to the man. "How many?" Raghnall asked while the messenger drank.

The man finished and wiped his mouth with the back of his sleeve, still breathing hard. "A thousand, Lord."

"A thousand," Raghnall said and spat on the ground. "Vengeful bitch. She really means to destroy us, doesna she?"

He looked back at Bryanna, his mouth twisted in a pained grimace. Then he looked around the estate and shook his head. "Tigh na Abhainn is on the enemy's way to Eilean Donan. We canna hold this against a thousand, nae with fifty farmers."

Bryanna gently clapped the horse on its side, taking comfort from its presence. A medieval war was coming—swords and arrows...and blood. What could she do? It seemed her adventure here was coming to an end. She had to return to her time. If she stayed any longer...it was very possible she would die here.

The image of her body in the arms of a bloodied warrior flashed through her mind.

"We must retreat," said Raghnall. "Everyone, all my tenants, everyone from Tigh na Abhainn. Take everything we can carry, all horses and all weapons and every piece of food. All valuables. We'll be stronger as one, in Eilean Donan, which has proper defenses and trained warriors." He met Bryanna's eyes. "We must return now, lass. It seems yer wish is coming true."

Bryanna nodded, her heart still squeezing in worry but also sadness to end this time with him.

Raghnall turned to the rider. "Thank ye, man, but it seems yer journey isna over yet. Take a fresh horse and ride to Eilean Donan, and tell my brother what ye told me. And that we're coming, too."

"I'll bring you something to eat," said Bryanna as she hurried into the kitchen.

When the man had eaten and left, Raghnall informed Eanar and Teasag about the plan and asked Eanar to ride around to the farms and to tell everyone to pack everything they had and prepare to leave today.

It took several hours for people to prepare. With somber faces, they abandoned their livestock and fresh harvests of barley and oats, their only livelihood. Children, old people, and pregnant women sat on top of sacks and barrels in wooden carts. Pitchforks, axes, and the odd sword and spear stuck from the piles of things. The rest of the people walked or rode ponies and horses.

Bryanna saw the worry behind the mask of confidence on Raghnall's face as they rode side by side. A long line of people and carts followed them along the hilly road of the Highlands. As the hills and valleys spread around them like a giant blanket, she swallowed hard, suddenly feeling light-headed. She hadn't had much of a lunch, just a piece of bread.

"Are you okay, Raghnall?" she asked.

He glanced at her quickly, frowning. "Aye, lass, 'tis nae me that ye need worry about."

"I mean, you just got your lands back, right? And now you have to abandon them."

His jaw muscles moved. "If this is my land, 'tis my responsibility as the lord to make sure my people are safe." His eyes darkened. "That my wife is safe."

His voice broke on the last word, and Bryanna frowned. There it was again, that ache, that pain she'd heard in his song. And he had no idea how dangerous everything was for her here. Being in a world with no insulin readily available was life-threatening for her. Not to mention the additional dangers of the war.

"I'm sure I'm perfectly safe with you," she said. "And your tenants are lucky to have you as their lord. Your first thought was about them."

He snorted. "My brother was right. If he wanted to educate me about responsibility, here I am. The responsible lord."

They rode for hours, and the longer they kept going, the surer Bryanna was that she was really not doing well. The symptoms of high blood sugar were crushing on her from all sides. The thirst, the dizziness, the headache, the weakness, the muscle tremors. She needed to get tested, but she couldn't stop the whole procession just for her sake.

She asked Raghnall for water and drank everything from his waterskin, getting odd looks from him. When the darkening woods and hills around her began swimming, and she felt like she was about to slip from the horse, they stopped to give the horses a rest and to eat.

When she tried to stand up in the stirrups to put one leg over the horse's back, all she could do was slip to her side. She tried to hold herself up by clenching the reins, but she was only clasping the empty air. The dark ground was heading straight at her when strong arms caught her and she was pressed against a hard chest, and the most mouthwatering aroma of man and pine and musk was in her nostrils.

"Lass, ye're unwell," Raghnall murmured in her ear as he set her on the ground. "Some water? Wine?"

"No...my purse."

He crouched on the ground in front of her. "Yer purse is on yer shoulder, lass."

"Oh." Her head was swimming, and he was going all blurry. She looked at her shoulder, and he was right, there was her purse in all its bright-purple glory. She let it slide from her shoulder and unzipped it, then began rummaging, not understanding what she was looking for.

Then she remembered.

The strips. The testing kit. Her pens...

She found her black carrying kit and undid the zipper. Stored in the little pockets were her monitor, her lancing device, and the box with the testing strips.

"Lass, what is all that?" Raghnall asked, alarmed.

She strained to see him clearly. "My kit...for low blood sugar."

"Yer...what...? For what? This all looks like...witchcraft. What are all these boxes and cases?"

She really didn't have time to explain everything. "Can you help me, please?"

She looked up at him. She could barely hold the box with the testing kit. He eyed it wildly, as if she were holding a snake to him.

"Aye," he said. "What do ye want me to do?"

She took out the lancing device, which was a cylinder, and unscrewed it, revealing the small white halter where the lancet would be loaded. Only, her hands shook so much, she would have a lot of difficulty putting the lancet in right, let alone not hurting herself with the needle while she did it. The little purple lancets were small plastic cylinders that contained sterile needles inside.

"We both should have washed our hands, but there is no soap or clean water or time. Just please wipe your fingers with these..." She broke the wrapping of the alcohol wipes and gave him one and wiped her own hands.

He smelled it and proceeded to wipe his fingers dubiously. "'Tis *uisge?*"

"Kind of. Pure alcohol. Now take one of those small purple cylinders," she said. "And insert it in here."

He looked at the lancets like they were angry hornets. "Aye." He went into the net pocket of the kit and took one out, then took the lancing device from her. "What is this made of? 'Tis smooth like a polished wood, but very light...almost weightless."

"It's plastic."

"What is plastic?"

Oh shoot...how did she explain what plastic was? It had become such a normal part of life in the twenty-first century, it was hard to imagine times when it hadn't been used or even invented.

"It's...um...do you mind if I explain it later when I can think more clearly... Just insert it into this white thing...line it up with the grooves..."

He fiddled with the lancet and the device. "And how is that going to make ye feel better, lass?"

"Careful, there's a needle in there..."

While he was doing that, she undid the cap of the plastic bottle with her testing strips and took one out. With her hands still shaking, she managed to slide the strip into the monitor and it turned on. The screen blinked, and Raghnall froze, barely breathing. And as he stopped pushing too hard, the lancet finally found its way into the grooves and snapped on.

"What is that?" He pointed at the device, backing off a bit, his eyes wide.

"It's a glucose monitor," she mumbled automatically. Part of her understood how confused he must be, but she just couldn't get into the lengthy explanations and "I told you so's" right now. "Can you just please break the cap? The little circle on top of the purple thing?"

With a stoic expression, he broke the cap, and she took the lancing device and screwed the lid on top of it. She then rubbed her fourth finger to get more blood into it, put the lancing device to the side of the finger and pressed the button. The needle prick made her wince, and when she put away the device, there was a small drop of blood.

"Lass! Ye're bleeding!" Raghnall put his hands around hers in a protective fist. "What are ye doing?"

"Testing my blood for glucose. It's fine." Through the fog in her head, she knew he was sweet and worried about her, and she was probably freaking out this huge, beautiful warrior like nothing else.

She freed her hands from his and wiped the first blood away just in case there was still any alcohol left, which would dilute her glucose reading. She then pressed on her finger again to release the new blood and picked up her glucose reader and put the testing strip against her fingers and it sucked the drop of blood in.

"Lass, why are ye feeding that yer blood?"

She didn't reply, watching the screen flashing as it calculated her glucose level.

"Is this blood magic? Are ye a witch? What are ye trying to do?"

He sounded mad, sounded like he was about to lose his mind.

It blinked: 267 mg/dl.

"Oh, shoot," she whispered. She'd already gone six days without an insulin shot, trying to save them, to stretch them out. "See this?" She showed him the monitor. "See the numbers? It says I have way too much blood sugar in my body. I need insulin."

Without insulin, her body accumulated too much sugar and couldn't deal with it. Her head spun even more. There it was. The danger. Real and as serious and right within her body.

Suddenly, the earth slipped from under her legs, even though she was sitting, and she had to lie down. The grass was soft and the small stones hard and uncomfortable under her body. A vague silhouette of a tree waved its branches above her against the darkening sky. Raghnall was studying her with an open mouth. "Ye have sugar sickness?"

She waved at her purse. "In there, find a black plastic cylinder, thin like a twig, with an orange cap. Quick. Hurry."

He did as she asked, frantically dumping the contents of her purse.

"This?" He showed her the pen.

"Yeah." Everything was very blurry, but she saw the orange blot of the cap. "Undo the cap." She heard her own words slurring, long, like she was drunk. She tried to find the edge of the skirt of her dress to pull it up. "The best place is the belly, it acts the fastest."

"God's arse, lass!" Cool air chilled her legs as he raised her dress up. "Please forgive me... What do I do?"

"Pinch my lower stomach, prick me with the needle, and press on the button once."

She could barely feel anything, but there it was, the pull and then a pinch. Then her legs were warm again, and someone was saying something, but it was all just echoey sounds.

And then she sank into darkness.

CHAPTER 15

I AM FROM ANOTHER TIME. Bryanna's voice echoed in Raghnall's head as he stared at the unconscious woman and the strange, thin cylinder that looked like a black reed, with a needle at the top of it.

The needle he'd just stabbed his wife with...after which her eyes had rolled and she'd slipped into oblivion.

Pale, with dry lips.

Another woman ye killed, said his father's voice in his head. *When ye left, yer mother wouldna listen to me like she should. Because of ye, I had to put her in her place. Had ye stayed, she might be alive, dinna ye think? I told ye the only thing ye're good for is...nothing. Ye bring death wherever ye go, lad. And now ye brought death to this one.*

Of course, these weren't truly his father's words. He hadn't spoken to the man since he'd been cast out. But anything bad Raghnall ever thought about himself sounded like his father's voice.

Cold sweat broke through his skin as, without knowing if he was right to do so, he closed the cap over the needle and dropped it on the ground.

"Lass!" He shook her shoulder. "Lass!"

She didn't move. He leaned over her chest and listened to her heart, trying to ignore the feel of her small, soft breasts under his ear. This wasn't the moment to think about her breasts...even though he'd never forget the long, slender legs, and the soft curve of her belly, and something he'd never seen before that covered her intimate parts—something short and silky.

Aye, all that could confirm indeed that she could be from the future... Her clothes, the bloodsucking metal thing, the needles that injected things into her...

Her bright-purple purse lay in the grass...perhaps it held something that would wake her up. Rummaging inside, he found another small purse. It was made of hard, snakelike leather. Within were rectangular objects of different colors and some sort of letters painted on them—very straight letters; he'd never seen anyone write letters like that. He wished his father had allowed him to learn his letters so he could read what was written there.

Then there was a small blue book, with more strange words written on it. As he opened it, the pages had beautiful images and colors, and on one page was Bryanna—a painting of such incredible skill and beauty that it looked exactly like her.

He stared at Bryanna, stunned. These all looked like things from another time. Mayhap she was telling the truth. When they'd met, she'd thought this all wasn't real, which meant she probably hadn't believed it herself that she'd traveled to another time.

That was why she'd married him.

Everyone knew there was no treatment for the sugar sickness. People went blind from it, lost the feeling in their limbs, and, eventually, died.

Ye bring death everywhere ye go, lad, came his father's voice again.

Darkness was consuming him, thundering in his chest, raging in his limbs. Desperation, grief, and sadness were rolling over him like a black blanket. "Shut up!" Raghnall yelled.

A few of his people who were setting up camp in a small

grove raised their heads at his yell. They were situated on top of one of the mountains because it was a better defensive position —just in case. Young lads and lasses had been sent to collect dry sticks and branches for firewood, while a few campfires were being started here and there. Teasag had put a field pot with water over the first campfire. He knew Eanar rode out to scout the surroundings, to make sure there were no unpleasant surprises.

"What?" Bryanna said as she rose to her elbows and looked around. "Did I say something?"

Raghnall dropped her things back into her purse and shifted to sit next to her. "Lass! Are ye all right?"

Gently, he supported her with his arms and pulled her into a hug. It was so good to feel her, warm, and moving, and alive. She smelled like something fruity, a pear perhaps. He remembered hearing somewhere that people with sugar sickness smelled fruity and their urine and blood tasted sweet.

"I'm fine. Thanks for helping me there. You might have saved my life."

"Saved yer life? Nae, lass. If anything, I am probably the reason for yer fall. I kidnapped ye and dragged ye away from the rock that would take ye back home."

She looked up at him. Her eyelids were heavy, but her eyes were alert. "So you believe me?"

He sighed. "Aye. Despite everything that I ken, I do."

She blinked at him several times. "Why? What made you change your mind?"

She seemed like she wasn't even breathing. "I looked through yer things. Yer strange wee plates with numbers and letters...the painting of ye made so artfully, there aren't any artists these days that have the precision and the talent. The materials on ye, yer wee needles, and this...thing...that drinks yer blood. Everything about ye, yer speech, the way ye carry yerself... Ye're a stranger, an outlander. Despite what I kent before, aye, there are things that are hard to explain and ye're one of them."

Teasag came to stand next to them and stared with wide eyes at Bryanna's black case and strange cylinders still spilled in the grass. "Lady, are ye unwell? May I be of help?"

Bryanna shook her head. "I'm fine, thank you for your concern. My husband is all I need now."

Teasag nodded and walked away, still throwing puzzled glances at them. With some small good fortune, none of his people had been close enough to see her fall or watch him push up her dress and use the strange needle on her. Now they were too busy setting up camp to pay the new lord and his wife much notice.

My husband is all I need now... Her words brought warmth into his chest. When he met her eyes, he noted how much more relaxed she looked, how she sagged against him in relief.

She rubbed his arm with her thumb. "You're not going to put me on a stake for witchcraft or something? Or put me in a dungeon?"

He chuckled. "Nae, lass. I..." He cleared his throat. "I wilna. It turns out, ye're the perfect wife."

Color returned to her face, lighting up her cheeks like a flame. "What do you mean?"

"Well, Angus wanted me to marry to prove I can settle down and be responsible. But I never wanted a wife. And I accepted that condition only to get my lands back."

"You never wanted a wife? Why? Isn't that what everyone is expected to do during this age?"

"Aye. But I... I just never wanted a family or bairns of my own. I like being alone."

Ye bring death with ye everywhere ye go, rumbled his father's voice inside his head. *Imagine if ye fathered a child. Poor bairn.*

He shook his head, willing for the voice to go away, then continued, more to shut his father up than to explain things to Bryanna. "And ye told me ye want to return home, aye?"

"Yeah."

"Well, then, I wilna stop ye. If ye tell Angus and my family that our marriage is real, that is, that we consummated it, he wilna have a choice but to accept ye as my wife. And then nothing will make him take Tigh na Abhainn back from me. Then, ye can leave this time and go home. I'll help ye clear the rubble if 'tis nae yet done."

Although he said that, part of him wasn't so eager to help her get back home. He liked her, he admitted to himself. Despite his resolve not to develop any feelings towards her, he had. That sense of joy and sunshine he had around her was addictive. He'd come to enjoy sleeping in a bed with her, despite his struggles to keep his hands off her. He enjoyed teaching her to ride and singing to her. She always took in information like she was starving for it.

And once or twice, she'd hummed along to his songs, and her voice was beautiful.

"What do ye say, Lady Bryanna?"

She raised her eyebrows. "Sure, I don't mind telling Angus that we consummated our marriage. But I'm pretty sure he already knows I'm from the future. I think I'm not the only one."

Raghnall blinked at her. "What do ye mean?"

"Well... It's not my secret to tell. But I'm sure you probably had your suspicions."

Raghnall frowned, thinking. Sir James...with his odd English and his odd mission to find Lady Rogene and David... Claiming he was an officer of the law or something... Was he from the future?

And if he came to look for Lady Rogene and David—he knew them. Only, if he was from the future that would be where he'd know them from, right? So, were they time travelers, too?

Raghnall shook his head. How could Angus and Catriona have kept it a secret? And David himself, who'd become a friend and a sword brother.

"Aye. I do have my suspicions," he said darkly. "I'll need to have a serious conversation or two once we arrive."

Woodsmoke from more campfires filled the air. The sounds of people talking quietly reached Raghnall's ears. He saw Eanar return, and as he jumped off the horse, he approached them. "Are ye all right, Lady?" he asked Bryanna.

"Thanks. I'm fine."

Despite their initial misunderstanding, Raghnall came to like the man more and more. "Is everything clear, Eanar?"

"Aye. We should be all right. Though people are worried. Uprooted from their homes like that... Bairns are scared."

Raghnall nodded. "Aye. I ken."

That was how he had felt as a fourteen-year-old lad being forced out of his home. As Eanar walked away to the camp, Raghnall studied Bryanna, looking for any signs of her being unwell. "Are ye truly feeling better?"

"I am." She sat straighter and looked around, then began gathering her things into her black case. "Insulin keeps me alive. It's the hormone that my body doesn't produce. Thankfully, they found a way to make it in the future, so my life depends on it."

He sucked air into his lungs. "And if ye stay here, without that...insu...lin...ye will die?"

She nodded without looking at him. "Yep. Pretty much." Then she gave a small chuckle. "It sucks."

It sucks... That probably meant it was shite. Poor lass. His heart ached for her. Living with a constant threat that didn't come from an enemy but from your own body... And especially this woman, so full of light and life.

"Ye dinna deserve it, lass," he said as he helped her put back her odd purple cylinders. Their fingers touched, and their eyes met. He could sink into the golden green of her eyes, bright and sparkling. "Ye should have a full life in front of ye...anything ye want. Anyone ye want."

Her skin was so smooth under his fingers, and she was so close to him...soft and bonnie and feminine. There were her lips, half open, calling for him.

Resist the call, he commanded. *She's not yer real wife and she's going to leave soon.*

What harm would one little kiss do then, if she was going to leave soon?

His body agreed. He reached to her, cupping her jaw, and, as though she had the exact same thought, she moved towards him, too. Like a hammer and an anvil, they came together, their mouths connecting, their arms wrapping around each other's bodies.

Unlike their previous kisses, there was no hesitation, no shyness, no holding back. Her lips met his with the same level of hunger that had been torturing him for days. They were soft, and her tongue tasted sweet, and it stroked his, caressing, playing, coming together and retreating. The taste of her, the scent of her filling his nostrils, the feel of her feminine body in his arms, brought fire deep within his veins.

He wanted her, aye. He'd wanted her for days. But it wasn't just lust. It was the need to bathe in her light, to own her by giving pleasure to her, to watch her fall apart deliciously under his careful guidance. Never had he felt this need, this hunger, this ache for a woman. Not even with Mòrag.

He was ready to tear her clothes off and take her right here and now—and she wanted him, too. He could tell from her grinding, and the small whimpers of distressed pleasure that came from her throat and drove him mad.

But he couldn't. Not after she'd been ill like she had just now. And not under the trees of a forest somewhere in the Highlands, when all his people could see them.

No. This woman deserved silks and a bed of feathers.

And no stolen glances from strangers.

With the effort of will that compared to tearing his own arm from his body, he stopped the kiss and leaned away from her. Her chest was heaving, her eyes were bright, and her lips were red and swollen from his kiss.

He wanted to see her beautiful folds swollen and red like that, too.

"I can tell ye one thing, lass," he said as he cupped her face. "I like the idea of having ye as my wife more and more. 'Tis going to be very hard to let ye go."

CHAPTER 16

BRYANNA HELD a wooden bowl with her dinner—stew made of oats boiled with parsnips, wild garlic, and onions. Not particularly appetizing, but she was grateful to get something warm and comforting into her stomach. It was dark around them, and only campfires were chasing the night away. Families and neighbors sitting around the campfires were talking and eating their food.

Raghnall was by her side, staring into the flames, mindlessly chewing a piece of bannock that Teasag had packed earlier that morning. Eanar and Teasag sat across from Bryanna, talking about something and clearly teasing each other. The air was filled with the scents of woodsmoke, stew, and roasted bread.

Even though the fires and the smells were comforting, the sense of danger, of desperation and fear, hung over the camp like a dark ceiling.

Bryanna looked over her shoulder to the next campfire, where a mother had her two children, ages six and eight, in her lap and was rocking them, repeating something that was no doubt supposed to be comforting.

Only, her voice sounded tense and worried.

Bryanna touched Raghnall's shoulder, and his dark gaze was immediately on her, sharp and focused like the scope of a sniper's gun. A shiver ran through her. How could he be so warm and worried about her one moment, saving her life, and then the next be a cold, distant man.

"Um…" she said. "I just wanted to ask if you have your lute with you."

He twisted his torso away and patted something on the opposite side. "Aye, I do."

"Everyone seems to be really on edge. It's a terrifying situation, to abandon their homes, especially for children. I teach music to children where I'm from, and I was thinking, maybe you could play and sing to them? That might help them to calm down."

His eyes lit up, sparkling with red-and-orange flames reflected from the fire. "Ye teach music?"

She picked up a small twig and fiddled with it. "I do."

His whole face changed—from a man with dark secrets and a burden on his shoulders, he transformed into a grinning boy. "What do ye play?"

Bryanna's own stomach tightened in excitement, as though he had infected her. She felt like a shy teenage girl who just got the attention of the most popular boy in school. She tucked a lock of her hair behind her ear and stared at the ground, a stupid smile spreading on her face.

"Not a lute, but something similar, in a way… Have you heard of a guitar?"

"A guitar? Nae."

"It's also a stringed instrument, but the sound is different. Louder, I think. And depending on what the strings are made of, the sound can also be more intense. I also play piano, of course. Every music teacher must."

"And ye sing?"

"Yes."

*Please, don't ask me to sing…*she begged him in her head.

"God's feet, ye may be the most perfect woman that has ever

walked this earth..." he mumbled, as though to himself, making heat burn her cheeks and neck. "Please, sing to me."

But shyness didn't want to let her go, and although she sang and played for work, she shook her head. What if he didn't like her voice? What if she sang the wrong note? Could she even remember a single song under his burning gaze?

"If ye wilna sing to me, then sing to the children."

"I don't know any medieval songs."

"Then sing something from yer time. I'll try to pick the melody with my lute."

She bit her lip. This might actually work. She could sing him something super easy, like "Twinkle, Twinkle, Little Star." The melody was basic and beautiful and soothing. This would be perfect.

"Okay," she said. "Let's do it... Though it's been a very long time since I sang when someone else played along."

"Twinkle, twinkle, little star," she began, quieter than she would have liked, and Raghnall stilled so completely, he could have been a statue.

"How I wonder what you are..." she continued, braver now, letting her voice gain strength.

Teasag and Eanar quieted and listened to her, open-mouthed.

"Up above the world so high..." She felt it now...that place within her, where she was safe, where she felt her soul pouring through her voice, where she knew she was connected with her audience, where she knew she brought beauty.

"Like a diamond in the sky," she sang, forgetting that anyone was watching her, or judging her, or listening.

She kept singing the song, and distantly realized that more and more people gathered around the bonfire and that children stopped whining and crying. She saw Odhran, Eamhair, and their kids and smiled at them. The beautiful chords of the lute joined in, softly and hesitantly at first.

And when she looked at Raghnall playing, he was watching

her like she was his sun and his moon, like she led him and he was happy to follow.

At some point, she didn't know where his music began and her voice ended. When she sang the last word, she didn't want to stop, so she started "Twinkle, Twinkle, Little Star" over again. Children watched her with bright eyes and open mouths, women smiled dreamily, men wore thoughtful expressions.

And then, once they started the song for the third time, Raghnall joined in the verse. He sang the first chorus with her, and then only hummed, but his voice was lower and hers higher, and the two of them intertwined beautifully.

If voices could make love, this would be it. They were perfect. His, velvety, seductive, the baritone of a troubadour, and hers, a perfect mezzo-soprano, as she'd been told by her own music teachers. They complemented each other, teased each other, and created something unique, something beautiful.

Something she never wanted to end.

When they finished "Twinkle, Twinkle, Little Star," their audience demanded more songs. For the first time since they'd left Tigh na Abhainn, Bryanna saw smiles on the faces of the children. And so she sang "Itsy Bitsy Spider," and "Ring Around the Rosie," and "Are You Sleeping, Brother John?" Finally, when the children were tired and, one by one, left Bryanna and Raghnall's campfire, they stopped singing. Only, Bryanna didn't want the night to end.

Raghnall put his lute away. "Lass, ye have a bonnie voice, like a nightingale. I could listen to ye all night."

She chuckled. "Thank you. I love your voice, actually."

The word *love* hung between them, heavy and loaded.

"Ye ken, I can barely get my mind around the fact that ye're from another time. I dinna think I'll ever recover when ye're gone."

She wished she could say, *Then don't lose me... Let me stay... Let me be with you...*

But there was no way a diabetic could live in the Middle

Ages. There was truly no future for them. Staying here with him meant death.

She took his hand in hers and put on a brave smile. "Whatever happens, I will never forget you, either, Raghnall Mackenzie. I think it's safe to say you'll always have a piece of my heart."

Not just a piece. He'd own her heart.

And once she returned to her own time, she'd once again live a half-life.

A life without him.

CHAPTER 17

THEY ARRIVED at Dornie early in the morning. Raghnall's heart eased at the relief and hope on his people's faces as they gazed upon the impenetrable walls of Eilean Donan.

On the way, Bryanna had asked him once if he thought the rubble covering the time-traveling stone had been cleared, and he'd said he hoped so.

But truth was, he didn't.

She'd be gone eventually, but having her near was like a sweet nectar that made his days brighter. Like she was giving him hope without even saying a word.

Last night, after they'd sung her songs around the campfire, they'd settled down for the night, wrapped into his traveling cloak, her back pressed against his torso. He'd asked her about the future and she'd told him miraculous things. She'd told him about flying carriages in the sky, about medicine that cured deadly illnesses, about how women were equal to men.

And he liked that. It was reassuring to hear that humanity would move towards a safer, better, healthier future with more freedom and opportunities. It was good that bairns didn't die as often, that women could learn writing and reading and could be as skillful as men in all sorts of crafts. He liked the idea of machines doing regular chores—weaving, washing, even cooking.

He watched her with different eyes. From a potential threat, she became someone wondrous. A miracle that had happened to him.

When they stopped at the Dornie quay to board the barge, his people started unloading their carts. As he carried sacks, he wondered if these were his last moments with her. What if the rubble *was* cleared, and she'd be gone very soon—today—what then?

Melancholy spread through his soul like a black cloud, and he felt like a wolf who wanted to howl at the moon. He'd never see her again, and that prospect tore his heart apart. He wanted more with her—more time, more talk, more...*love*.

Aye, if she did leave now and never appeared again, he would regret not making love to her. He knew it would be the last piece of happiness before the rest of his life.

But war was coming. Death was real, and it might take his own life, not to mention hers. Especially since she had that sugar sickness that was so dangerous without her...needle medicine.

While the barge moved towards the castle, rocking on the small waves, Raghnall watched the wind playing with Bryanna's honey-colored hair. "Would ye come to the great hall with me first, before ye go?"

She smiled that smile of hers that wrinkled the skin around her eyes. "Yes, of course, to tell them we consummated the marriage, right?"

Ah, that. He'd forgotten that he needed her to secure Tigh na Abhainn.

Now, he needed her, period. He wanted her to come with him so that he'd have more time with her. They could eat and talk, and mayhap she'd sing to him again. "Aye," he said. "Right."

When Raghnall looked back at Dornie, he saw more of his people embarking on wooden barges with sacks and chests and boxes, taking their cattle and sheep. He nodded to Odhran and

Eamhair and their children, who were on the barge, and they nodded back, pressing out brave smiles. He hoped no harm would come to them or any of his people. As the barge approached Eilean Donan, he saw men working on the outer walls and roofs, spreading mortar into the cracks, nailing fire-proof animal hides to the roofs.

The castle was clearly preparing for a siege.

Raghnall watched it all, his hand curled around the handle of his sword. "Actually, lass," he murmured. "'Tis best ye leave right away."

When they docked, Raghnall directed his people where to go. As they passed through the gates, he explained to the guards who they were and was told they were expecting people from Tigh na Abhainn thanks to the messenger who had arrived yesterday.

The first inner bailey was packed with people camping in tents. Animals bleated, chickens squawked, and geese honked. Campfires burned here and there. People's faces were somber, worried. Mothers huddled with their children, stirred pottage in cauldrons, and turned bannocks frying on cast-iron pans. Young lads and older men trained on swords. In another corner, James trained several men and women to shoot arrows into hay dummies.

In the second inner bailey, Raghnall noticed several lean-tos. Nothing more than four posts and a roof, they wouldn't last long but were a quick solution to keep food away from rain and sun. Several men whittled wood for arrows and bows, and three blacksmiths worked in the smithy, repairing swords and making arrowheads.

A dark worm of worry churned in Raghnall's gut. He'd never been in a besieged castle before.

And then a thought struck him—what about Seoc? Would the boy arrive right in the middle of the siege? Could Raghnall get Iòna a message to stay away for now?

His heart sank in worry. He couldn't be responsible for the deaths of both Seoc and Mòrag. *Nae.*

When they were a few feet away from the main keep, Angus emerged from the door, his face a mask of determined concern. Rogene hurried after him, saying something. She was now four moons pregnant, and with her sickness passing, she'd finally gotten that glow many expectant mothers had about them.

Raghnall wondered how he hadn't noticed how different she was from everyone he knew, how those little habits of hers—like eating with a small pitchfork, and cleaning her teeth, and insisting on boiling water before drinking, and many more little things— were different. She knew how to write and had been appointed as scribe to write up the marriage contract between Angus and Euphemia, even though most scribes were monks. Men.

His reflections were interrupted when Rogene and Angus stopped abruptly before them.

Rogene beamed. "Ah, our newlyweds! How are things? How's marriage?" She looked Bryanna over carefully, then her eyes narrowed on Raghnall.

For a moment, he thought he wouldn't be able to hide anything from his sister-in-law, but it was Bryanna who replied, "It's fine. He knows."

"He kens?" Angus's dark eyes landed on Raghnall.

"Aye."

"And what do ye think about that?" said Angus.

"I think the lass needs to go back to where she came from, right away. The enemy is on our doorstep. I didna ken she's from the future, or I wouldna have marrit her. So she needs to go."

Angus crossed his arms over his chest. "So ye want to annul the marriage?"

"There's no need for that," said Bryanna. "The marriage happened, if you know what I mean."

Angus's and Rogene's dubious gazes locked with Bryanna's. But, giving credit to the lass, she didn't waver. After several moments, Rogene relaxed and exchanged a knowing glance with her husband. For a split second, envy towards his older brother burned in Raghnall's chest. Just for the blink of an eye, part of him wished he had someone to exchange a knowing glance with and agree without a word.

Not just someone.

He could imagine a glance like that passing between him and the strange woman he was married to. And he liked the idea of that more than he wanted to admit to himself.

Angus cleared his throat. "I am sorry, lass, but ye will have to stay in Eilean Donan a wee bit longer."

Rogene pressed her lips together. "Unfortunately, the pile isn't cleared yet. It's as though someone, like a certain faerie we all know, really wants you to stay."

Bryanna paled a little, then gave a stern nod. Her shoulders straightened, and her chin rose. "Then I guess I'm going to help here as much as I can."

Rogene squeezed her hand. "Thank you. Let me show you where you and Raghnall can sleep."

As Raghnall watched the small, thin figure of Bryanna walk towards the main keep, relief flooded his body, lifting him like a gust of warm air. He hated himself for liking that the lass would stay with him longer.

As she reached the door to the keep, she turned and met his eyes for a moment, and something stirred in his loins. Because instead of regret and fear, there was that light in her eyes again, and even a small smile curled her lips.

He'd share a bed with her for God knew how long.

He'd be damned, but she looked like she liked the thought of that, too.

CHAPTER 18

ONLY TWO INSULIN pens left and no way to get through the pile of rocks...

Bryanna's hand curled around the hard surface of the torch as she stared at the pile. She had spent the afternoon helping Raghnall's people to settle. They had just had dinner in the great hall, which was packed with people, and Bryanna wanted to see the situation in the underground for herself before she went to sleep.

"Sure looks like it's miles away, doesn't it?" said a female voice behind her.

Rogene came to stand next to her, her hand on her small baby bump. Raghnall had told her earlier that Rogene was pregnant. If Bryanna didn't know any better, she'd never have thought this was someone born in her time, in her home country. The woman looked as medieval as she could be: the simple dress hugging her waist and streaming down to the floor in a straight cut, with long, angel sleeves lined with fur. No makeup —her face was pretty in its natural, beautiful features. Long, curly eyelashes cast shadows on her skin, and long, thick, dark hair shone in the light of the torches. If not for Rogene speaking plain American English with her, Bryanna wouldn't even know this woman belonged to a different time.

Could anyone say the same about Bryanna?

"Worlds away," said Bryanna, dropping her gaze to the pile of rocks.

Judging by the fact that the pile had been reduced in size, some attempts had been made to clear it. But now huge boulders lay on top of the time-traveling rock, and Bryanna knew it would take several people and at least one lever to move them.

"Sorry, it looks like you're stuck with us for a bit longer," said Rogene, her voice remorseful. "I know it must be hard."

Bryanna nodded and chuckled. "You're the woman who disappeared with her brother, aren't you? All the media's talking about you. Eilean Donan is now opened only for a couple of hours per day. They still don't know what happened to you, your brother...and now me."

"What about James?"

Bryanna shrugged. "Nothing about James, though I'm not sure why. I suppose the story of a missing policeman would really scare people off. So, what happened?"

As Rogene started telling the story, describing how she was at a wedding and went exploring the castle, then met Sìneag, Bryanna's heart beat like crazy. Sìneag had told Rogene that Angus Mackenzie was the man meant for her. There were many obstacles that seemed to be impossible to overcome, but their love withstood everything. It was easy to see how happy the two were. Their eyes glistened every time they looked at each other, and their bodies moved in harmony.

Then there was David, who, despite everything that they knew about time travel, had come through the stone when he had touched Rogene. And now he wasn't able to return.

And, finally, James, the Oxford detective who had been investigating Rogene and David's disappearance and vanished from the twenty-first century himself. Although he had been able to save Laomann's life and those of many other Mackenzies,

Euphemia of Ross was still clearly determined to obliterate the clan and get her revenge.

Rogene, David, and James were all time travelers who now lived in the Middle Ages. How could someone sacrifice all the freedoms, medical care, and conveniences of the twenty-first century to live in another time, love or no love?

"Did Sìneag say there was someone destined for you on the other side of that rock?" Rogene asked.

Bryanna really didn't want to discuss this with anyone, not even Raghnall. What did it change that Raghnall was supposedly her destiny? Sìneag had also told her he could be her demise.

Bryanna turned and walked out of the dark room filled with heavy desperation. "Yeah, she said something about Raghnall, I think."

They walked through the large underground area, fire from their two torches bouncing off the rough stone walls and carved wooden chests, as well as the spare swords, axes, and bows and arrows hanging on the walls.

"But obviously you don't think he's the one. I mean, how can you—this is all absolutely insane, isn't it? All this time travel, the medieval world, the war, the castle, the faerie...all of it."

Add diabetes and just two insulin pens left, and the prospect of death that she saw in one of her prophetic dreams...

She kept walking, avoiding Rogene's eyes. "I mean...no." Tears burned at the backs of her eyes. She wished she could open up to Rogene and tell her all her worries. "No, he's not the one. He can't be."

"Well," Rogene said. "You just wait and see."

As they reached the narrow stairs leading to the ground floor, Bryanna glanced back at Rogene, who walked behind her. "Can you spare anyone to help clear those rocks, please?"

They were climbing the stairs now, the stone steps polished and smooth under Bryanna's shoes. "Yes, of course," Rogene said softly. "We didn't get much done because the masons were busy with other parts of the castle... And, to be honest with you, I think Sìneag doesn't want you to go back so easily. I believe that's why the collapse happened in the first place. But I'll have Angus free up a few men to help clear the rubble."

Bryanna's heart squeezed in appreciation. "Thank you."

But as they reached the storeroom on the ground floor, someone was descending the stairs and, in a moment, the massive frame of Bryanna's Highlander stood before her, his long, dark hair ablaze with shades of bronze and auburn from the light of the torches.

Like always, he fixed her with his unblinking, dark gaze that seemed to penetrate right into her soul.

"I lost ye," he said, not even acknowledging Rogene's presence. "I thought ye may have returned..."

His voice was low and crackling with tension.

Bryanna inhaled sharply, a momentary anger blazing through her. "What if I had?"

Rogene raised her eyebrows, clearly uncomfortable. "Okay, you two. I'm going to see if Angus is ready to go to bed, because I sure am. My nausea is gone now, but my lower back is killing me."

As Rogene climbed the stairs, probably to the great hall, Raghnall narrowed his eyes at Bryanna. She raised her chin. "Raghnall, you can't expect me to stay when I clearly said I need to go."

"Always tell me where ye are. I canna stand people disappearing."

There it was again, that edge in his voice that chilled her soul. But she wasn't his possession or his anyone, except for a pretend wife.

"I don't owe you anything." She brushed past him towards the stairs, heading to their bedroom, which was next to Catrìona and James's bedroom on the floor above the great hall. "I told Angus and Rogene that our marriage is legal. You're all cleared."

As she climbed, she heard his footsteps behind her, barely

audible against the stairs despite his considerable weight and height.

"Rogene promised to spare some people to clear the rubble so that I can leave as soon as possible. So you won't need to worry about me at all."

They passed by the great hall and kept climbing. Her body felt good, despite her episode from last night. Although she had been mismanaging her blood glucose, she felt like she'd gotten stronger since coming to the Middle Ages. Daily exercises on the horse, walks, and other physical activity were good for her health. Now, climbing the narrow stairs, she barely broke a sweat, her heart beating faster, feeling healthy and strong.

When she entered the small, dark bedchamber, Raghnall followed her, closing the door behind him and leaning against it. He grabbed her by the arm and turned her to face him. The light of the dying sunset and the early starlight were illuminating his face, intense and tormented as he caught her gaze.

What demons did he fight in his soul? Why didn't he let anyone in?

"But I worry about ye, lass," he said, bringing her closer to him. The feel of his hard chest against her breasts spread sweet tingling through her. She gasped as her soft stomach brushed against his hard one. He was so warm—hot, even through the layers of his medieval clothes—and so broad-shouldered, his muscles like boulders. "I dinna want to," he breathed out, "but I do."

Thoughts couldn't even formulate in her head as she was caught in the dark prison of his eyes, just now realizing they were alone, yet again, with a single bed that was so inviting and suddenly so big it seemed to have the gravitational force of a planet.

His gaze dropped to her mouth. "Tell me one thing, lass. If ye leave tomorrow morning, and never see me again, is there anything ye'd regret?"

The answer stole her breath. All her life, she'd been nothing but careful. She followed a strict diet, she did the safest exercises, she avoided relationships because she didn't want to become a burden for yet another person besides her family.

This had been the craziest, wildest, most incredible experience of her whole life. She'd been so light and so free when she'd thought she was in a wonderful, vivid dream. She'd been stripped of fears, of caution, and of worry. And, underneath all those layers, perhaps for the first time in her life, she'd become herself.

And she freaking loved that person.

That person wanted adventure, wanted to taste life, drink it in handfuls, taking risks and making mistakes.

That person had been awakened by Raghnall Mackenzie.

"I wouldn't regret a lot," she whispered, wrapping her arms around his neck and watching with satisfaction as his pupils dilated and his eyes darkened. "But I would regret not doing this."

She pushed the cautious part of her aside, lifted her face, and kissed him.

CHAPTER 19

BLOODY HELL, the woman's kiss melted him like sun melted honey. Her lips, delicate and soft and velvety, stroked and caressed. Her mouth opened, inviting him in. As his tongue dipped in and made the first stroke against hers, small bursts of pleasure exploded through his body.

Hunger for her took over. As he wrapped his arms around her waist, a low growl escaped the back of his throat. She was so fragile and feminine in his arms, he had to stop himself from crushing her.

Her taste—sweet and flowery and delicious—and her own smell of a woman—musky and beautiful—brought his blood to a boil. Desire coursed through him in a quick, all-consuming rush, like a fever. He deepened the kiss, licking, stroking, longing to join with her, possess her, have her all to himself.

The woman who was bound to disappear.

The woman with an untreatable disease that waited to kill her without magical medicine from the future.

The woman whose blood might be on his hands if he didn't help her.

He almost pulled away, but she didn't let him.

To his surprise, she ran her hand down his chest to the girdle belt at his waist. As she started undoing it, his skin burned, her touch scalding him like she was the sun itself.

His girdle landed on the floor with a soft thud, and she slid a hand under his tunic. When her fingers smoothed up his torso, caressing his old, aching wounds, it felt like he was coming back to life. Like a frozen cave that had finally received the light of spring after centuries of winter.

And he wanted more.

With a groan, he picked her up, letting her wrap her legs around his waist, and carried her to the bed. They both landed there awkwardly, painfully, but he didn't care. He was hard and aching for her, all soft and sweet, spread under his weight with her legs wrapped around him, right where he wanted her.

He withdrew and looked at her face. She was so incredibly beautiful, her lips full and dark and swollen from his kiss, her eyes luminous, lids half closed, a slight blush on her cheeks.

This was just the beginning. She'd look even prettier with his name on her lips as he drove her higher, showing her all the sweetest pleasures her body could have.

He lowered his head to her neck, inhaling the scent that made his head spin. "I kent ye'd come to me, asking to be in my bed."

As he planted soft kisses down her throat, moving to her collarbone, she pressed her head back into the mattress, exposing her neck to him. The vein there beat violently against his lips.

With a throaty moan that made him even harder, she dragged her fingernails down his back, grinding the apex of her thighs against his erection.

He let out a groan that sounded pained, agonized, and she continued to tease him.

"I didn't," she managed. "I didn't ask you anything."

He chuckled as he bent his head to her chest, and found one of her nipples, biting her slightly through the fabric of the dress. To his satisfaction, she gasped and arched her back.

He cupped her breast with one hand and pressed his fingers slightly, making the nipple stand out. "Oh, but ye will, in just a moment, lass. Ye wilna just ask. Ye'll beg."

He took half her breast into his mouth, wetting, sucking, massaging her sensitive flesh, enjoying the small pleasure-tortured whimpers that came from her mouth. He wanted to see her naked, that sweet, soft flesh of hers exposed and ready for him, that silky skin so smooth under his fingers. She dug her nails into the muscles of his back.

"That's right, lass," he whispered. "Show me how much ye want me."

"Ahh…" was all she managed as he grasped her other breast and repeated the same treatment with her second nipple while circling the first one with his thumb. "Oh, good God!"

He loved hearing her calling for God and making all those sounds of sweet distress. He'd had enough women in his life to know how to please one, but most of his connections hadn't meant anything beyond mutual physical pleasure. With anyone but Mòrag.

And now, here, with Bryanna, this was nothing like what he'd experienced with anyone at all.

He wanted to please her, wanted her to squirm and call for more. As he moved down her body, while reaching to the edge of her dress, he noticed she was shaking ever so slightly, and when he ran his hands up her long, smooth legs, exposing her to him, she grasped his head, sitting up.

"Raghnall…" she said, a slight warning in her voice.

"Ye're so beautiful, lass," he said as he dragged his lips up her inner thigh, already inhaling the mouthwatering, intoxicating scent of her aroused sex.

"Raghnall!" she repeated, louder now.

"Are ye begging, lass?" he murmured as he spread her folds, covered with soft, dark-blond curls.

But before she could reply, he sealed his mouth with her sex, and there it was, the moan he'd been anticipating all this time, a deep, throaty call for more.

"Are ye begging?" he murmured as he leaned back for a short moment.

"More!" She gave up. "More!"

"Hmmmm," he hummed right against her softest spot, knowing it would add to her pleasure, and a shudder went through her.

He kept caressing her, kissing her where he knew she'd love it the most, and his own body was ringing with a hot desire for her, like a church bell calling a warning. Urgent. Loud. Impossible to ignore.

"Tell me what ye want, lass," he murmured.

"You..." A moan came. "Inside..."

He chuckled against her folds and gave a lick. "Say please, lass."

Her only reply was a moan as he added more pressure.

"Say please."

"Ahhh..."

An urgent pounding sounded against the door. Damn it! She was so close, he could feel her flesh tight and hot and ready.

"Go away!" he yelled.

But the pounding resumed. "'Tis Iòna, Lord! I am back."

Somewhere at the edge of his consciousness, he remembered that he had sent Iòna for Seoc. He straightened his back, trying to focus and ignore the hot need of arousal in his body.

Iòna's voice came again. "I have the lad, Lord. He's here."

CHAPTER 20

ILLUMINATED by the flames from the fireplace in the great hall, Seoc devoured chunk after chunk of bread, almost without swallowing, eyebrows drawn together in a perfect, somber line. He'd grown up so much in the past four years that Raghnall might not have recognized him if he'd met the lad somewhere on the street. He wasn't tall, though, and looked malnourished—the bones of his skull protruded through the thin muscles of his face, and dark circles shadowed his golden-amber eyes.

There was so much of his mother in the lad. Mòrag had been a fierce woman, a woman who had been protecting herself and her son for years before Raghnall had appeared. And this lad, no doubt, had her determination and her bravery.

Raghnall swallowed what felt like a rock with sharp edges as he chased away the dark melancholy that bit him in the middle of his chest. "Ye grew up," he said into his cup of uisge and threw the fiery liquid into his throat.

The lad didn't even look at him, the loud chewing, almost slurping sounds the only response.

"He..." Iòna cleared his throat. "He didna want to come."

Aye, why would he? The lad knew even better than Raghnall who was responsible for his mother's death. But the lad didn't know what was best for him. Raghnall was the only one left to take care of him. Had he not been too late and had married Mòrag, he'd have been the lad's stepfather by now, responsible for his life and well-being.

"Ye take me away from my aunt and uncle," Seoc grumbled and spat out a small bone onto the floor. "Ye send a man I've never seen in my life…"

"I sent ye yer mother's engagement ring," Raghnall said, staring at the piece of bone on the floor like it was the piece of his own heart.

"Aye, but the day she died taught me nae to trust anyone," said Seoc and locked his eyes with Raghnall for the first time.

A chill ran down Raghnall's spine as he realized how much older the lad seemed for his ten years of age. He didn't have the eyes of a child whose only concerns were to run around and play with sticks and stones.

This boy had to grow up earlier than he should have—all because of Raghnall.

"Aye, rightly so," said Raghnall, his voice cracking. "But now ye're with yer clan." He paused, letting the contractions in his throat pass, then added at the edge of his breath, "With me."

God, Angus was right—the responsibility, the weight of taking care of someone besides himself was the hardest thing he'd ever had to do. He felt his fingers tighten around the smooth surface of the bone cup. "And I will take care of ye."

For better or for worse, he now had a wife with death sitting on her shoulder and a young lad who looked more like a barely domesticated wolf cub than a human.

And, somehow, the cub wasn't impressed at the opportunity to be Raghnall's responsibility at all… Mary and Joseph, help him.

"Well, hey there!" Bryanna's voice even sounded like sunlight, illuminating the great hall with the energy and warmth of summer. "You look hungry." She entered, almost flying like a faerie, looking weightless.

She sat at the bench between Raghnall and the lad, who watched her with wide, careful eyes. Raghnall noticed that the lad trusted her more than him, even though he was seeing her for the first time.

Earlier, when they had been so abruptly interrupted by Iòna, Raghnall had barked out that his son had arrived and left, ignoring her open-mouthed surprise. Shocked to hear Seoc and Iòna had returned so soon and worried about the lad, he had never even given her a kiss or said how much he regretted the interruption, how he didn't want to leave her and would rather stay and finish what they had started.

Worried everything he'd sacrificed would be ruined, he'd left his wife, warm and beautiful and trembling.

And now she'd returned, not even giving him a second glance.

"Ah, you must be tired from your journey," she said. "Are you glad to see your father?"

Seoc just kept chewing and shrugged one shoulder. "Havena seen him for years. So...nae."

She raised her eyebrows and threw a quick, worried glance at Raghnall, then picked up an empty bone cup and poured more of the uisge standing on the long table. Without acknowledging anyone, she threw back the contents of the cup. "Well, your father is a mystery, isn't he?" she mumbled without looking at Raghnall, but he had the distinct feeling the words were like a dagger intended for his chest. "He might abandon people from time to time when they least expect it."

It was like he felt the smoke and the ash on his face again.

He abandoned people...people abandoned him...his father, chasing him away, screaming at him that he was a slug not worthy of his boot, that he was an insult to kitchen waste, and that he'd be better off dead.

That was what Raghnall had been doing until he'd met Bruce and his army...trying to die.

When he'd met Mòrag he'd been a mercenary for hire. And

then, just when he'd decided to be a better man and marry her... just when he'd lost her...he'd heard the Highlanders were uniting under the rule of the true Scottish king. And something within him knew that if he wanted any salvation, any chance in life, that was it.

He had to fight for the right thing. For freedom. For Seoc's future and the future of the country he loved so dearly.

His whole life had been for this moment, so that this little human, who wasn't even his son by blood, could sit by the fire, eat bread and meat, and be safe.

Seoc raised his head, his eyes narrowing at Bryanna. "Who are ye?"

"I'm..." She pursed her lips. "I'm Raghnall's wife, I suppose."

Seoc's curiosity was replaced with a hard stare. "Ye suppose?"

She chuckled and covered Raghnall's hand lying on the table with hers. The gesture, Raghnall knew, was just to convince Seoc of the truthfulness of what she said, but despite himself, it meant more for him than she'd ever know... It spread warmth and tingles and made him feel lighter, like the sunlight within her spread to his every cell.

"I am his wife," she said, the tremble in her voice short. "It's new, so I'm not yet used to it... And I didn't know he had you."

Seoc shrugged. Good Lord, how did the lad manage to look like he was a sixty-five-year-old man in the skin of a ten-year-old?

"He didna have me. My mother did."

Bryanna's throat moved as she swallowed, and she looked at him. "Right. Your mother. Who was she, anyway?"

"Her name was Mòrag," said Seoc proudly before Raghnall could add anything. "I was a wee lad when she died. I'm nae a wee lad nae more, mistress."

"Who's the lad?" boomed a voice somewhere by the entrance. Angus.

Raghnall's shoulders tightened as he realized he should have told his family about Seoc. He should have opened up about such an important part of his life...

But Seoc wasn't his son, not even his stepson.

So how could he have trusted Angus to recognize the lad Raghnall was determined to make his heir?

He had to lie.

Raghnall stood up, and so did Iòna—ever loyal, ever kind Iòna—but Raghnall stopped him with a gesture of his hand.

"'Tis my son and my heir," said Raghnall. "He came to live with me and is part of the clan now."

Angus's dark eyes lay on Seoc who had a tiny expression of surprise and, just as Raghnall had feared, distrust.

Angus narrowed his eyes on Raghnall. "Whether he will be part of the clan or nae remains to be seen. Why havena ye ever said a word about yer son? All these years we fought for the Bruce together...and ye returned to Eilean Donan months ago."

Why hadn't he said anything? Because even the thought of talking about Mòrag and his own cowardice that led to her death made him want to take a dagger and cut his own chest open. That would be less painful.

Raghnall felt his fist clench till his short fingernails bit into the skin of his palm. "If ye wouldna even accept me, how could ye accept my son?"

Angus walked farther into the hall, closer to Seoc. A few moments later, two more figures appeared in the doorway— Catrìona, rubbing her eyes, her long hair in braids, and James by her side, looking like he was ready to launch at any potential threat to her.

"What is going on?" Catrìona said in a thick, croaky voice.

Angus rubbed his chin thoughtfully. "I just learned that Raghnall has a son." He looked at Raghnall. "We accepted ye, brother."

Catrìona stared at Seoc with wide eyes. "Raghnall, ye have a son?" Then she looked at Bryanna. "Did ye ken?"

Bryanna shook her head. Raghnall felt his blood churn. "Ye

accepted me? Ye didna want to give me my lands. Ye didna trust me."

Angus made a sweeping gesture with his hand in the direction of Seoc. "Can ye blame me? How could ye hide yer lad? Do ye think that wouldna have changed my decision about yer lands? The lad needs a home and a future."

A sharp pain of regret slashed across Raghnall's chest. "Ye would have given me the lands without making me marry anyone?"

Angus shrugged. "Mayhap. Where is the lad's mother, anyway? Is yer marriage to Lady Bryanna even legitimate?"

And this was the moment of truth, the moment that Raghnall was dreading. Even mentioning her name was like casting a spell of desperation and pain.

He felt the heavy gazes of his family, of Iòna and of his wife. Even Seoc was glaring at him.

Tell them what happened. Tell them the truth. Tell them the woman ye loved is dead because of ye.

Moments dragged by, and the crackling of wood consumed by fire was the only sound in the hall. Raghnall was opening and closing his mouth, fighting to get the words out of his throat, but it was as though a rock was blocking everything.

Finally, help came from where he didn't expect it.

His wife laid her hand on Seoc's shoulder. "Our marriage is legitimate, Angus. Unfortunately, Seoc's mother died."

This woman was loyal and brave.

He didn't deserve her, and the right thing to do was to tell her the whole truth.

Even if he had to open the door to a creepy, freezing dungeon full of demons that might kill him.

CHAPTER 21

THE LAD WAS PUT in Raghnall and Bryanna's bedchamber, which would stop his plans to continue what they had started earlier. Standing in the open door, Raghnall watched Seoc huddle into his bedroll next to the fireplace. Behind Raghnall, Bryanna stood in the dark landing of the stairs, and he felt her eyes on him.

When he turned around to meet her gaze, there wasn't judgment or anger or disgust. There was something he didn't feel he deserved.

Sympathy.

Something a real wife would offer to her husband.

And just like in a real family, the lad slept in the same bedchamber with his parents. This would have been his life with Mòrag.

"Come," Bryanna whispered, her voice insistent. "Let's talk."

He owed her that. And if he was going to open up to anyone, it would be to her.

They went downstairs, but when Bryanna turned to enter the great hall, he caught her hand. The touch of her skin, like always, created that burst of sweet energy that invigorated him and gave him strength.

"Nae there," he said. "I dinna want anyone to interrupt us. If ye want me to talk, I have much to tell ye."

Without breaking contact, he led her down the stairs, feeling like she'd just given him a second wind. Her hand was smooth and silky in his rough, calloused fingers, and he remembered how smooth and soft her thighs were, and how delicious she tasted against his tongue.

They exited the tower and went across the inner bailey.

Raghnall led her up the narrow stairs running along the curtain wall, up into the crisp air of the Highland night. As they walked towards one of the towers at the far end of the wall, Raghnall wondered how he would ever begin telling her his story.

He wanted to be away from the confinement of enclosed spaces and close to the sky. They passed by a few sleepy sentinels. As he entered the tower and took another flight of stairs to the highest level, he knew based on the thin, pale golden line of light on the horizon to the east, the night shift would soon change with the morning shift.

He told the guard he could go now and that Raghnall would stay and keep watch, and the man happily took the offer. When the guard left, Raghnall took a lungful of air. But it didn't help to soothe the trembling in his hands.

He was about to open the door to the most horrific day of his life.

He had to face the demons that kept him awake at night, the demons that were at the bottom of every uisge cup he'd emptied since then. The demons that were at the edge of the blade he used fighting the enemy and at the depths of every nightmare he had. All he did was try to forget them, keep them away until the moment when he couldn't run from them anymore.

That moment was now.

∼

BRYANNA'S HEART WAS RACING. SHE KNEW HE WAS ABOUT TO open up, to tell her the worst thing that had ever happened to him. The night was still dark, even though the horizon was starting to lighten. The air was lush and crisp from the scents of the loch mixed with the scents of the forest.

Bryanna's hand was on the parapet of the defensive tower, the rock rough and cold against her fingers. A slight breeze played with her hair and tickled her cheeks.

Raghnall, Mr. Mystery and Darkness, had a son, who looked nothing like him, by the way. And Raghnall had thrown that information at her, spoiling the best sexual experience of her entire life, leaving her confused and shaking, trembling, mindless from desire.

He'd wanted her to beg him... She had been ready to plead him to stay with her and keep doing whatever he was doing to her.

When she had found him in the great hall, his face ashen, like he'd seen a ghost, she just knew this boy and that sad song Raghnall been singing about a woman were connected. The man with no heart had brought only demise to the woman—she must have died. And since the boy's mother had died, too, it wasn't hard to put the pieces together.

She could be wrong, of course, but that was her gut feeling, and she knew by now to trust her gut.

So would she now hear about how the woman had died? And why Raghnall couldn't even talk about her in front of his family?

"After my father chased me away from the clan," he said, "I didna ken what to do with myself. No money, no sword, nothing to my name but the clothes on my back and a warm cloak to keep the cold away." He leaned against the parapet and stared into the darkness. The sole torch on the wall illuminated his thoughtful face, making fires play in his eyes. "I went down south, with no purpose, no one to turn to, and nothing to achieve. The only people who wanted me were reivers in the Lowlands. I joined their band. We robbed travelers, raided

lonely farms, kidnapped noblemen's daughters for ransom, and killed for coin."

There, she realized, that was where the darkness came from. That readiness for anything, that look that told her nothing anyone said or did could be worse than what he had already been through. A shiver went through her and something cold crept across the muscles of her back.

"I wasna proud of that, but I also didna want to do any of that, nae like many men in the group. I was never raised a thief and an outlaw, but there wasna another option for me to survive. The chief of the band was called Daidh—the man made my father look like an innocent bairn. If ye talk about a man with nae soul, 'twas Daidh. Though he never did anything to me personally, I kent he was dangerous to those he wanted gone."

He kept silent for a moment and looked at her. It was quiet, and only the waters of the loch rustled somewhere down below. The horizon was lighter now, and she could see the hurt in his eyes, the regret. And Bryanna's heart ached for him, something sharp stabbing her right in the middle.

"After years of surviving there, I had a good sword I got from robbing men, and I'd saved enough coin to get by on my own. So I said goodbye to the band of thieves, to Daidh's great displeasure."

He shook his head, a muscle along his cheekbone twitching.

"I traveled by myself and earned coin with my sword in England, France, and Flanders. Years later, I decided to go back to Scotland and was on my way to Carlisle. It was late and I knocked on the door of a small farm to ask for shelter for the night. A woman opened the door, a lad of six years clutching at her skirts, that same, fearless, stern look in his eyes, like he was ready to throw himself on me like a wolf cub."

He chuckled and wiped his mouth slowly, thoughtfully. Despite herself, Bryanna's nerves flared with jealousy, like acid eating her tissue away. She knew she shouldn't. How could she be jealous of a dead woman?

136

And yet, Bryanna clung to every word, both dreading and longing to hear how he fell in love with that woman who opened the door at night and gave him shelter. Bryanna longed for him to look at her like that, the way he was staring into the Highland night, seeing the woman his heart ached for, the woman whose loss made him sing songs of love and longing years after her death. The woman whose child he was living for.

That must have been quite a woman—she'd managed to capture the heart of this lone wolf.

How could Bryanna compete with someone like that? Bryanna, who was a diabetic and literally incapable of living in the Middle Ages? Bryanna, who was constantly afraid for her health and life? Bryanna, for whom *careful* was the word to live by.

Raghnall's eyes watered, glistening in the light of the torches. "'Twas Mòrag. I remember she casually laid her hand on the dagger attached to the belt at her waist, before she proceeded to question me about who I was and where I was going. She demanded I pay her for the lodging, and I agreed. I must say, I didna have much, but the scent that came out of that house made me want to sell my soul to stay there. So I paid. And then I stayed there for sennights."

Bryanna kept nodding, more to distract herself from the dull ache in her middle at the image of Raghnall in the arms of another woman. A healthy woman, a woman single-handedly running a farm and raising a child.

"I helped her on the farm, first to earn my keep, then because I liked her and she liked me. She asked me to stay and mentioned marriage." His hand clenched in a fist and he bumped it against the surface of the merlon softly. "Daidh's band attacked a moon later. I managed to stop them together with Mòrag's field workers, who were a tough lot. Mòrag had a temper and she insulted Daidh. I saw her death sentence in his eyes, but I didna want to believe it. I should have killed him there, but I made him promise to never come back, and I let him go. Although I had taken lives before, I still didna like to kill a man in cold blood."

He paused and rubbed his chin covered with short beard.

"But he left and we didna see him again and things settled down at the farm. With time, Seoc warmed up to me, and she... the more I got to ken Mòrag, the more I fell in love with her. I didna acknowledge that to myself and especially nae to her, and I'd been avoiding giving her an answer to her suggestion of marriage. And when she started to insist...I ran."

Bryanna stopped breathing, everything sinking within her. "You ran?"

"Aye, lass, I ran like a bloody coward. I just left her, nae a word. The truth is...I left her before she could break my heart. I felt like a shite. I'd been alone and outcast from the clan since I was a lad of fourteen, lass. I had no clan. I had no one, and I had thought I didna need anyone. For most of my life, I've been caring for myself."

He sighed and shook his head. "Three days later, I came back. I changed my mind. I kent I was being a coward. I kent she deserved better. And I realized just how much I loved her. A goldsmith made a ring... A simple one, but still. I went back to the farm..."

His voice broke, and his face crumpled in a tearless grimace of grief. Bryanna laid her hand on his shoulder and squeezed. Looking at the lightening horizon, he breathed for a moment.

"Daidh raided the farm again, lass. He came for revenge. He murdered her because of me!"

Bryanna gasped and blinked. She reached her hand out to him but stopped herself.

Raghnall swallowed, his throat working. "She lay in the dirt, in a pool of her own blood...dying. I asked her to marry me, and she said yes. I promised my dying betrothed that I'd always take care of Seoc. But truth is, lass, I'll never be able to relieve my guilt. She died because I didn't have courage enough to be a man and marry her like she'd asked me to. Had I not run, I'd have been able to protect her against the man who wanted me. There's something so wrong about me, lass. I should never have a family, never marry. I should never have children."

"But why, Raghnall?" Bryanna asked carefully, her voice coming out deep.

He looked at her, and at that moment, she knew all his walls were down. His defenses had crumbled, and she was looking right into the very core of his soul.

And she saw no darkness there.

There was only light. Light, dimmed for years and years by pain.

"Because 'tis better to be alone than to hurt anyone again, lass. Loving means hurting people, losing people. How can any relationship in my life be any different?"

She couldn't stand the raw, blistering pain saturating his raspy voice. She closed the remaining distance between them and cupped his jaw, the touch of his rough stubble burning her fingers.

"You're so wrong, Raghnall," she said. "You don't hurt people. You protect them. And there are people who wouldn't hurt you..."

His eyes softened. "Aye, I've seen that from ye, lass. Why have ye been so loyal to me, when I kidnapped ye and held ye in my house against yer will?"

The vision of him blurred as tears welled in her eyes. "Because, my fierce Highlander, we may be separated by centuries, but we're not so different, you and me. I have secrets of my own, and I know what it is to feel alone. And no one has ever made me feel so alive as you do..."

CHAPTER 22

HE KISSED HER THEN, sealing his mouth to hers. His lips were tender and hard at the same time. He wrapped his arms around her, crushing her against his chest, locking her in the steely, hot embrace of his arms.

There was salty wetness on her lips—tears, she realized, though if they were his or hers, she didn't know. There was an ache, as well, the desperation of two wounded souls that sought refuge in each other.

And found it.

They were connecting, coming together and falling apart, and aching for each other as their tongues glided and moved, loving. Soon, pained groans were coming out of his mouth, and kitten-like whimpers out of hers. She was hot and needy, every cell in her body alive and vibrant with him...her Highland warrior with a broken soul of gold and demons that begged to be released.

And suddenly, she knew without a shadow of a doubt why Sìneag had sent her here. Maybe it was the psychic in her; maybe it was just that her heart had finally been tuned to the right tone.

But she knew.

She had come for him. He was her soul mate, even though

they'd never be together. Even though he'd never love her like he loved Mòrag. Her time would come to an end here, but they were still soul mates.

And as his soul mate, she would heal him.

She stopped the kiss and leaned back and took his head in both her hands, her eyes searching his. His were wild, as dark and as shiny as wet obsidian, and so full of desire she shuddered.

"I'm yours, Raghnall," she whispered. "Whatever happens, no matter how much time we have together—and I may go back to my time tomorrow—no matter for how long destiny has brought us together, I'm your wife now, and I'm yours, and I won't abandon you."

He blinked, and the desire mixed with another emotion—ache...gratitude...wonder.

Bryanna swallowed the ache in her own throat and said, "You wanted me to ask you to make love to me. Here I am. Asking."

He exhaled, his eyes bottomless. "Are ye certain, lass? After everything I told ye?"

"Especially after everything you told me."

With a wolflike growl, he returned to her and crushed his mouth to hers, his lips taking hers completely. The kiss changed. From tender and sensual, it became hungry, lustful, craving. Like a starved man, Raghnall was devouring her, his tongue lashing and caressing, claiming and owning her.

His hands went up and down her body, stroking the curve of her waist and down to her bottom. Grabbing two fistfuls of her butt, he lifted her up and sat her on the crenel. Bryanna felt the emptiness of the air behind her, the danger of the twenty-foot free fall strangely exhilarating.

And yet, she felt no fear of falling. She completely trusted him, as though they were on the ground.

"What if someone comes in?" she whispered against his lips.

"I'm going to tear them apart like a rag," he growled back. "Hold on, lass..."

And before she could say anything to protest, he shifted her to the edge of the crenel, sank to his knees on the ground before her, and raised her skirt up to her waist, exposing her legs completely. She gasped, heat burning up her cheeks like boiling water.

"'Tis an interesting garment, lass," he said, pushing her panties to the side. "Do ye mind terribly if I tear it?"

She'd been washing her panties every night and putting them before the fire to dry. Sometimes they didn't dry if the fire died in the night, so she had to go some days without underwear. But, as she'd learned, medieval women didn't wear underwear at all.

"I don't mind if you do anything you want with me..." she whispered.

The growl he gave out could have belonged to a predator. She felt his hot fingers against her thigh, then heard the wrenching sound of fabric being torn and felt a cooling wisp of air against her heated flesh.

Raghnall brushed the inner side of her thigh up to her sex. "Oh, God almighty, ye'll be the death of me, lass."

And then his mouth was on her—there... She gasped from the overwhelming pleasure that spilled through her veins and all through her thighs. He held her hips and placed her legs on his shoulders, wrapping his arms around her pelvis.

He was moaning, making a feast of her, giving her the most intense sensations she'd ever felt. Liquid heat spread through her in quick bursts. Teasing, licking, sucking, he was giving and giving to her, making her lose her mind with pleasure.

Cool wind was brushing against her cheeks, against her heated lips, against her naked thighs, and the cold stone on which she sat was cooling her enough to keep her sane.

And then, she was close, so close to the edge...

"Raghnall..." She tugged at his hair gently. "Stop, I'm... I'm..."

He raised his head, his face as satisfied as a cat that had just enjoyed a bowlful of cream. "Aye, lass, come. If ye think 'tis the last time for today, ye dinna ken me at all. I havena even started."

"No, no, I want this... I need you...inside... Please..."

He rose to his feet, the significant bulge in his trousers making her shudder again.

"What are ye doing to me, lass... Begging me..."

She sat up and leaned forward, undoing the belt that held his breeches and letting them slide down his legs, exposing a pair of muscular thighs and an erection that sprang at her, big and pink and beautiful. And she swallowed, wondering how he could fit inside her and craving him.

"Oh God..." she managed.

He leaned forward and picked her up, making her wrap her legs around his waist, then moved with her to the crenel and leaned her against the wall.

Oh wow...he was going to take her against the wall of the castle... She clenched in response, feeling herself getting even wetter.

"I want you, Raghnall Mackenzie," she whispered, looking into his eyes. She reached down and found his erection, which was poking at her entrance, and let the tip slide right there. "I'm yours."

With a moan that was half ache, half impatience, he pushed, burying himself completely within her. She gasped as she was stretched inside so completely, so fully that there was an edge of pain. He froze for a moment, panting wildly, staring into her eyes. "Aye, mine, lass." He rasped. "My wife. My soul. My woman." He dove inside her again. "Mine to protect." Slowly, he retreated and then plunged in again, sending a burst of sparks through her veins. "Mine to love." Another thrust and she was right there, at the edge again. "Mine to please."

She saw he was at the edge, as well. At the edge of madness, of wild pleasure, at the edge of letting himself go, at the edge of saying something he wouldn't be able to take back.

And then he began to pound within her, thrust after thrust of the wild, primitive ride of a man who wanted his woman. But he didn't look away. With his head tilted back, his dark eyes were on hers, holding them captive.

"I will protect ye, lass," he groaned, pounding within her like mad, driving her insane with pleasure. "Whatever it takes, I will protect ye... Ye're safe with me... Ye're the wife I never thought I needed. Ye're the wife I always wanted. Ye're...everything..."

The last word came out in an animalistic groan, and this was his undoing as it was hers. She fell over the edge of sanity, bucked, and was coming and coming and coming, shuddering, moaning, trembling. There, above the ground and close to the sky, among the first rays of sunlight, deep in the Scottish Highlands, waves of sweetness were washing over Bryanna—with the man she could never have, the man she was falling in love with.

CHAPTER 23

THEY SAT FOR A WHILE, leaned against the cold wall of the merlon, right on the floor of the tower, watching the sky lighten up. It was colored in soft gold and pink, blending into a pale manganese blue and then indigo on the other side of the sky.

There was a new awareness in Bryanna. Raghnall's arm was wrapped around her shoulders, and something about that gesture made her believe he, indeed, meant it when he'd said he'd protect her, he'd make sure she was fine, even though it had been said in the heat of the moment.

She felt protected and secure. This man...she tangled her fingers with his, and he brushed the side of her thumb with his, sending soft tingles through her skin.

They connected on a whole different level—somewhere beyond words, beyond time, and beyond her comprehension. There must be something about that soul mate thing. She'd never felt anything remotely like it with the three boyfriends she'd had in the past.

Raghnall...

She looked up at his calm, peaceful profile. "You make me feel alive."

He shook his head and chuckled. "Lass, ye dinna ken what ye talk about..."

"No, listen. You're wild. Pure in your rage, in your pain, and in your love. Like a true Highlander, you never do anything by half, do you?" He frowned and watched her, completely still. "You always dive into everything wholeheartedly, whether it's for your own good or ill. Don't you?"

He cleared his throat. "Aye, lass, I suppose, 'tis the correct explanation."

She shook her head and gave out a bitter chuckle. "I've been just the opposite. My diabetes...the sugar sickness...it made me careful. Always watching my diet is one thing, but I also have to keep track of my blood sugar and always have insulin handy. I'm like a ticking bomb, Raghnall. Yes, I'm manageable in the twenty-first century, but I'm completely dependent on medicine. You saw it yourself. And my family has always been worried I'll injure myself doing sports because it's always more dangerous for the diabetics to get hurt and go through surgeries. That's why I've never been allowed to ride a horse, and you made me so happy when you taught me. And this..." She gestured around at the castle. "This adventure, overall...nothing has ever made me feel so afraid...and so alive. It showed me I can do it, that I'm not a fragile wallflower. I'm strong and I'm capable of more than I thought I was." She cupped his face. "You showed it to me, Raghnall."

He smiled. "There ye are again, the sun."

"What?"

"When ye came to me by the church, I thought I'd never seen anyone that had more life and energy than ye. Ye...brightened everything around ye. Ye made me feel like there was hope, like I could be happy. Just yer presence brought me joy."

The corners of her mouth tightened and threatened to spread in the broadest smile. "Really? That was when I thought I was in a wonderful dream and that I was invisible...and diabetes-free."

"'Tis who ye are, lass. 'Tis the true ye. Nae ye bent by sickness." He placed his palm in the middle of her chest. "The sunlass."

Her eyes welled with tears. "I wish I could stay with you forever. If I didn't have diabetes, I would stay. Truly. I'd live in this crazy medieval world with you and Seoc, and I'd face any hardships and embrace any adventures." She whimpered. "But I can't. You know I'd die without insulin."

He turned away from her, his jaw muscles working under his short beard. "Aye, lass. And I canna have another woman die because I failed to protect her. Ye're going back. 'Tis the end of it. Ye wilna die here, I swear."

Suddenly the vision of her dead body being carried out of the castle by a warrior flashed in her mind. Tall...muscular...dark-haired...

She couldn't see his face, but it really could be Raghnall.

Sìneag's words came to mind, *He may also be yer destruction.*

She didn't believe he'd kill her, and she knew he'd do everything to protect her...so how could he be her destruction?

No. She chased the thought away.

"You know, I still might die here." She looked at her hands and picked at one fingernail with another.

"Aye, but—"

"I've...I've never told this to anyone. Not to my sister or my mother or my dad... But I see things."

Raghnall turned to her, suddenly more serious than she'd ever seen him. "Ye see things?"

"Yeah...I think I have psychic abilities. Well, I'm pretty sure I do. And I've seen my own death... here."

Raghnall stopped rubbing his thumb against hers. "What did ye see?"

She licked her lips. "My own body, carried out of the castle by a medieval warrior. I don't see his face, so I don't know who he is. But I know I'm most certainly dead in his arms."

He blinked several times. "Lass, how do ye ken 'tis true?"

"I've seen other things that came true." Suddenly the memory of her vision of her dad slapped her mind, and the pain of guilt and grief pulled her under like an ocean wave. "I saw my dad having a heart attack... I woke up, and I almost told him to call his doctor and ask for an appointment to check his heart. But I was afraid everyone would think I was crazy, that they'd start to worry about my psychological well-being. So I did nothing..." She choked on a sob. Tears ran down her cheeks, burning her skin. "I was a coward. I could have saved him, Raghnall. Why am I having these visions if I can't put them to good use?"

She sniffled, wiping her cheeks, and Raghnall pulled her close, wrapping his arms around her. There he was, her safe haven, this man with whom she could never stay.

He was stroking her back up and down. "Ye wilna die, lass," he said firmly. "I swore to ye I wilna let this happen. And one thing ye didna mention about a Highlander—he always keeps his word."

And as she sighed a relieved breath into his chest, she looked up and met his eyes. "But Raghnall," she whispered, "what if that Highlander in my vision is you?"

His eyes widened, and he blinked faintly as he looked into nothingness, fear and pain on his face.

She knew then that she should have never said it. Because he said nothing, and that said everything to her.

It was exactly what he was afraid of, too.

He broke the connection and let go of her, then stood up, his expression somber. He opened his mouth to say something but then turned to look away from the castle.

And his face went rigid.

Bryanna jumped to her feet to see what was happening, and there, approaching Dornie, was a medieval army with troops as far as the eye could see.

CHAPTER 24

"Ye must leave, Bryanna, now!"

Raghnall's voice was ringing in her ears as she stood on weak legs, not knowing how she'd made her way back to their bedroom. Her chest contracted, struggling to get enough oxygen, and her hands shook as she opened the door.

Yeah, no shit, Sherlock, you have to get back! Of course she had to get back, right freaking now. Only nothing had changed and the damned rock was still under a huge pile of rubble.

And while Raghnall had run into the barracks in the inner bailey, calling all archers and warriors to arms, she had run like a coward into their bedroom to get her purse. Then she would go to the basement and try to lift those rocks and clear the way out until her fingernails split and her fingers bled.

But as she opened the door, a wave of shock hit her like a concrete wall.

In the middle of the room was Seoc, standing amid shards of plastic and two transparent pools of liquid shining on the wooden floor, early-morning light reflecting from the insulin.

A sound came out of Bryanna's throat, something that resembled a pained bird's cry...

Her purple purse was in Seoc's hands, and her things were

scattered on the floor—her wallet, her cards, the pack of tissues... Her diabetes kit was open and hung from his other hand.

He looked up at her, his eyes big, confused, afraid...

And then the wolf cub Raghnall had described was back. His eyes turned narrow and wild, eyebrows as rigid and straight as a line, nose wrinkled as he reached to his belt and stepped back, pointing a small knife at her.

Her heart broke. How could a child have been treated so badly that this was his response to having been caught breaking something? What must he have gone through? He was probably just curious and didn't think to ask if he could look in her purse. And of course he didn't know what he was looking at—the pens, the kit, everything else.

"Get back, witch!" he cried.

But that little wolf cub, with no ill intent, had broken the only chance she had to survive for much longer here.

Fear and dread squeezed her gut like a vise.

"Oh, good Lord..." she whispered as the image of her carried in the arms of a Highlander flashed in her mind. That image became bigger and brighter and, if it was possible, more real. The vague, blurry features of the Highlander's face became clearer, as though emerging from the fog, and she could see the dark, obsidian eyes and the battle scars and that dark beard under high cheekbones.

As she'd suspected for a while now, it was Raghnall who carried her.

He may also be yer destruction.

So far, it seemed, his sworn stepson was.

"It's all right," she said to Seoc, feeling anything but. She remembered she'd been a teacher back in the twenty-first century, and she knew how to calm ten-year-olds down and get them to behave. "You're safe. I'm not going to hurt you."

The boy blinked and let his arm fall, the knife pointing

downwards. She knew her voice sounded soothing and teacher-like, and every child had an immediate reaction to it.

Even a medieval one.

Seoc looked around. "I'm so sorry, mistress. I was just curious, and it all fell out, and I stepped on these wee things, and they broke. I didna mean to... What is all this, mistress?"

Her life being smashed against the floor...

But she had to appear strong and capable. Before she could reply, steps sounded from behind her, and Raghnall appeared in the room, panting, his eyes wild... And then they grew wilder when he looked at the floor.

"Oh, lass..." he managed. "Is that yer...insu—"

Bryanna closed her eyes and nodded solemnly.

"Oh, God's arse! Seoc, what did ye do?"

She shook her head. "He didn't. It was me, I...I was too clumsy. Don't blame him. It was me."

The boy had gone through enough, losing his mother, moving across the country with a man he didn't know—and he was clearly malnourished and uncared for. What he needed was love. What he needed was care.

Raghnall took her by the arms and shook her a little, his face a mask of desperation.

"Lass, ye ken what this means!" he shouted right into her face. "Ye must leave, now. The enemy is right at our door."

She felt her legs beginning to shake. She looked at the medical supplies and other stuff scattered around the floor. Was her glucose monitor even whole? Did it even matter if she couldn't get more insulin in any case?

She swallowed, hard.

"Ye must leave, at once," Raghnall insisted.

"But how?" she whispered.

"Let's go, I'll help ye clear it."

She saw the hesitation in his eyes, the conflict. The pause, the frown between his eyebrows told her everything.

"You can't help me. You're needed to protect your family..."

She looked at Seoc, who was staring at them wide-eyed. "Your son."

Raghnall's chin jerked, decision hard on his face. "My family has enough men to protect them, including Angus, who is the best warrior I ken. And ye have no one."

He looked at Seoc. "Come, lad, help me get Lady Bryanna's things back into her purse."

As Raghnall rushed to the floor, the boy stood forlorn, blinking. "I am sorry, mistress," he whispered in a small voice.

Bryanna, who had knelt to pick up her wallet and, one by one, her ID card, her credit card and her other cards, looked up at him. Suddenly, he was so small and vulnerable, she ached to reach out and wrap her arms around him.

"It's okay," she said firmly. "What's done is done. All you can do now is help."

The boy nodded and picked up the black case of her medical kit and handed it to her shyly. She took it from him and smiled, then put everything back into her purse.

When all was done, she straightened up, and Raghnall was already on his way.

She followed him, catching the shouts of distress coming from beyond the tower. The great hall was empty, and on the ground floor, men were rushing in and out of the basement, holding swords, crossbows, and bows and arrows.

Everything had changed. And everything might change even further—if she managed to free the rock today, she could be back in her hotel, hugging her mom and sister, tonight.

Only, as Raghnall and she worked together on removing the rocks, the image of her dead body in the arms of a medieval man whispered in her ear that there wouldn't be a happy ending today.

That she may never see her family again, after all.

She didn't know how long they worked. Her fingers became bruised and scratched, her fingernails chipped and torn.

Raghnall had had to change two torches already, and she felt even guiltier that she was taking him away from fighting for his family.

But then Seoc appeared in the basement. "Raghnall!" he cried, and both Bryanna and Raghnall looked up at him. "Yer brother the laird, he is asking for ye... Dornie fell. And now a whole fleet arrived...and they have fire arrows."

CHAPTER 25

"WHERE'S ANGUS?" Raghnall barked at Seoc, looking wildly around the inner bailey.

The lad and he had just come out of the main keep, and daylight hurt his eyes. Many Mackenzie warriors crouched behind merlons on the walls as arrows, some of them aflame, rained down on the castle. This was not a place for a lad.

"Damnation. Stand behind me," he commanded, pushing Seoc between himself and the wall of the keep. "Tell me where Angus is and go back into the keep."

Seoc picked up a small, wooden shield that was propped against the wall and showed Raghnall his dagger. "I'm nae going to hide. The laird is on the outer wall, on the tower facing Dornie."

Raghnall spat out an oath as he grabbed Seoc by the shoulder and dragged him back into the tower. When the door behind him closed, sinking the storage space into semidarkness, he pulled a shield down from the wall and a bow and a quiver of arrows.

Then he looked the lad straight in the eyes. "Stay here, I say."

Seoc's gaze shot daggers at him. "Why? Because ye're my da? Ye're no one to me, nae even my stepda."

There, two small eyes in the darkness, burning with the anger of two coals, declaring all the hatred and all the blame he had for Raghnall.

He wasn't grateful. He didn't think Raghnall was helping him.

He didn't want to do anything with Raghnall.

He blamed him for his mother's death, too.

Darkness opened up deep in Raghnall's soul. "I wish I could turn back time, lad, and save yer mother. I wish I could have been yer da, yer true da. But 'tis impossible to go back and change things. And so I have to live with my guilt for the rest of my life, hoping it will be a short one. But nae matter what ye think of me, I am here for ye, and I will provide ye with the future ye deserve. The future I should have always given ye."

Seoc's eyes watered. "I dinna need anything from ye. Ye canna bring my ma back to life."

Raghnall's head hung. "Nae, lad, I canna. But I can make sure ye're nae following her into the grave. Stay here."

When Seoc didn't say anything, Raghnall took it as the lad's quiet compliance, nodded, and sprinted out of the keep. The sounds of a battle assaulted him as he loped through the inner bailey: cries of pain, clashing swords, urgent commands. It smelled like smoke and singed animal skin—no doubt fire arrows had landed on the hides covering the roofs. As he ran, he raised his shield above his head, and arrows thunked against the wood and stabbed the ground around him.

But just as he crossed the inner bailey to run through the still-open gates and into the outer bailey, he stopped dead. In the outer bailey, Mackenzie men were retreating. They descended from the outer walls, supporting their wounded sword brothers. And those who could, turned around from time to time and sent arrows into the Ross army.

Ross warriors poured through the gate into the inner bailey, chasing the Mackenzies. The enemy had taken Dornie and the outer bailey.

As the Mackenzie warriors took refuge in the inner bailey, Raghnall saw Angus among the last of them. The laird hurried, supporting a wounded man and holding his shield over their heads.

"Retreat!" Angus yelled. "Retreat!"

"Retreat!" James echoed. He was up on the inner wall, his bow in his hands, shooting one arrow after another. Catrìona stood next to him, shooting, too. Then Raghnall spotted David, who was one of the last warriors, making sure the rest were in front of him. Even Eanar hurried back inside, holding his shoulder.

And then Raghnall saw through the open gates that the enemy had climbed the outer walls.

"How did they get in?" shouted Raghnall as warriors were passing by him, but no one bothered to reply. "What happened?"

Still, no one replied. Guilt churned in him—if he hadn't been making love to Bryanna in the tower, he would have seen the enemy coming sooner and sounded the alarm.

As the men closed the inner gate, Raghnall saw with cold, slippery horror that hundreds of enemy warriors poured through the outer gates like they owned the place.

He saw Odhran run past him, a bloody sword in his hand, and Raghnall stopped him.

"Where is your wife?" Raghnall asked. "Where are the women and children?"

"All in the great hall, Lord," said Odhran, panting. "Safe for now."

"Good. 'Tis good. Can ye make sure Seoc is there, too? He should be in the main keep. Tell yer wife to keep an eye on him, aye?"

Odhran nodded. "Aye, Lord."

Raghnall squeezed his shoulder in gratitude and watched him sprint into the main keep. Relieved that Seoc would be taken care of and that the women and children were as safe as possible,

Raghnall ran to Angus and supported the warrior from the other side.

"What the hell happened?" Raghnall demanded. "How could they have gotten in so quickly?"

"She's too clever, brother. She distracted us with Dornie while her ships came from the sea gate, and before we knew it, they sent men from there. They have some sort of new ladders with hooks, and it was as though she knew exactly where they needed to throw them to get in."

"Ah, goddamn it. How could no one have seen the ships? It's not like they're moving fast."

"They saw them, but she was burning the village down...the church..." Angus's voice broke. "I dinna ken if Father Nicholas is even alive. He refused to leave the house of God. And I didna think the ships would be a threat at all, we're so well defended..."

"How many men does she have?" Raghnall asked.

"A thousand at least." They reached the barracks and went inside. Angus and Raghnall let the warrior lie down on one of the beds, then they turned and left.

"What do we do?" Raghnall said. "If they have those strange ladders, they can use them again for these walls, too."

Angus stared at the walls with a cold determination as they walked. "What do we do? We fight like hell. I wilna let them harm my wife and my unborn child."

Raghnall's blood chilled at the thought of the pregnant Rogene. "Euphemia wilna let her live," he murmured. "Or ye."

Angus shook his head once. "I'm nae so sure about that. Death may be my best option if she gets a hold of me. But if it would allow us to stop this..."

Raghnall frowned as they marched towards the walls. "Brother, ye're nae seriously thinking of surrendering."

Angus climbed the stone stairs that were built along the inner curtain wall. "Right now, I'm thinking to give her hell," he threw over his shoulder.

Raghnall followed him, and when they both stood on top of

the wall among other archers and warriors, they hid behind the merlons. The inner wall was thicker than the outer one. Here and there, sand was being heated in the cauldrons. Men carried rocks up the stairs, and many were throwing them onto the assailants below.

Thick gray clouds rose from Dornie on the other side of the loch, bringing the scent of smoke and of disaster. A volley of arrows swooshed past overhead, followed by the sounds of iron arrowheads knocking against the rocks, and moans and cries of pain from the wounded in the inner bailey.

Raghnall's heart sank at the sight of how many enemy warriors were in the outer bailey. Ross archers stood on the outer wall and shot at them.

And then he saw the new ladders. They were rope ladders with iron hooks on the ends... Ross men threw the hooks at their wall. Many times, they didn't catch. But they were trying again and again. Mackenzie archers worked hard, sending arrow after arrow into the rows of men below, but there were too many of them...someone else was always catching the hooks and throwing them again.

Raghnall took out his own bow and began sending arrows into the enemy. Someone picked up a large bowl of hot sand and poured it down. Agonized yells of pain sounded from below. God, that must hurt as sand filtered through the gaps between the armor and reached their bodies. The scent of singed hair and flesh tickled Raghnall's nostrils.

After a while, he noticed cries of pain and screams from his left and saw that the enemy had managed to hook the ladders to the wall on the other side of the gate and were climbing up. They were being pushed off, and more hot sand was being poured on top of them. But nothing could stop so many men. Not rocks. Not arrows. Not hot sand.

And then Raghnall's heart stopped as he saw a lad launch himself at an enemy warrior and stab his small dagger into the man's ankle.

Seoc!

The warrior yelled in pain and raised his sword, about to strike Raghnall's son.

The scent of smoke, of singed flesh and hair, plus seeing Seoc in mortal danger, flashed the image of four years ago into Raghnall's mind. How the farm burned, and the woman he loved took her last breath, and how he swore to protect Seoc and take care of him.

He couldn't let Seoc get hurt.

He darted, weaving around the fighting warriors, seeing no one and nothing but the boy whose life he had to save.

Or he wouldn't be able to live with himself.

Seoc ducked and avoided the blade, but the man raised it again, ready to strike. Raghnall managed to put his claymore against the enemy's sword just in time.

Sassenach warrior, he noted distantly. Their swords clashed together again and again, ringing. The man's blade slashed against Raghnall's shoulder—a scratch.

Seoc dodged in again and stabbed the man in the thigh. As the man yelled, distracted, Raghnall managed to stab him right in the eye and send him to his death down the wall.

Breathing heavily, Raghnall leaned closer to Seoc. "What did I say, lad!" he yelled. "Ye must remain in the tower."

"Why do I have to remain in the tower when even yer own lady isna?"

"Bryanna?" Raghnall murmured as he looked around...and saw her down in the inner bailey, putting rocks into a wooden crate.

Their eyes locked, and he was immediately struck by the intensity of her fierce gaze, and that sunlight of joy and strength that he knew she radiated when she was herself.

She must have brought rocks from the underground area, he thought.

Did she manage to clear the stone?

But he couldn't go to her because more warriors appeared

from the ladders. A sword flashed right by his neck, and he barely ducked. He raised his blade. He had a child, a wife he loved to protect as well as his whole clan. A family that loved and accepted him.

He raised his sword.

Only, unlike many battles before, he didn't chase death at the edge of a blade.

He chased life.

CHAPTER 26

A few minutes earlier...

Bryanna stared at the now cleared rock, the carvings dancing wildly from the jumping torch light. Raghnall had helped her so much, but at some point, she'd smelled a whiff of freshly cut grass and lavender, and after that, the work on the rocks had gone much easier.

It was as though the glue that had held them together had crumbled, and they'd become lighter.

After Raghnall had had to go to help in the battle, she'd gone on removing the smaller stones with a shovel and pushing them aside with her bare hands.

And now she could see it, still covered with dust and small rocks, but free enough for her to put her hand in the handprint...

And leave.

So why was she hesitating?

Because she'd never see Raghnall again.

And that thought brought an anguish so heavy, she couldn't breathe. She could return here at any moment and leave now.

She would just take one last look at him, make sure he was okay...and whisper her goodbye, even if from a distance.

When she stopped outside the main keep, her whole body went numb.

Men with spilled guts and bloody gashes were lying on the ground. Dead... Wounded... Clashes of swords were mixed with screams of pain. And the smell...oh God, the smell! Smoke, burned flesh, and something acrid and ironlike.

A real war.

The Mackenzies, the Ross clansmen...they were all men. And this was real—as real as a heart attack.

She had to do something to help! She couldn't fight. But she saw people on top of the wall throwing rocks on the climbing enemy. And they needed more. She had more.

Pushing the shock into the back of her psyche as much as she could, she went back into the basement to get rocks—the rocks she'd been clearing for hours now.

When she descended, she felt dizzy. This must be from the sheer exhaustion of hard physical labor. She might normally need the insulin injection. Fear scraped at the back of her mind. She had no more insulin, but the way home was clear, and she'd be careful.

So she got back to work, with shaking hands, putting more rocks into a crate she'd found in the basement. And then as soon as it was heavy enough to bring an efficient load—but light enough for her to be able to carry it up into the inner bailey—she headed up there.

But every load brought more and more exhaustion. She wasn't doing herself any favors, and she knew it. It was getting worse, with every step that she took, with every stone that she put into the crate. Under normal circumstances, she should be resting and taking her insulin...

Bryanna stopped in the doorway of the storage room, looking at the bailey. Dead bodies, men and women fighting... There were people she'd met, the man she was falling for...maybe even had fallen for...swinging his sword up on that wall, protecting her, protecting his family, protecting the boy that wasn't even his.

How could she hide somewhere and wait until others risked their lives for her?

She couldn't fight and she couldn't take care of the wounded...but she could do this simple job. She could bring rocks up onto the wall, there, where it wasn't breached. She could help defend the castle.

Raghnall had said she had sunlight about her...that freedom when she had thought she was invincible.

Well, maybe she could pretend she was. Just for some time. Even though she was anything but.

Shaking her weakness and dizziness off, she shifted the crate with rocks to relieve the pain in her fingers from the side of the board digging into them.

Then she walked through the bailey and up the stone stairs that ran along the curtain wall and led onto the wall. Maybe it wasn't the best idea, because the dizzy spell made her feel like she was on a helicopter spinning out of control.

There, on the right side, where the archers were shooting— including James and Catrìona and even David—the protection was still working. And other warriors were throwing rocks onto the attackers who were trying to climb the walls.

But to the left of the gates, on the wall, Mackenzie defenses had been breached, and the battle was going full speed ahead. There was Raghnall swinging his sword, his face a mask of fury and battle rage, and her heart squeezed in worry and fear for him. But he seemed to be invincible, taut muscles playing under his tunic as he fought.

He was death itself—merciless, efficient, and cold-blooded. And next to him, ten-year-old Seoc was trying to jab Raghnall's opponent in the thigh.

Bryanna gasped. How could she have forgotten about the boy? She put the crate next to one of the warriors who was busy throwing rocks. He gave her a grateful, curt nod before returning to his defensive work.

With her feet cold, and feeling like she was flying, she hurried to Seoc, avoiding the fighting men.

"Seoc!" she cried. "Seoc!"

But the boy didn't turn to her, didn't hear her.

She kept going. A movement flashed to her right, and a man who had just thrown one of the Mackenzie warriors off the wall was suddenly right in front of her—just a step away.

The enemy's eyes were wild with battle rage as he stared at her, panting, upper lip curled in a bloodthirsty snarl.

She saw the thought flash through his mind—an unprotected woman, he could kill her, or kidnap her, or drag her away and rape her if he wanted. But before he could do any of that, someone else jabbed a sword into his face, and he had to duck and forget about her.

With fear chilling her limbs like ice, she kept sprinting along the wall. Good grief, this was not a place for children!

"Seoc! Seoc!" she kept calling.

Like a small wolf cub helping a grown wolf, he was fighting another enemy warrior with Raghnall. With a knife in his hand, Seoc dashed left and right, throwing jabs into the man's waist, legs, lower back—anywhere he could reach.

"Seoc!" she called. Finally, he turned around. throwing an irritated glance at her. "Stop this right now! Come on, you can help me—"

Raghnall turned his head to her, too.

But not the man they fought. He used the opportunity to slash Raghnall across the chest, cutting through his *leine croich* to flesh...

All the blood drained from Bryanna's body at the sight of red saturating the edge of the slash, spilling down the *croich*.

Raghnall winced, not moving for a moment, probably from shock. Sensing his close victory, the enemy warrior raised his sword in a final, victorious slash.

It would be too late. Raghnall wouldn't have time to defend himself. Or duck. Bryanna didn't hesitate. She grabbed a rock that lay close to her feet and smashed it with all her might against the man's head. He was wearing a chain mail coif, which absorbed most of the impact, but it was enough for the man to stop and turn to her.

That gave Raghnall an opportunity. He stabbed the man in the stomach. The enemy grunted, holding on to the blade that was sunk deep in his gut.

Strong arms caught her from behind, and the stench of male sweat, blood, and bad breath invaded her senses. Then the man dragged her away, Raghnall's panicked face receding into the distance.

CHAPTER 27

GOD'S BLOOD, *they got Bryanna!* Raghnall pushed the man he'd killed aside as he hurried towards the place where Bryanna had just stood.

Before he could chase after her, she managed to wiggle out of the man's arms. She backed away from him and the other enemy warriors. Then, cornered and panicking, she climbed up onto a crenel.

Working with his elbows, Raghnall pushed men away to get to her... But in the heat of the ongoing battle, a warrior was pushed against the wall, knocking into her.

She gasped, and for a moment she waved her arms, trying to grab on to something. The skirt of her burgundy dress flapped in the air... Then she was gone into the vastness of air behind the wall.

"Aaaaaaahhhhh!" Raghnall roared.

The door in the middle of his chest that had been sealed for years dissolved. In its place there was a dark, bloody gap.

And out of that gap, things burst forth. The horror, the guilt, the terror of the worst thing that had ever happened to him in his life. Something irreversible, something that had rent the deepest cracks in his being...a wound that would never heal.

The loss of someone who, despite his best efforts to keep her away, had become the matter of his very soul.

"Naaeee!" On numb legs, he rushed towards the wall. He pushed someone aside, avoiding the swoosh of blades and thuds of fists around him.

He looked down into the swarming warriors below, expecting to see her body sprawled and broken.

But somehow she yet lived... Bryanna had landed in the midst of the men waiting to climb the ropes and two men were dragging her down from there. Given that the inner wall wasn't as tall as the outer wall of Eilean Donan, the fall wasn't as high as it would have been had it happened out there.

"She's a Mackenzie, looks like a noble lady, nae a milkmaid or a servant!" yelled someone below. "Lady Euphemia told us to bring every Mackenzie we could get our hands on. She wants hostages."

Aye, Euphemia must want to exact her vengeance upon Angus by bringing pain to everyone he loved. She must especially want to get to Rogene and Angus's unborn child.

Raghnall itched desperately to get to Bryanna, to tear the enemy throats out like a wolf and take her back to safety.

But he still had Seoc to think about. Helplessly, he was watching the kicking, screaming Bryanna being dragged somewhere... Someone tugged him, and he looked down.

Seoc, his eyebrows drawn together, eyes big. "Where is she? The nice lady?"

Raghnall's eyes watered. This was just like then... The woman was gone, and only he and the lad remained. He felt the edge of mad despair like he was standing on top of a cliff, nothing but blackness and chaos beneath.

This was what he had been so terrified of all these years, and even before Mòrag. To lose people he loved.

It would be so easy, to let himself fall apart, let the madness take him. Let the chaos win.

Or take the easy way out. Death was everywhere around him,

yearning to take his life. Engage one of the enemy and not duck. Let the blade bite deep. Hang his head and let the sword do what it was supposed to do.

Only, this wasn't the end, and Bryanna was still alive. The battle hadn't been lost yet.

And Raghnall could do what he'd learned to do best when he was one of the reivers.

Deceive and kill.

Wary of the enemy around them, he sank to his knees and looked straight into Seoc's eyes. "Ye must promise me something, lad. I canna worry both about ye and about her. So if ye want to help her, please, for the love of God, go and hide in the safety of the keep. Can ye promise me that?"

Seoc's eyes watered. "I only wanted to help. I saved yer life."

"Ye did. And now 'tis time to save hers. Promise me. A warrior's promise, aye?"

Seoc nodded, solemn and serious. "Aye."

Raghnall nodded and they proceeded down the stairs to the inner bailey. As he watched Seoc run into the tower, Raghnall felt bad leaving his sword brothers to fight without him, but he had to discuss his plan with Angus.

Mackenzie warriors were racing towards the places in the wall where the enemy had managed to push through. Raghnall climbed up the stairs to the part of the wall where he saw James and Catriona shooting arrows, and Angus and the rest throwing rocks.

Raghnall touched his arm, and Angus turned his head to him. It was clear from his face how tired he was, how worried. Sweat caked locks of hair to his forehead.

"We are about to lose, brother," Raghnall said. "And both ye and I ken we canna afford that."

Because that would mean not just their deaths but the deaths of everyone they knew and loved.

"We're still holding," said Angus. "But there's just too many of them."

"Aye, which means we must do the one thing that'll stop them."

Angus stared at him for a moment. They both knew what that thing was—killing Euphemia or, even better, taking her hostage.

"So here's what I suggest," Raghnall said. "She wants the Mackenzies. She wants us. Everyone that's dear to ye—and ye, she wants ye most of all."

"Ye want me to go there?"

"Nae just ye alone. Ye and me. Ye distract her. I'll take her hostage. Make her stop the fight and have them retreat."

"What if they wilna stop?"

Raghnall felt his throat work. "Then I'll kill her."

Angus gave out a long sigh. "If ye kill her, ye're gaining a very important enemy, just as strong as Euphemia herself. Her brother. He may never stop fighting us."

Raghnall swallowed. "Aye. But if he can take his justice upon me, he will be satisfied. The Earl of Ross is a rational man, unlike his sister. He may take me to the king and the king would have to give his judgment. I hope Bruce wilna forget how I fought for him all these years."

Raghnall squeezed Angus's shoulder. "Ye and me, brother, let's stop this. What do ye say?"

Angus nodded. Of course he would, this big, powerful man as solid as a bear, and as deadly.

Raghnall told him briefly about his plan, and they agreed on details. Then he hurried down the stairs and back onto the part of the wall where the battle was still in full swing.

He fought his way through the little battles between men and to the only way he knew how to get down—the rope ladders that hung from the wall.

As more men were climbing up, he got to the hooks of one of them and yelled down as loud as he could: "'Xcuse me, lads! Give way! A Mackenzie's coming through!"

The men froze in surprise, and as he climbed over the wall

and started descending, one of them yelled, "Ye get back there, ye bastart, or I'll stab ye in the arse!"

"Have a message to Euphemia from Angus. He may be ready to surrender. But I guess she wilna ken of that, since ye'll stab me in the arse and I'll bleed to death like a pig."

The Ross warrior mumbled dirty curses but looked down to his clansmen. "Go down! Now! Down, I'm telling ye!"

Finally, one by one, they descended and gave Raghnall way.

As he kept descending under the heavy, malicious gazes of the enemy warriors, he thought this must have been the stupidest idea he'd ever had. Here he was, walking over ground moist with the blood of the dead and the wounded, and everyone he saw had something to kill him with.

And yet, they stood as if stunned, just watching.

And then he saw her. By the opposite wall, behind one of the household buildings, was a woman on a horse. Her long, golden hair and straight back were unmistakable. Although she looked quite pale and thin, Raghnall thought, remembering that Catriona had wounded Euphemia several sennights ago.

She might still be unwell, Raghnall thought, which he could use to his advantage.

But where was Bryanna?

And then he saw her, being held by two guards in front of Euphemia, who was seemingly talking to her.

His heart sank at the sight of Bryanna. She was looking fierce, staring into the eyes of someone who wasn't even her enemy. Her back was straight, her head held high.

As Raghnall approached, he heard Bryanna say, "I'm not going to tell you anything."

"Ye're an interesting one... Like Rogene aren't ye, with yer odd accent, and yer perfect skin, and yer youth..."

Her words were slurring a little, as though she was drunk...or maybe just exhausted.

"Ye're a Mackenzie, also, even though just because ye marrit one. But they'll come for ye, I ken, especially if we entice them a wee bit."

She signaled, and one of the guards raised his giant arm and slapped Bryanna.

A guttural yell burst out of Raghnall's throat, and he ran to put himself between her and the guards.

CHAPTER 28

THROUGH THE RINGING in her head and the explosive pain, Bryanna heard a man roar.

She turned her head, both worried and hopeful it was Raghnall, but could see only a blurry spot running at her.

She hated herself right now. For being weak. For being so useless. For letting that man back on the wall knock her over.

For being her.

She was the weak link. She wasn't the brave woman that Raghnall had told her she was…a woman full of sunlight.

She was a woman full of misfortunes.

But at least if she did die today, it would be while she was having the biggest adventure of her lifetime. She'd take it every time over dying alone in a hospital bed while on life support.

She blinked trying to make herself see sharper, and finally could distinguish Raghnall, running at the guards with his sword raised.

"Ye will be sorry, ye bastart!" he roared.

Euphemia blinked at him. "Stop him, right now!"

The guard standing by Euphemia lifted his sword and met Raghnall's, the ring of metal against metal loud and bright.

Raghnall kept thrusting his sword. "I came. To deliver. A message. From Angus."

Euphemia came to life. Her whole body straightened, her head rose higher, and a blush even seemed to hit her pale cheeks. "Stop! Let him speak!"

The guard froze, still pointing his sword at Raghnall, a look of warning on his face.

Raghnall stopped also, his chest rising and falling quickly. Despite the acute danger both Bryanna and he were in right now, she couldn't help but admire this man. He'd been wounded in several places, clearly, but he kept going. His eyes met hers, and there was everything she needed to know... He'd come for her. He was afraid for her.

He was here for her.

"Yer wife was useless," said Euphemia. "Ye Mackenzies have nae taste in the women ye marry. What's Angus's message? Would he like to surrender now or a wee bit later, when half of his men will be dead?"

"He wants to negotiate," Raghnall said, returning his gaze to Euphemia.

Euphemia shrugged one shoulder. "If he wants to negotiate, why didna he come himself?"

"He wants ye to meet him, one-on-one. Nae warriors. Nae weapons. Just talk."

A shiver ran through Bryanna. Euphemia kept her cool exterior, but something had shot through her—something that might have been curiosity or even desire. Bryanna didn't know the whole story and she didn't know what Raghnall was playing at, but she knew this meant something to Euphemia. She knew Raghnall was on the right track to change this losing battle.

"There's nothing to discuss," Euphemia said, her voice emotionless. "Ye've almost lost. I only have to wait, and my men only need to keep pushing. 'Tis nae in my interest to talk."

"What do ye want?"

"Ye ken what I want."

"Kintail?"

She straightened her back, but there it was, that barely noticeable wince of pain, and scowled at Raghnall. If Bryanna had ever seen a look that could kill, this was it.

Raghnall kept staring at Euphemia, too, but not a word came out of her mouth.

"What if I told ye," Raghnall said, "I can deliver what ye want. If ye go and speak with Angus."

She cocked her eyebrow. "I ken ye, Raghnall Mackenzie. Word around is ye're nae to be trusted. Nae by yer clan. Nae by anyone. So why should I trust a single word that comes out of yer mouth?"

Raghnall was losing now. Bryanna knew it, and he knew it, and so did all the guards standing around them. For the first time, Bryanna saw Raghnall at a loss, not knowing what to say or do. Whatever he had come up with, it wasn't working.

She had to help. She had to act.

No, she told herself. What she needed to do was be careful. She was in real danger here, and not just from the swords and axes and the fists of real killers who would snap her neck in a second, but from her body. She was on her last reserves, and she knew it. She felt it. That headache, her vision blurred and her muscles as weak as spaghetti, and that tingling that spread throughout her body.

Goddamn diabetes. This wasn't fair. How was it fair that she was so sick she lived a half-life? How was it fair that she couldn't help the one man who made her feel alive?

And that was why she had to risk it. She had to do something. Her whole life, she hadn't done anything. She was a teacher instead of a musician. She avoided relationships. She lived with her parents.

She never said a word about her psychic abilities.

Had she been braver, she might have saved her dad's life.

But she could be brave now.

All Raghnall needed was a little help. A little distraction.

"I see death in you," she said, looking straight at Euphemia.

Euphemia's eyes darted to Bryanna, sharp like the fangs of a snake. "What?"

Bryanna felt Raghnall's worried gaze on her, his eyebrows drawn together in a deep frown. Those thick, black, masculine eyebrows that made him look like Aidan Turner.

"Bryanna!" Raghnall said in warning.

"I see death," said Bryanna, using her eeriest voice and making her eyes go unfocused, looking somewhere beyond. "A black, black curtain of death before you. The curtain that will consume you."

Euphemia blinked. "What are ye talking about? 'Tis nonsense."

If Bryanna was going to burn, she'd burn brightly. "I am a witch, I see things. I saw my father's death—" Her voice broke. "I've seen my own death, 'tis nae far away." She met Euphemia's steely blue eyes. "And I see yours."

Euphemia was pale now, so pale, her skin appeared grayish. "Wh-what do ye see?" she asked, blinking rapidly.

"Tell the guards to let me go and come to me, and I'll tell you. Or do you want your enemy to find out?"

Euphemia's eyes darted to Raghnall for just a moment, then she jumped off the horse, wincing. She wore thin chain mail, but no doubt it was solid and well made. Euphemia retrieved a dagger and walked towards Bryanna, holding it casually, but the edge of the blade pointed upwards in a warning.

When she was two steps away, she stopped and showed her the blade. "One wrong move and I wilna hesitate to use this. Aye?"

The blade was so sharp it glistened in the dull light of the day. Bryanna nodded. "Clear. Tell them to let me go and come closer."

Bryanna didn't have a plan, not really. She didn't know if she could grab the dagger from Euphemia, but she could try. And then what? Would she really be able to kill another human being? She couldn't afford even a glance at Raghnall, not while Euphemia's eyes held her in their gaze with the intensity of tractor beams.

Euphemia made a small gesture with her head, and the guards stepped aside.

You wanted adventure? her own voice asked her in her head. *Here it is. More adventure than you can stomach.*

Her heart slamming against her ribs, Bryanna swallowed hard and took one step closer to Euphemia, who raised the dagger higher and let it point at Bryanna's stomach. "One wrong move..."

Hot sweat broke through the skin of Bryanna's back, and adrenaline ran through her, making her shiver all over.

Kick her! Grab that knife! Do something!

But her arms felt boneless, and her mind was getting as cloudy and thick as a milkshake.

And then from somewhere behind Euphemia, a big, tall figure with a sword dripping blood was approaching. Even though she couldn't see straight, and everything was blurry, Bryanna knew it was Angus.

"You'll die in the arms of the man you love..." she said, but it came out as weak as a whisper.

"What?" Euphemia asked, wincing in confusion. "Ye spoke so weakly. What did ye say?"

Lifting her hand that felt as heavy as cast iron, Bryanna gestured with her index finger for Euphemia to come closer.

Curious, impatient, Euphemia leaned forward, and Bryanna locked her eyes with the woman. From the corner of her eye, as if in slow motion, she saw Raghnall drive his forehead into the face of one of the guards. Angus raised his sword, blood flying through the air like raindrops.

There was a movement from her sides—perhaps her own guards realized what had happened.

But Bryanna had to keep Euphemia distracted for a moment

longer. With as much strength as she could muster, she said, "You will die in the arms of the man you love."

As Euphemia's eyes widened, and her pupils dilated—from fear, no doubt—Bryanna knew she'd gotten to her. Her mouth opened; her pretty, arched eyebrows drew together in an upside-down horseshoe.

And then she turned around and saw...

Raghnall had just slit the throat of one of her men. Angus, who had just killed another guard, pulled his sword from the man's stomach and looked straight at her.

Euphemia glared at Bryanna, fury in her eyes. "Ye bitch..."

She drew her hand back for a deadly strike. With her last bit of strength, Bryanna stepped back, but she staggered and fell. Her head knocked against something hard and sharp, pain exploding in her skull.

Stars were bursting behind her eyelids, bright and golden. And as everything was fading into black, and she was growing cold and disappearing into the air, she desperately commanded herself to get up, to live, to keep fighting.

But her vision had gone completely dark.

Only one image remained.

Her, dead, in a medieval dress, dirt and bruises on her pale face and hands. A Highlander carried her body, grief stricken and mournful.

Only this time his face was crystal clear.

CHAPTER 29

As RAGHNALL WATCHED the life slip from the woman he loved, he went cold and immobile.

And not just his body. His heart. While a moment ago it had beat, warm and alive and whole, now it stopped. Every ounce of blood and tissue turned into ice. And as moments flew past, and Bryanna, as pale as death and as unmoving as a corpse, didn't show a sign of life, the ice in his chest was cracking...

And breaking into millions of tiny pieces.

"Nae!" he yelled. "Nae!"

She couldn't be dead. She'd told him about that vision and about her sickness...but he'd done everything to prevent it.

Nae!

A sword swooshed, aiming for his face, and he stepped back in the last moment, sending his own blade into the shoulder of his attacker, cleaving his arm off. The scream of pain did nothing to Raghnall—he barely heard it.

While fighting with another man, he kept throwing glances to see if Bryanna would move or breathe...or something—but she remained as still as the earth she was lying on.

"Nae!"

Angus was fighting his own battles, and Raghnall saw from

the corner of his eye that the rest of Euphemia's troops had seen them, and a huge wave of men were coming at them.

Now or never, they had to finish it.

And he would. Because now he had his own reason to get even with Euphemia. Bryanna wouldn't be in this situation if not for Euphemia attacking the castle and then taking her hostage.

A wave of pure, white-hot rage broke through Raghnall's body in an all-consuming blast. He stabbed his opponent in the face, piercing his eye, and let him fall.

Then he looked at Euphemia, who stood, helpless, furious, panting wildly. The two men who had been guarding Bryanna stood protectively around Euphemia, but no one would stop Raghnall now. He would not let the same thing happen to Bryanna as had happened to Mòrag. He would not let her die.

And if Euphemia and anyone else stood between Raghnall and Bryanna's chance to live, he'd do anything.

Anything.

He'd gladly give his own life.

Roaring, he launched at them, scything a wide horizontal arc as he ran, slashing the air before him like a madman. Forgetting all caution, his logical mind slipped into darkness. And all that was left of him was this raw, pulsing rage.

He was that rage. That ancient, marrow-deep call for life and death that every man had to face.

He was the spirit of Morrigan, the Celtic goddess of war and death, and the Celtic god of war, Neit.

His own war cry rang in his ears. The world stopped existing. There was only slashing, jabbing, piercing, and striking. There was blood and broken bones and torn flesh.

And there was steel.

And then the two piercing icy-blue eyes found him. He stood, panting. Men were coming—he saw the wall of them approaching—and if they reached him, it was all going to be over. The two guards were dead, and Raghnall tasted blood on his tongue, and he thought that he had, perhaps, bitten into one of their throats like an animal. He spat the blood, and with three giant steps he walked to her, his sword ready to strike.

Euphemia unsheathed her own claymore and lifted it, and their blades clashed. But her arms were weak, and there was pain in her face. Raghnall pressed his sword down, and beat her sword out of her hands as though she were a child.

He raised his sword, pointing it right at her throat, naked above the armor and completely unprotected.

She was done; he saw it in her eyes.

"Raghnall!" Angus called as he ran towards him. "They're coming."

Raghnall grabbed Euphemia, clasping one arm around her shoulder and pressing her back to him. He held his blade to her neck.

He turned to where Angus was pointing. From two sides— the side of the inner wall that was still held by the Mackenzies and the outer wall—Ross men were coming.

"Call them off," yelled Raghnall. "Tell them to go back. Ye're the Mackenzie prisoner now. Tell them to stop!"

He felt Euphemia shake in his arms. "Nae."

"Tell them to stop, Euphemia!" roared Angus as he looked at her. "'Tis over."

She swallowed, her neck moving against Raghnall's blade. "Nae. no one humiliated me like ye have. I will never stop."

"Ye dinna have a choice, Lady Euphemia," Raghnall said. As the men stopped before them, Raghnall thought there must be two or three hundred of them still. Too many against just two.

"Turn back!" said Angus. "Go away, and we wilna hurt yer mistress. Move one finger—"

"Shoot him!" yelled Euphemia. "Archers, ye have the perfect shot! Shoot him!"

"Stop!" Raghnall yelled. "Dinna even think of it! Or ye will return with the body of yer mistress, and how would ye explain it to the Earl of Ross? Ye think he'd take it kindly?"

The men's hands were on their swords, and their bows and crossbows.

"Stand behind me, Angus," said Raghnall. "Turn and leave," he called to the Ross warriors. "We dinna want yer deaths."

And as he said that, a war horn sounded from somewhere beyond the outer wall...

"Stop right now, in the name of the king!" sounded the call from beyond the wall. "Yer king commands ye to stop!"

Angus and Raghnall looked at each other, their faces masks of relief.

"He came..." Angus whispered. "I asked the Cambels to call for his help since he favors their clan...and he came!"

Raghnall nodded. "Bruce wouldna have forgotten that ye hid him in Eilean Donan and saved him when he was alone and weak."

The Ross men were exchanging glances and lowering their weapons. "Dinna stop!" yelled Euphemia.

Raghnall felt relief flooding his body like a warm bath. He relaxed his grip on Euphemia, looking at the gates, through which the king himself, Robert the Bruce, and a large group of warriors were coming. He saw Cambel banners, MacDonald banners, and the banners of other clans that he vaguely recognized.

At that moment, the snake was ready to bite. Using his negligence, Euphemia twisted out of his grasp like a slug, grabbed a knife hidden at the back of her belt, and launched at Angus with a yell. Angus stood with his back to her, looking at the king. She was silent—no victory cries, no war cries.

A snake striking from behind.

She was aiming for Angus's kidney—a sure way to bleed him to death. Raghnall reached forward, yanked her by the hair, and before he could think, slit her throat with his sword. Angus turned, surprised, only to catch her dying body. Her eyes locked on Angus as the last moments of life were still beating in her, and she saw, perhaps, that Bryanna's prophecy was right, and that she was dying in the arms of the man she loved.

He'd done it unthinkingly, instinctively. Did he need to kill her? No. He could have restrained her probably.

Had the years as a mercenary and on the battlefield made him so cold, so able to take a life when needed and then move on to the next thing?

No. Mòrag's death had taught him not to let dangerous people walk away. This woman had tried to kill his family numerous times.

She wouldn't have stopped, and he couldn't lose his brother, one of the dearest people he loved.

Bryanna!

Raghnall couldn't wait another moment, couldn't stay and greet the king and explain why he'd just committed the murder seen by Robert the Bruce himself as well as hundreds of witnesses.

He sprinted six steps to Bryanna and dropped before her unmoving body.

"Bryanna..." he whispered, stroking her face. It was cold, too cold, but not the cold of a corpse. There was still life in her. He dropped his head to her chest, listening for the *thump-thump, thump-thump* of her heart...and heard it. It was very weak, but it was there.

She wasn't dead.

She needed her medicine, her insulin. And he had to take her to a place—a time—where that medicine existed. The future. He put his sword back in the sheath on his belt and picked her up. God's bones, how light she was, like she weighed nothing. He hurried to Angus.

"Take care of Seoc, Angus. Promise ye'll take care of him. Tell him I'm sorry, but I must make sure Bryanna lives. I have to take her to the future. There's medicine there that'll keep her alive. Here, she'll die. If I dinna come back, promise ye'll give my estate to Seoc."

Angus's serious eyes locked with his, and he nodded. "Of course, brother. Anything. Ye ken Seoc is safe with us. Go. Save her."

They nodded to each other, and Raghnall knew he'd never felt closer to Angus than he did now. Not losing any more time, he ran towards the keep. His shoes sank in the wet ground, soft and slurpy from blood. Ross men, who knew that the king had come, were stepping aside and letting him pass. "Open the gates!" yelled Raghnall. "Open the gates! We won! The king is here!"

Slowly, the gates were open, and he ran through them, followed by surprised eyes. As he ran, he noticed that someone had joined him—James, he realized, Catrìona, David, and Rogene...they all followed him. They all knew what it meant.

They had to make sure Bryanna was sent back to her time or she would die, just like she had predicted.

The way downstairs felt like it took forever, even the steps under Raghnall's feet felt slippery and dangerous. Holding his precious woman like a gift from God, he prayed in his head, for the first time ever—prayed for God to help him. He knew he had had no chance with Mòrag.

But he felt so much stronger now, with Bryanna. Somehow, deep within, he was ready to fight with time itself, or with a million demons or Highland faeries if needed, until his dying breath.

He'd do everything—*everything*—to make sure she survived.

And if it meant crossing hundreds of years, let it be so.

Down in the underground room, he was amazed to see that Bryanna had managed to finish the job and the rock was cleared.

James looked at Bryanna with worry. "Time is of the essence. She must be in a diabetic shock."

Raghnall nodded and crouched with her in his arms next to the rock. David sank to his knees by Raghnall's side.

"Listen to me, when you go through there, you'll be in a museum. Ask for help. Ask for museum workers and tell them they must call an ambulance right away because this woman is in a diabetic shock and is dying. Got it?"

Raghnall blinked, the words mixing like a porridge.

"Repeat what you need to do," said David.

"Um..." Raghnall blinked. "Museum. Find workers. Tell...call ambu..."

"Ambulance. Doctors. A healer."

"Ambulance," Raghnall repeated.

"What are you waiting for, go!" cried Rogene. "Put your hand in there."

Raghnall's jaw muscles worked as he looked around at his family, perhaps for the last time in his life. He met Catrìona's eyes. "Please, take care of Seoc," he said. "I'm such a shite for leaving him—again."

Catrìona nodded solemnly, and squeezed James's hand. "Dinna even worry, brother. no one is going to let Seoc be sad or lonely for a moment. Go. Save her."

His heart cracked open, and he felt like one half of it fell off and rolled on the floor, but he didn't allow himself to think anymore. His stomach flipped like he was about to jump into a dark abyss.

Cradling Bryanna's limp body to him, he leaned forward and put his hand into the handprint.

Distantly, he noted the carvings glowed. It felt like he didn't touch the stone, but as though his hand went through empty, cool air, and then there was no rock at all, and he was falling and falling into darkness. He held on to Bryanna, but after some time he couldn't feel her anymore.

He couldn't even feel himself.

And then darkness took him.

CHAPTER 30

RAGHNALL WAS cold and his whole body ached. Rising up on his elbows, he struggled to remember where he was and what had happened. Rough stone walls and a vaulted ceiling were illuminated by a single source of light that hung suspended by a black rope. Was it some sort of an oil lamp? But it couldn't be fire as the light didn't move, didn't blink, and didn't dance.

Then the next thought came.

Bryanna...

Her name was like the air he needed to breathe, her presence as necessary as the blood in his veins.

He looked around and his gaze fell on the unmoving body lying next to the rock with the handprint and the ancient carving. And suddenly the memories of what had happened and what he had to do came back.

She was dying. He had somehow fallen through that rock and traveled through time. It must have worked because the rock was the same but there was no rubble.

He scrambled to his feet, aware of numerous sources of pain in different parts of his body—the bruises, cuts, and wounds from the battle of Eilean Donan. He still had his sword and was still dressed in his *leine croich*, though it was cut and torn and caked with drying blood.

"Bryanna, I have ye, lass," he whispered as he leaned over her and cupped her face with one hand and found the vein in her neck with the finger of the other hand. There was no pulse. There was no movement, no sign of life he could find under his fingertips.

"Nae!" he cried, dropping his head to her chest...but he couldn't hear her heart. "Nae!"

Fear rushed over him like an avalanche of icy rocks, crushing his very soul, tearing his heart into a bloody pulp. He lifted her into his arms and ran.

He couldn't be the reason for her death. He couldn't be that man from her vision.

He couldn't lose the woman he loved.

He ran without seeing where. Instinctively, he knew he had to go through the door, and then up. As he left the small underground room behind, he rushed through a dully illuminated space with tables and some sort of large chests and chairs. Those were completely unfamiliar objects and things, but then he saw something he recognized.

The stairs that he'd known from his time.

As he ran, it felt like his feet moved slowly—just like in a nightmare, where the ground was dragging, sucking him in, trying to stop him.

Up the stairs, and then there was a small door, and he stopped before it on the small landing and kicked it with his foot.

It opened up with a swoosh and a crack when the door hit a wall.

There was no storage room like in the Eilean Donan he had known. No firewood, no sacks of oats, no weapons that hung on the walls. There were no sounds of the castle that he'd known— no pounding of the hammer against the anvil, no laughter and talking of warriors coming from the great hall, no squawking of geese and chickens from the outside. It smelled different...like something fruity and like old wood and dust, but also...clean.

There was a narrow corridor with some sort of square panels hanging on the walls, beautiful paintings on them the likes of which he'd never seen in his life. The corridor was illuminated by a small green lamp with a sign of a fleeing person that pointed to a heavy arched door. He hurried down the hallway, clutching Bryanna's body to his.

And all he could think was, *Please, let her be alive... Please let her be alive... God, I'll do anything. Take my life, if ye need one. Take me, just please, let her live.*

But his luck had run short. He pushed the heavy door with his shoulder, and it didn't budge. He grunted and fell against the door with all the power and weight that he could muster...

Shut. Completely closed.

"Heeeelp!!!" he yelled. "Someone! Heeeeelp! I need a healer!"

Nothing.

Then the scent of lavender and freshly cut grass tickled his nose.

"Ye need to hurry, lad," a female voice said, and a woman appeared by his side. A pretty, freckled face, a small nose, red hair under a green hood.

She leaned to the door, fiddling with the lock. This must be—

"Sìneag?" asked Raghnall. "The Highland faerie?"

"Aye," she said distractedly. "Ye have to forgive me for crashing the rocks in yer underground. It was necessary to keep the lass with ye... Och, these modern locks! But I will help ye now."

The door opened, letting the gray daylight in and blinding Raghnall.

"Hurry," Sìneag said, already stepping into the small, empty courtyard. The ground was made of rocks, and short, dark walls, towers, and more stairs surrounded Raghnall as he stepped into it. He looked back at the keep.

Lit by gray daylight, this wasn't the Eilean Donan that he'd known. This was a castle, aye. But it looked so different! It was smaller, and everything was made of rocks. The construction of the tower itself was completely different. There were more rooms, and more windows, and the roof...the roof was made of something he couldn't even describe.

In the meanwhile, Sìneag ran through the courtyard towards an arched gate—much smaller and much more impractical for warfare than he was used to. Again, fiddling with the lock, she looked at him over her shoulder. "Now ye must go over the bridge and towards the small buildings on the other side. Yell for help, and people will come. When all is done, ye will have only one chance to go back to yer time. Only one, Raghnall. If ye decide to go back to 1310, ye wilna be able to return to Bryanna."

He swallowed. He hadn't even thought about what would happen afterwards. "It doesna matter. All I care about is that she lives."

Sìneag nodded, and the big gate finally gave in. She stepped aside, opening the gate for him. "'Tis where I leave ye, Raghnall. Remember. One more time."

He didn't even nod, but ran through the gate and onto the long, stone bridge that led to the other side.

His feet pounding against the stone of the bridge, he glanced around. Lit by the clouded afternoon light, the same mountains and hills he'd known grayed around him. There was no Dornie—not the one he'd known, anyway. Hidden among the trees and on the hills, the buildings seemed to be made of pale yellow and white polished stone. No thatched roofs, no smoke coming out of chimneys... And that long bridge over the loch in the distance. There were no boats on the loch, but some sort of iron carriages of bright colors—red, green, black, silver—stood on the other side of the water.

His head spun. He commanded himself to stay focused and to only concentrate on the woman in his arms.

Finally, after what felt like an eternity, he was on the other side of the bridge. Marveling at how easy it was to run on the surface of the ground that resembled smooth, polished stone, he approached the buildings where he saw several people standing outside. As he skidded to stop, they all turned to him, and their conversations died. Standing in a line, about a dozen people were frozen, staring at him open-mouthed. They were all dressed so richly and so strangely. Thin, impractical clothes of bright colors and tight fits. Men with short hair, women with some sort of paint on their faces, and all in breeches... And then they looked at his waist, at his sword, and started to back away.

Aye, if he'd had any doubts before, he didn't have them anymore. He had traveled in time.

And he needed to ask for help. "Healer!" he yelled.

A woman shrieked, hiding behind a man.

Nae, that wasn't right... What had David told him?

"A doctor!" Raghnall yelled... God's bones, he was speaking English without even trying. "I need a doctor!"

They all looked around and one woman in her fifties stepped forward. "I'm a nurse." She looked back at a man who must be accompanying her. "Call the ambulance right now. Someone find a museum worker immediately." Then, looking back at Raghnall. "Lay her down on the ground. What's wrong with her?"

"A nurse?" He looked at the woman's chest. Could she still be able to nurse bairns at her age?

"What's wrong with you!" she cried out, covering her chest uncomfortably. "A medical nurse!"

Raghnall's throat contracted. Could he trust this woman? He was a stranger here, at a complete loss, and he didn't know how things worked in this time.

But he couldn't bring himself to trust anyone.

"I wilna let go of her," he growled. "She has the sugar sickness...and I...she may be dead..."

The woman paled, and while the man pressed with his fingers on a small, rectangular object in his hand and then held it to his ear and began talking, she walked towards Bryanna.

"She has diabetes?"

"Aye, 'tis the word she told me."

The woman took Bryanna's wrist, her eyes widening even more. "There's a pulse but it's weak." She looked at the man. "Tell them to hurry. She's in a diabetic shock. There isn't much time."

She locked her eyes with Raghnall, and he recognized the focused look that Catrìona had when she was healing someone. "Put her on the ground and turn her on her side. That will allow her to breathe easier."

Raghnall couldn't move. He couldn't imagine letting go of Bryanna. Somehow, letting go of her meant she'd die.

"Nae."

"You have to trust me, sir. You can hold her hand, but it will be better for her if she's on the ground."

"It's coming," said the man with the small black object. "The ambulance from Dr. Mackinnon Memorial Hospital is on its way."

Ambulance...aye, that was indeed another word David had told him.

Help was coming.

Raghnall sucked in air and commanded himself to calm down. He was a stranger here, in this time of polished stone buildings with windows made of glass so clear it was like water. The people looked at him strangely, like he was a wild animal and could snap at them with no warning. If this time did allow Bryanna to live with sugar sickness, he had to trust healers would be able to help her.

"Aye."

But before he could lay Bryanna on the ground, a plump woman in her fifties hurried out of the building. "Is someone sick?" She stopped dead before Raghnall and looked at him and Bryanna with wide eyes. "Who are you?"

"He carried her from the castle," said the nurse. "Running like crazy. Screaming healer, healer."

The plump woman slowly looked at Eilean Donan. "But the museum isn't open yet... How did you get in there?"

Raghnall didn't reply. Silence hung in the air, long and loaded, and only the distant rumbling and rhythmic swooshing of something from that bridge across the loch, the chirping of birds, and the rustling of leaves filled Raghnall's ears.

"I heard people have disappeared there," said someone from the small gathering behind them. "But that they also appear...?"

Raghnall didn't want or need to give anyone any explanation. "Ye wanted to help?" Raghnall said, his teeth clenched.

The plump woman came out of the stupor. "Oh, yes. I work in the museum. My name is Leonie Peterson. Come inside, there are chairs you can lay the lass on."

As they walked inside the building, Leonie kept staring at him, at his sword, at his clothes. She even leaned back to look at the back of his *leine croich*.

She gestured at a row of four chairs that were connected and made of some sort of iron or polished wood he had no name for. The nurse followed him, and she told him to lay Bryanna on her left side. She kept checking Bryanna's pulse, her hand on Bryanna's wrist as he walked. Raghnall dropped to the floor, which was made of absolutely perfect flat rectangular gray stones that had no doubt taken a lifetime to lay.

He took Bryanna's hand and kept praying, in his head, that he wasn't too late, after all. That the ambulance, or whatever it was called, would come any moment. He kept throwing glances at the window. The nurse and Leonie kept asking him questions—where he had come from, why he and Bryanna were dressed like that, if he needed help with his scratches and wounds—but he kept silent, ignoring them. Nothing mattered beyond getting Bryanna well.

They didn't know that before them sat a man who held on to his sanity by a hair. That he had made an impossible choice and crossed a barrier they couldn't even imagine. And that all he could do was pray that if God wanted to take someone today, He'd take Raghnall and not Bryanna.

After what felt like a lifetime, there was a wailing, high-pitched sound from through the door, and blue-and-red lightning flashed, but no thunder came...rather, he heard some sort of roar that was distant at first but came closer at an astonishing speed. He jumped up and unsheathed his sword, making both the nurse and Leonie jump away from him with shrieks of horror.

"Put that down!" cried the nurse.

"Why is there blood on it?" yelled Leonie.

The door opened and three people came in wearing dark-green tunics and trousers, holding small chests and rolling a stretcher on wheels inside. They stopped, frowning at his sword.

"Sir, please put that down," said a young woman in the green clothes. "We came to help."

Raghnall blinked. "Are ye the healers...? Doctors? Ambulance?"

"Yes, we are. Please put that down and let us look at the patient."

Raghnall commanded himself to put his sword in the sheath. Anything to help Bryanna, even though all his warrior's instincts screamed at him to not let his guard down.

David said ambulance. Doctors. They would help her.

He stepped aside. "Save her life."

They rushed to her, checked her, stabbed her arm with a needle as thin as a fish bone, and attached something to her that snaked up into a transparent bottle. He hated every moment of it, itched to push them aside and not let them pierce her, hurt her, do things to her he didn't understand... But he also remembered she had cut herself to drop her blood into that magical box that showed her the sugar in her blood. And then he himself had stabbed her stomach with something she'd called an insulin pen and that saved her life...

So he had to do the most difficult thing ever—nothing. Just stand back and watch, helplessly, desperately praying for them to not be too late.

As they put her on the stretcher and were tying some ropes around her, one of the healers turned to him. "Are you her relative?"

Raghnall cleared his throat. "She's my wife. Bryanna Mackenzie."

"Okay. You can come with us, Mr. Mackenzie. We have to take her to the hospital."

He frowned. "Hospi—"

"We have no time to waste. Your wife is in a ketoacidotic coma, and it's a matter of life and death. Are you coming, sir?"

"She's still alive?" he asked, realizing that he was asking something that had an obvious answer.

"Yes, she is, but her condition is critical."

They rolled her out of the house and towards a big white metal cart with a roof and a large stripe of bright-yellow and green rectangles. Inside, the cart of hell had small, blinking lights; white chests; transparent bottles; smooth black cords; and yellow-and-red things he had no name for.

He'd wanted to command them to stop, but now he knew better. She needed this. They'd help her.

They rolled her inside the hellish cart and the male healer attached more ropes to her—they connected to a black board that began to blink with colorful numbers and letters right away. The other two healers looked at him.

"Are you coming, Mr. Mackenzie?"

Nae, screamed everything within him. *Dinna get into that hellish cart. Dinna go deeper into this strange world ye dinna ken. Dinna let them take ye...*

But she'd come into his world, she'd stayed with him through everything, despite the deadly risk to her life.

And he'd do the same for her.

"Aye," he said, hopping inside the cart.

The devilish cart had nothing on him.

He'd give his life for her.

CHAPTER 31

Bryanna was in heaven.

She was warm, lying on something soft, and she was inhaling the scent of Raghnall—the male musk, and leather, and iron... and that barely detectable tang of the sea.

The scent that meant adventure. Being alive. Being fearless.

She'd been fearless. Unapologetic. She'd taken every risk that she could.

And she'd loved it.

But she'd died. She must have. The last thing she remembered was that battlefield. Raghnall, all bloodied and wounded, enemies all around, and Euphemia with her knife, so close, aiming to kill.

She must have killed her, and this must be heaven. And if so, that scent meant the man she loved was somewhere nearby.

But then...he'd be dead, too?

No! Not him!

Fear hit her system like a wall of knives, and the pain returned. She opened her eyes, and was blinded by white walls, ceiling, and furniture. She blinked rapidly to get her eyes to adjust to the light, trying to sit up, but she had no strength. She groaned.

"Lass!" came his voice, and a big, dark shadow was by her side, and that scent again...his scent. "Are ye all right?"

She blinked more as the blurry blotches of white and dark faded away. There it was, the dearest face she'd ever seen in her life.

The long, arched eyebrows were drawn together in a straight line. Underneath them, the black eyes were dark with worry but glistening with emotion. She stretched her hand out to him, needing to touch him, to make sure she was really seeing him.

He grasped her hand, his big, warm, and calloused fingers scratching hers.

Dried blood, cuts, and bruises decorated his face, and his *leine croich* was torn and cut in places, with caked blood on it.

He looked as medieval as ever, just like when she'd last seen him.

And yet... She looked around, not comprehending how it was possible. This was a hospital. She was hooked to an IV and to a heart monitor. The artificial light of the hospital lamps felt harsh and almost painful to her eyes.

No. A hospital couldn't be heaven.

She cleared her throat. "What happened? Where are we?"

"I brought ye to yer time, lass," he said simply.

To her time... Relief rushed through her like a gust of warm air, and she felt the muscles in her neck relax, her head sinking back into her pillow. She was safe. Her mom and her sister were here. There were no clan wars, no rocks to clear, and plenty of insulin available.

"Ye almost died," Raghnall continued. "I heard the word *coma*..."

"Oh no...ketoacidotic coma..." she whispered.

"Aye, that."

Tears welled in her eyes and the vision of him blurred again. She tugged him to her and then he was leaning over her in the hospital bed and grasping her in the tight, warm, strong hold of his arms. She buried her face in the crease between his shoulder and his neck, inhaling his scent like it was oxygen itself. "Thank you for saving my life..." she whispered.

"Dinna thank me. I couldna do otherwise. I promised I'd protect ye."

She leaned back and grasped his collar, then tugged him in for a kiss. His lips were warm and soft and tender, and his beard scratched her face. She could tell he was holding back. He sat and cupped her face. "Lass, ye're too weak for kisses. Ye were almost gone. Ye need to save yer strength and get better."

She let out a big sigh. "So what I saw in my prophecy... You weren't the reason for my death. You were the one who saved me."

Raghnall chuckled. "Nae, lass, I may as well be the reason for yer death. I should have helped ye sooner to clear those rocks. I should have never kidnapped ye away from the castle. I should have insisted Angus send men to free the rock."

"No. Don't blame yourself. Tell me what happened? The last thing I remember is Euphemia jumping at me with her knife and then me passing out. What happened after that?"

He told her how he'd fought the guards and gotten to her. How he'd made the Ross army stop by threatening Euphemia's life. How Robert the Bruce and some ally clans, including clan MacDonald, had arrived and put an end to it. How Euphemia got out of his grasp and jumped at Angus, intending to kill him, and how, instead, Raghnall had to kill her.

How he picked Bryanna up and ran to the underground, and how he got into the modern-day Eilean Donan where Sìneag helped him by opening the doors because the castle had been locked.

How Sìneag said she had made the rocks fall in the underground to give Bryanna more time.

"What a mischievous little faerie..." muttered Bryanna.

Raghnall proceeded to tell her how he ran across that bridge with her in his arms and found people and waited for an ambulance.

"That bloody cart of hell... I didna like it one bit. How can they move so fast? I almost shited myself."

Bryanna had to smile. "I wish I'd seen your reaction when you first saw cars...people...buildings. Must have been quite a shock for you."

He chuckled, the worried, pained expression relaxed and replaced by amusement for the first time. "Aye, ye can say that. 'Tis all...very strange, aye. The hardest part, love, is to let them do things to ye that I dinna understand or ken."

Love? He called her love? Her heart flapped like the wings of a hummingbird. But she shouldn't hope. She shouldn't even dare hope he went through all this because of anything but obligation to her.

She brushed his hand with her thumb. "You did everything right. I'm alive. I owe my life to you."

He shook his head. "Ye dinna owe me anything."

Her heart was drumming in her chest, tension between her ribs painful, and she realized she was holding her breath as one question was aching to come out. "But...you're here...so...what now?"

His dark gaze was long and full of emotion. "Now, lass, I stay with ye and make sure ye're all right."

His words released tension inside her, her whole being filling with lightness and sunlight, happiness spilling through her like stardust.

She couldn't stop herself. She tugged his hand, pulling him closer and wrapping her arms around his neck, and kissed him. This time, he didn't resist. This time, he was right there with her, and she knew the thought of even a moment more together brought him as much happiness as it did her.

His lips were gentle and tender, showing her all that he was feeling, all that he had in his heart for her, and suddenly, it was so clear to her, she stopped kissing him, and leaned back and whispered, "I love you."

He froze. Went so still, he could be a statue in human clothes. He sat back down, staring at her—glaring at her—making all the blood rush to her cheeks in a fiery wave.

"Ye canna love me, lass," he croaked.

Her back straightened and she sat up, anger suddenly giving her more strength. How could a person go through so many emotions in such a short amount of time? Confusion, relief, joy and happiness, love, embarrassment, and now anger. This couldn't be good for her blood pressure.

"You can't tell me what I can or cannot do. And excuse me, but that is not a great response when someone tells you they love you."

"I'm nae good for ye."

"Well, yes, we're perhaps the oddest couple one could imagine. I'm a modern-day American and you, a medieval Highlander... But time doesn't mean anything. Distance doesn't mean a thing. Background and history mean nothing. Despite all the differences between us, or perhaps because of them, I love you."

His eyes watered. "Lass, what are ye doing to me...?"

A thought occurred to her, and it was as though a knife was struck right in her core. She was pouring her heart out to him, while bringing her back to her time was just him fulfilling his promise to her, his duty. He was a Highlander, who'd rather die than betray his honor and his word. And she was torturing him with her love confessions. "If you don't feel the same way, that's fine—"

"'Tis nae that. Ye...ye're so beautiful, and I dinna just mean ye're bonnie. I mean ye're the most pure, kindhearted, and courageous woman I ken. How can ye love someone like me? An outcast? A man that fails to protect the ones he loves?"

She felt even stronger now and tugged him to her again, and when he sat closer, she climbed onto his lap and cuddled into his arms, making sure her IV didn't detach. His scent, his body were giving her the energy to live, to breathe, to want more.

"You're delusional, buddy," she whispered. "You just saved your clan and crossed hundreds of years to save my life. Now, be honest with me..." She looked up and met his dark gaze. It was soft and open, and she could look right into his soul. She loved it when he was like that with her, sweet and gentle and open and vulnerable. "What do you feel for me, Raghnall?"

He didn't answer for a while, his throat working, his eyes blinking. "I love ye, lass," he said finally, his voice croaking. "I had thought my heart was long dead, frozen in an eternal winter. But ye woke my heart up and filled it with so much love."

Bryanna's stomach flipped, and happiness burst in her, spilling through her nerves like warm honey. She whimpered a happy sound and was just about to kiss him when a voice made her jump.

"What's this?" a female voice behind her asked with a modern Scottish accent. "You, sir, go back to the chair, and you..." The doctor pointed an accusing finger at her. "You need to lie back and rest."

She looked at Raghnall. "You should have called a nurse the moment your wife opened her eyes. She just came out of a coma."

She tsk-tsked and shook her head as she approached Bryanna. She looked at the monitor, which was showing regular heartbeats. Retrieving a thin medical light, she leaned over Bryanna with a stern face and cast the light into one of her eyes. "Your husband told us your name was Bryanna Mackenzie, but he couldn't give us your ID, your address, or insurance information." She lifted her other eyelid and shined the light in that eye as well. "No hotel we could call, no other relatives that may know anything."

"Oh," Bryanna said. "I need to call my mom and my sister. They must be worried sick."

"Yer ma..." Raghnall said thoughtfully, rubbing his lip with his thumb. "Yer sister..."

"This man brought you from Eilean Donan... You're not that woman that disappeared not so long ago, are you? It was all over the news, all the people that keep disappearing there through the summer."

Crap. She completely forgot she'd also have to deal with the police and somehow protect Raghnall. They'd need to come up with a story. And now that he'd told everyone he was her husband...

"I didn't disappear," she said. "Long story."

The doctor threw a sharp glance at Raghnall, then leaned closer to Bryanna and lowered her voice. "You're not in danger from that man, are you?"

Bryanna blinked. "No, of course not! He saved my life."

The doctor narrowed her eyes. "Just give me a signal if you can't talk. You were insulin deprived and...quite honestly, you did almost die. And he...he looks very suspicious. Those cuts and bruises, the bloodied sword we had to force him to leave with security. And he's dressed like a homeless person and doesn't know much about you...or the world around him. Did he...force you? Keep you captive somewhere?"

Oh no, Raghnall may be in more danger than she had realized.

"No, Doctor. He's not a danger to me or anyone. We were in a bit of a trouble, yes, but he protected me and saved me."

The doctor didn't blink. "As you wish, but he won't even let us look at his wounds."

"He's entitled to decide whether he wants help or not, right?"

"Of course. Again, just signal me or one of the nurses if you want any help. And I have to call the police and inform them that you're here."

She sighed. "And I need to call my mom. Is there a phone I could use?"

As the doctor nodded and left the room, Bryanna met Raghnall's eyes, which weren't filled with wonder and love anymore but were cold, closed off, and full of darkness.

And just like that, her little bubble of heaven was burst by harsh reality.

Raghnall had had to protect her in the Middle Ages. It had never occurred to her that their roles would be reversed and she'd need to protect him from the modern world.

CHAPTER 32

THE NEXT FEW days were undoubtedly the maddest days in Raghnall's life.

At some moments, he found himself happier than he'd ever been, holding his wife's hand, watching her gain color and strength. At other times, people who called themselves the police interrogated him, questioned every word, every movement, even every detail of his appearance. And then came Bryanna's mother and her sister, who openly told him he should have nothing to do with Bryanna because he'd failed to take care of her.

And they were right.

Bryanna and he had agreed it would be best if they didn't tell anyone about time traveling. To the police and to her family, she told a story of how she went outside the museum and got lost in the woods. Raghnall had found her, but his car—the hellish cart that no doubt demons created—had broken down. Taking a lot of blame and guilt, she told them she hadn't wanted to be contacted for a few days and had just wanted to enjoy Scotland alone.

This had upset her mother and sister so much. Raghnall didn't blame them, but he also hated that he was the reason for

Bryanna's conflict with her family who loved her. They called her selfish and cruel. They also called her very reckless because she'd had only three insulin pens with her, and look what happened. And why didn't she go to a pharmacy and buy more? Why did she allow herself to become so insulin deprived that she went into a coma?

Raghnall itched to jump to her defense but told himself to stay out of it, to let the family solve their own problems.

The police had more questions and more doubts, and they clearly didn't believe any of the vague answers that Bryanna and Raghnall gave them, but Bryanna saved the situation by insisting that she'd been away of her own will, no one had forced her into anything, and she was not in danger. When they asked for something called IDs, Bryanna said they'd both lost theirs, and finally, the police left, though very unsatisfied. But, as Bryanna explained, they had no case since no one was pressing charges and everyone was well and alive.

Raghnall had been given modern clothes that his mother-in-law bought for him. He liked the blue braies Bryanna called jeans. They were thick, warm, and comfortable. The tunic they called a T-shirt smelled strange but felt nice and smooth on his body. But he didn't care much for the short braies called underwear. They were soft but too restrictive, and he decided hell if he'd wear them.

The next day, Bryanna was allowed to leave the chamber that they called the Intensive Care Unit and was taken to a simpler chamber of her own. Since he refused to leave the hospital without Bryanna, he was allowed to use the warm waterfall that Bryanna called a shower. The moment he stepped into it, breathing the warm clouds of clean water, he thought humanity had done right. All of the struggle, all of the progress were worth this miracle of turning a metal stick and letting warm water pour on him from the wall.

He didn't know how long he let the streams flow down his skin, burning his old—as well as his recent—cuts and wounds.

He even liked the smell of the liquid soap, something very foreign and fruity that made him think of distant lands and of flowers he'd never seen. It was heaven.

The only thing missing there was his wife.

Three days later, Bryanna was allowed to leave the hospital and move into a dwelling in Edinburgh with her mother and her sister. As Bryanna explained to him, she needed to get a new passport since her things had been left in the fourteenth century, and she couldn't leave Scotland and return home without it.

A heart-wrenching, five-hour trip in one of the demon-carts driven by Bryanna's sister, and they were in Edinburgh. It would have taken him at least a dozen days on horse with good weather, or four to five days of travel by sea. The Isle of Skye, where Bryanna's hospital had been, had belonged to clan Ruaidhrí, who'd always helped him if he needed...but Scotland wasn't ruled by the powerful clans of the past in Bryanna's time. There wasn't a king or a queen of Scotland. No fortresses, no lairds, and no war.

This was a strange world, Raghnall realized as he observed every human with a wee rectangular thing that allowed people to talk and even see each other from a distance, pay with invisible money, read, and even listen to music. And everyone seemed to be completely and utterly taken with the wee rectangles, spending more time with them than with their loved ones.

Edinburgh overwhelmed him with the number of buildings. It was as though castles with big glass windows stood side by side. Hundreds of people walked, rode the demon-carts, and the strangest thing he'd ever seen—a few iron rods with two wheels that were put into motion by rotating two stirrups with your feet.

The whole way there, the car engine revved like a deranged bee. They turned on the radio, and he listened with every fiber of his heart to the modern music. Some of it shot right into his soul. Those were called rock ballads, Bryanna told him. Others, like techno and house, he didn't understand. They were simplistic and lacked subtlety and poetry.

As Scottish hills, mountains, and lochs flashed by, he craved to open the window and let fresh Highland air in—the scents of grass and water and wet earth. But he didn't want to make Bryanna sick and instead breathed in the stuffy air of the car, which added to the feeling of being trapped inside a cart from hell moving with an inhumane speed.

When Bryanna's sister stopped the demon-cart by one of the castles, he wondered if everyone in this time was so wealthy that they could own one. But it turned out, they weren't. People owned three to four chambers in the castle and called them apartments or flats, and they lived near one another, with just a thin wall separating families.

When he stepped out of the car, Edinburgh was loud with the whirring of the car engines, people talking, music being played on the streets in the downtown. It smelled of burned metal and bitter smoke, and Bryanna told him it was gasoline, the liquid that made cars move. There was also the smell of fresh bread, perfume, and wet stone.

Bryanna explained to him that this was the flat where they, and her mom and her sister, would stay until she got better and got her passport to be able to return home. Her country's embassy was in Edinburgh as well as the airport. The airport sounded especially strange to him, like a giant field for dragon-like metal creatures to fly people into the sky. But he couldn't imagine that dragons, something from the myths and legends his mother used to tell, would come alive in the future.

As they settled into the apartment, and Bryanna was well and fine again with the use of her insulin, he started enjoying himself as she showed him around the city. Drinking water running from the tap, and a clean and hygienic latrine were luxuries that made life here very pleasant, indeed. The chest, or fridge, that kept food cold, the stove and oven that heated up with no fire, the lights that came alive with just a press of a finger made life godlike.

He liked whisky, something that Scots had invented much later than his time. The wine, the ale, the food were exquisite. The convenience and safety of this society made him a little uneasy, but after a few days, he started to get used to that, too. Everything was faster, brighter, cleaner. Women didn't hide behind layers of clothes, though he did find both male and female fashions here quite questionable.

Every day he watched Bryanna stab herself in her lower abdomen with that needle, and every day he thanked God for this medicine that kept her alive.

But every time she pricked herself, he winced, remembering what it was saving her from.

What he had saved her from.

Death.

He remembered the feel of her limp, lifeless body in his arms, the pale skin, the scent of her breath—sweet, like overripe pears—that meant she had much too much sugar in her blood, and it was killing her. Every time, that image brought the memory of another woman dying in his arms—Mòrag.

And the lad who was waiting for him to come home. Who waited for him to finally keep his word and take care of him.

Who wanted a father, which Raghnall was supposed to be for him.

Every day he saw that unasked question in Bryanna's eyes... What would happen to the two of them?

It must have been two sennights after Raghnall had arrived in Bryanna's time that they went to visit Edinburgh Castle. Raghnall had been amazed by the structure, the grandness of it, what humanity had added to castles with time. He'd never been to Edinburgh in his time, but the strongest castle in Scotland, Stirling, couldn't compete with this.

Visiting the castle, seeing the rough stone walls, the thick gates with massive hardware, the familiar furniture from his time, smelling the old wood, and hearing the medieval ballads being played in the background, made him feel for a few moments that he was back in the fourteenth century.

The guilt, the ache to do the right thing weighed on him like a boulder.

When they came out of the castle on the esplanade, the sun was already setting and the city of Edinburgh was lit in orange and pink. They walked towards the rough stone parapet that surrounded the large open area with many tourists walking, talking, taking pictures in front of the castle and the view of the city.

As they walked, he looked back at the castle. It was dark, almost black...and so familiar. In front of him was the sunlit city, most of it modern.

He felt as if he was stuck between the past and the future—in his body, his mind, and his heart.

Losing Bryanna would destroy his very soul. Her diabetes ran in her veins like a wild predator waiting to crush her, only sedated by regular medication. But she was still sick.

She was always in danger.

And so was his heart. He loved her. If anything happened to her, the pain would crush him. He wouldn't be able to survive it.

When they reached the parapet, he turned to her, lit by the golden-orange sunset, the stone rough against his hip. Her dear, bonnie face was worried. "What is it, Raghnall?"

"Love... Ye're well, aye?"

"Yes."

He kept silent, not knowing how to say this. "Then my mission here is finished."

She blinked, her eyes watering. "What?"

"I brought ye here so that ye'd live. But I never intended to live in the future."

Her head shot back as though he'd slapped her. She turned her face away and stepped back.

"Love..." He stepped towards her.

"I shouldn't be surprised," she said, her voice hoarse. "But it feels like you just kicked all the air out of me."

"I never promised ye I'd stay."

"I know you didn't. And I'd never ask you to. But I was hoping you'd want to stay with me. That you'd see I'm not broken and that you don't need to protect me here, that I can manage fine by myself. That you'd want me more than your life back there."

Her words lashed him like a whip. He reached out his hand to her, the need to soothe her made his fingers hurt. "Lass, 'tisna fair."

"I know. I'm sorry. Mom's right, I am selfish. You have your family there. You have Seoc."

"But I dinna have ye."

She nodded, her eyes watering, and watched him without saying anything.

"I only have one more chance to go through the stone, 'tis what Sìneag said. And now I must make a choice whether I spend the rest of my life with the woman I love as a selfish man with no honor. Or do my duty, keep my word to a dying mother, and give Seoc the best life he can have."

Bryanna's eyebrows drew together, her lips pursed in a pained grimace. "And the woman you love might die, even with modern medicine, even with careful insulin management…because diabetics always have complications."

This hit him like a war hammer. The image of the two women he'd loved in his life invaded his mind. Mòrag and Bryanna, both on the verge of death.

She was right, he knew. He was terrified to give his all to her, to be with her, body and soul, only for her to be taken away from him by some illness.

And so, it was better to keep being the lone wolf he'd always envisioned himself to be. Even if his heart would never heal or love again.

Seagulls soared over their heads in the dying light, their cries mournful. A young couple with a child five or six years old passed them by, the wee lass with two dark ponytails playfully skipping across the concrete in her pink shoes, squealing in delight when her father picked her up and whirled her from time to time.

"I'm right, aren't I?" she whispered. "It's my diabetes. Even with you here, where I have the best chance to live, it's still keeping me away from living a great life, the full life of a healthy person."

"I'm sorry, lass. Like I told ye, I've never wanted a life with someone. I love ye and always will. Time with ye is the most precious gift this life has given me. But ye were right from the start. Our story would always have an end. We were always meant to love each other, but never to be together forever. And this is where we part."

CHAPTER 33

THE NIGHT before Raghnall left Edinburgh, Bryanna had made sure his clothes were cleaned in one of those incredible washing machines and then stitched the rips herself. She drove him to Eilean Donan in the morning, and the whole way there, his hand was on her knee or wrapped around her small hand.

They barely talked, but he tried to stretch every moment in her company into a lifetime. A hundred times he asked himself if he was really doing the right thing or if he was committing another irreversible mistake and losing his only chance at happiness.

Since Bryanna, the last missing person, had been found, there was no official case anymore, and a healthy crowd of people stood before the ticket queue. Bryanna had been worried they might be forbidden from entering, but no one stopped them. In their modern clothes, it was possible no one even recognized them.

Unfortunately, a museum employee guarded the door to the underground. For a moment there, relief settled in Raghnall's stomach—that his difficult choice had been taken for him. That he had to stay with Bryanna and tell himself for the rest of his life that this was why he'd had to break his word to Mòrag and to Seoc.

He saw the same glitter of hope in Bryanna's eyes, only it lasted a mere moment. "Do you want me to help you to get rid of the guard?"

Tell her nae. Tell her ye changed yer mind.

But he couldn't stay with her. He couldn't be with her for the rest of his life. He couldn't lose her. And so, painfully, heavily, he nodded, even though it killed him inside.

"Excuse me," Bryanna said to the guard, "I'm not feeling well... I have diabetes. Do you have somewhere quiet I could sit?"

Of course, the guard believed her and left his post to show her a quiet spot somewhere. As she was turning the corner, she threw a last glance at Raghnall, and he could read everything in it—all her love, all her pain, and her goodbye.

Goodbye... As he descended the familiar stairs, he thought that the worst was he didn't get to say a proper goodbye. He didn't get to give her the last kiss that would get him through the rest of his life. He didn't get to whisper to her how he imagined a life with her... how he'd teach her the lute, and how she'd teach him modern music, how he'd take care of her and protect her and let her show him her world.

The world that he'd actually come to like, despite its strangeness, despite the number of people and the noise and the demon-carts and the rectangles called phones that everyone loved so much.

In the underground, the door to the room with the stone was unlocked. He changed into his medieval clothes, though he couldn't take his sword with him as Bryanna had told him they wouldn't allow it and he couldn't attract more attention than needed. But he was glad to leave it to his wife. Something dear to him that, perhaps, would remind her of him and protect her in the rare instances that she might need it.

He kneeled before the stone, watching the carvings and the

handprint like they were filled with poison. He turned around at the door, hoping, waiting for Bryanna to come... Or for Sìneag to appear and plead with him not to go. She was on the side of love, right?

But love wouldn't win in this story. Love wasn't everything.

Love didn't mean anything when death looked someone right in the face. Love wouldn't resurrect Mòrag, and it wouldn't one day save Bryanna.

And as moments passed and no one came, Raghnall knew that he couldn't wait any longer. He wouldn't stay, so what use was it to wait?

Putting his hand into the handprint sucked him into the cold, dark nothingness that brought him back into his time, just like it was supposed to.

For the last time.

He opened his eyes in complete darkness. Crawling on all fours, he bumped into sharp rocks and slowly found his way out through the door. There was light somewhere ahead, and he recognized the narrow stairs leading up.

He climbed them and opened the door, all doubts disappearing when he saw the medieval storage room. Sacks, crates, chests. The scents he hadn't smelled for a while: smoked and dried fish, dried corn, the barely noticeable whiff of animal dung that must have come from the outside. Swords and bows hanging on the walls.

From up the stairs, he heard voices and laughter, probably people in the great hall. From outside, the sound of the blacksmith hitting his hammer against the anvil, the squawking of chickens, bleating of the sheep, sticks knocking against each other, and men grunting as they no doubt trained on practice swords.

All that sounded and felt familiar. But, surprisingly, not like home.

When he climbed the stairs to the great hall, he stopped in the entrance. Had he ever noticed how small the great hall appeared? How wee the windows were, how dark the space?

After seeing the big, bright world of the future of Scotland, he was back to his old life. But instead of relief and joy at being back home, it felt like he was like trying to put on a shoe he'd long outgrown.

The scene before him was peaceful. Angus and Rogene were leaning over their meals together, heads close, whispering something. Their faces were alight with love and shared secrets. Laomann and Mairead were playing with their son, who was greatly entertained by the hound. Warriors of the clan sat around the tables, talking, some eating, drinking. David leaned over a book with such ferocity on his face, as though he was determined to murder it.

Fire played in the fireplace, and he realized the scent of woodsmoke now seemed foreign to him. Despite the fire, the room was cold, and a chill spread through him, reaching his bones. Houses in Bryanna's time were much warmer, more practical, and he missed so much light coming through the windows and lamps.

And then he saw Seoc, his son. Sitting on the floor between Catrìona and James, he was building a castle with small, wooden cubes... The look of a bristled wolf cub was gone, the wildness, the fear had disappeared from his eyes. He was...

Smiling.

James said something to him, then put a longer block between two towers, creating a bridge. Seoc beamed and put a wooden horse figure on top of the bridge.

It didn't even look like they missed him. Raghnall's heart did something like a lurch—of relief...and some sort of ache. He could have had that, too. He'd wanted Seoc to learn from him. He'd wanted that happy, peaceful home, full of love and support...with Bryanna, and with Seoc, and with more children.

All heads turned to him. David jumped up, looking as though he'd just seen a dead man return to life. Rogene gasped. Angus narrowed his eyes, as though trying to see more clearly.

"What are ye doing here, brother?" Angus crossed the great hall and hugged Raghnall in a bone-crushing embrace. "I thought ye were gone..."

Laomann and Mairead came, hugging him, greeting him. Catriona, James, and Seoc approached, wide-eyed and looking like they were a little family.

David came to him, too, carefully looking him over.

David's intense brown eyes were on Raghnall. "Is she alive? Did you find the doctor?"

Raghnall clapped him on the shoulder. "Aye. Bryanna's well. Thank ye for the words ye gave me, they might have saved her life."

James narrowed his eyes. "Then why did you come back?"

Laomann stared at them with confusion, but at that moment, Ualan let out a loud fart and burbling noises came from him, and the unmistakable smell of a child's poo. Laomann and Mairead hurried out of the great hall.

Raghnall looked around at his family and then his eyes landed on Seoc. "I came for ye."

Seoc blinked, his expression softening for a moment but then returning to his usual distant apprehension that hurt Raghnall. What did he expect? A hug? Tears of joy? The lad didn't owe Raghnall his love. Raghnall had been the source of Seoc's misfortune in the first place.

Angus frowned. "Why didna ye tell us he wasna ycr real son? Do ye think we'd have treated him any differently than if he's yer adopted son?"

Raghnall sighed. They knew. "How do ye ken?"

"I told them," said Seoc. "Pretending and lying didna sit well with me. And I like it with Catriona and James."

In the two sennights that Raghnall had been gone, the lad had grown some meat on his bones, looked healthy and well. And there was something else Raghnall had seen only when Mòrag had been alive.

A child's carefree joy.

Catrìona's cheeks reddened. "Not much time passed, brother, but James and I took a big liking to Seoc. He's been inseparable from us. And, forgive me for assuming that ye wouldna return, but since we ken he isn't yer real son, we were thinking to adopt him."

Raghnall blinked, pain stabbing him in the guts. Adopt him? Seoc, for whom Raghnall had lived ever since Mòrag?

James laid his hand on Seoc's shoulder protectively. "Everyone assumed you'd stay with Bryanna. Clearly, Sìneag intended for the two of you to be together, so..."

Raghnall let out a loud exhale. "I dinna intend to break my word. Angus, ye wanted me to be responsible, are ye happy now? I bloody crossed the river of time for my responsibility, leaving the woman I love, the woman who loves me, behind."

Silence hung in the group, then Seoc's quiet voice was like a hammer that broke Raghnall's world. "Ye didna have to return for me, Raghnall. I want Catrìona and James to be my ma and da. They want me, and I never had both."

Raghnall felt his jaw muscles work. "I promised—"

"Ye kept yer promise to my ma. Ye brought me here. Ye dinna have to stay and punish yerself and suffer for my sake. Ye promised her to take care of me and protect me. Ye did."

Raghnall's stomach dropped as emotions he didn't know he had gushed within him from an open wound. The wound of being rejected and abandoned. The wound of having left the woman he loved, of having wasted the only chance he had at real happiness.

"Only if 'tis all right with ye, brother," said Catrìona. "Truly, we didna mean to steal yer lad away. Ye ken that, aye?"

Raghnall nodded, though tears were burning his eyes. He

dropped to his knees in front of Seoc and squeezed his wee shoulder. "I am proud of ye, lad. Ye fought like a wee wolf at the battle. Ye have more courage at ten years than many grown men. And ye deserve to have both a ma and a da, and I will never be able to give ye that because I will never marry again. The only wife I ever wanted since yer ma is somewhere I can never go. Tigh na Abhainn is yers. I dinna need it. Catrìona, James, ye both can have it and then pass it on to Seoc once he's old enough. I never wanted an estate to manage for myself. Treat my tenants well, they're good people. Eanar, the tacksman, will be yer right hand."

James frowned. "Are you sure, mate? You don't have to make this decision right now. You can still think about it."

Raghnall sighed. "If 'tis all right with Angus and ye, Rogene, I'll stay for a while here in Eilean Donan. Now that the whole purpose of everything I did for the last few years is accomplished"—he patted Seoc's head—"I need a wee think about what to do. Where Bryanna lives...it changed quite a bit the way I see things now. And I dinna ken yet what that means for me."

Angus clapped him on the shoulder. "Of course, brother, stay as long as ye wish. Yer whole life, if ye want. Now that the Ross clan is nae more a threat, we can finally rest and enjoy a wee bit of peace. Though Bruce told me there are still skirmishes and war in the south."

"I've yet to see if he's going to hang me for killing Euphemia."

"He wilna, he told me." Angus pulled Raghnall into a big hug. "And Bruce managed to find a way to work things out with the Earl of Ross. The king granted him an estate that had belonged to the Comyns. Apparently 'tis all it took for him to forgive us for the death of his sister. I'm nae so sure he'd been supportive of her war action towards us anyway."

"I'm just glad the clan wilna need to carry the consequences of my actions."

"I'm glad to see ye, brother. And I'm sorry ye canna be with yer wife."

Raghnall hugged him back and then proceeded into the great hall. But instead of feeling like he'd arrived home, he felt like he was heading right towards the edge of an abyss.

CHAPTER 34

Two weeks later...

Bryanna held her new passport in her hands, looking at her photo and not recognizing herself.

Not because she'd been thinner and had darker circles under her eyes when the photo was taken, right after she'd been discharged from Dr. Mackinnon Memorial Hospital.

But because the woman in the photo was not her.

That woman, as sickly and skinny as she looked, was happy. There was that sparkle in her eyes, the almost feverish excitement...and love. She'd just gone through the worst and the best time of her life at once. She'd just died and come back to life.

Yes, she was different. Before Raghnall and after Raghnall. Before death and after death.

Perhaps part of her had died the moment her head hit that rock. And as Raghnall had carried her through the threshold of time, perhaps the old Bryanna had never crossed that invisible border. Perhaps when she'd opened her eyes in that hospital, it was the new her.

A shadow appeared behind Bryanna's shoulder. "Oh, honey, thank God you don't look that thin anymore," her mom said.

Bryanna paused just for a moment. The old her wouldn't say anything, wouldn't want to contradict her mom or make her mom's life any more complicated by starting an argument.

But now, she said, "I actually think I look happy."

A car passed, rattling loudly over the cobblestoned Regent Terrace, the street the American embassy was on in Edinburgh. The street was quiet, a long row of light-brown, three-story Georgian houses ran opposite a thin strip of trees, bushes, and vegetation that separated the small street from a busier road.

Mom cast a shadow on Bryanna's passport, shielding the rare autumn sunrays as she moved to stand in front of her. "You look delusional, that's how you look."

There it was again, Mom's voice loaded with guilt and hurt, with one goal—to make Bryanna understand how wrong she was and to convince her to never be so reckless with her health again. And Raghnall was the very representation of that reck- lessness.

"Mom, come on," said Kris. "She knows she was wrong. She told us."

Yes, Bryanna had apologized, and she really was sorry for making her family so worried, only this wasn't exactly fair.

Mom sighed and shook her head, her short, strawberry-blond curls moving. "Let's go back to the hotel. I'll call the airline and ask if they can put us on the next available flight. Now that you have your passport, we can finally leave." She adjusted the edge of the black turtleneck showing under her padded navy jacket. "I can't wait to get home where I can keep an eye on you. No disap- pearances there, miss. And I'm so glad that husband of yours left you."

Kris gasped, her mouth making a perfect, peach-tinted circle. "Mom! Now that is mean."

It was mean, and it did hurt. But maybe it was the pain

Bryanna needed to stand up for herself and finally tell the whole truth.

"You know what, Mom?" Bryanna said, pushing her passport into her new purse—bright purple again because the color reminded her of her adventure. "You think you know me so well?"

"Of course I know you well."

"Well, did you know that I have psychic dreams?"

Mom frowned.

"Yeah," Bryanna kept on, "I dreamed of Dad's death. I dreamed of the teaching job opening. And I dreamed of Raghnall."

"You dreamed about Dad's death?" asked Kris, tears in her eyes.

Bryanna met her sister's gaze, tears welling in her own eyes. "I did. But because I was afraid everyone would think I was insane, I never said anything. I could have told him to go to the doctor that day and get his blood pressure checked. But I was too much of a coward."

Mom shook her head, also tearing up. "That doesn't mean anything, hon. Dreams are just dreams. We dream all kinds of crazy things..."

"I saw how it would happen, Mom. What he wore. What he did. Every little detail happened just like I saw it."

Mom took a step back, hurt and confusion on her face.

"And I saw my own death in Eilean Donan. How Raghnall would carry me out of the castle, unmoving and unconscious. And that was exactly how it happened."

Mom's fingers shot to her mouth. "Oh dear God..."

"But there's something else." Bryanna was unstoppable now. She'd just told her family her deepest secret, the deepest regret that had eaten her alive for years. What would another piece of shocking news be? "I didn't just go for a walk in the woods. I actually traveled back in time. That's why I couldn't call or send an email or come back. That's why I didn't have access to pharmacies. My insulin got smashed and that was it. And Raghnall is a medieval Highlander who crossed time to bring me to a hospital and save my life. He's my husband. We're married. And now..." She sobbed. "He's back in his time, and I'll never see him again."

People walked past them, cars swooshed by, but both Mom and Kris were staring at her with a deafening silence.

Bryanna let out a laugh that sounded on the verge of hysteria. "You think I've lost my mind, don't you?"

"Um...honey..." Mom used the calming, careful tone of someone who was talking to a dangerous person. "Let's just go somewhere and have a cup of coffee...no, perhaps chamomile tea would be better."

"Kris?" Bryanna looked at her sister, who was staring at her with the same expression her mom had.

"I—I'm not sure I know who you are anymore..."

Bryanna sighed and scoffed. "That's interesting. Because for the first time in my life, I actually know exactly who I am. Raghnall was right. I do feel like sunshine, I do feel invincible, and I don't need anyone else to tell me when to be careful and how to live my life. You know, Mom, I learned to ride a horse. I got married to a stranger. I was in a medieval battle. And I almost died. I love you, and I appreciate everything you've done for me, but the purpose of my life can't be to make your worries and anxieties go away. I don't need to be a music teacher and live with you, Mom. I'll always love you, both of you, but I can take care of myself, and I don't want to live my life in fear. I'm going to live it unapologetically, responsibly but fearlessly. So if you two can't wait to go back home, I understand. I kept you here longer than you ever wanted, but I'm not finished with Scotland yet. It's my husband's country, a phenomenal place to explore, with history and culture you can't even imagine, and I'm going to stay."

Mom's mouth hung open. "F-for how long?"

"I don't know."

"If you think I'll leave you alone after the tirade that you just went on...about time travel and about your psychic dreams...we need to take you to a neurologist!"

"You can stay, Mom, if you want. But I'm not going to a neurologist. I'm going to rent a car and go back to the High-lands. Maybe get a job somewhere and learn Scottish music."

Mom and Kris exchanged a flabbergasted look. "Bryanna!" Mom started.

But Bryanna did something no one expected. She placed a gentle kiss on her mom's cheek and hugged her. "Thank you for everything you did for me, Mom. Thank you for worrying, thank you for loving me, and thank you for raising me into who I am." She looked at her mom, whose pale green eyes were bloodshot and watery. "I think you feel like I'm still small and still need protection. But your job is done now. I'm raised. It's time for me to live my life and for you to live yours, knowing that your daughter will be fine."

Without saying anything else, she kissed and hugged Kris, turned around, and walked down the street.

But even though she felt strong and meant every word, she knew that she'd lied to her family with her last words.

She'd never be fine, not completely, as long as Raghnall wasn't in her world.

But she'd need to live with that.

CHAPTER 35

TEN DAYS after arriving in his own time, Raghnall threw a pebble into the handprint illuminated by the dancing light. It didn't go through. Like its ten predecessors, it bounced right off, this one rolling under the edge of the boulder he was sitting on. The rock was now completely clear, and the masons had been working on repairing the wall but were finished for the day. Raghnall didn't know how long he'd sat here today.

Every morning, the first thing he did was come down here and press his hand into the print. And every morning, cold, hard rock didn't let him through.

"You know, I heard Èibhlin turned up, married to a cousin or something," said David. "Sends her apologies to you."

Raghnall looked up. His young friend stared at the rock with the same stern, careful expression as a hunter tracking a wolf. His arms were crossed over his chest.

"I'm happy for her."

"Are you? Don't you wish she'd have come to the church, and you'd have married her and not Bryanna? At least you wouldn't be sitting here staring at a piece of rock for days."

Raghnall threw another pebble. "No. What I wish is that I hadn't left the future."

"Welcome to the club. I've been doing the same thing you're doing for months now."

Raghnall sighed. "Well, at least I'm a man of honor. A very unhappy man of honor."

David picked up a pebble and threw it into the handprint. Like Raghnall's pebbles, it bounced off.

"How did you like it there? In the future?"

"I liked it fine. Strange, of course, with the cars and electricity and those big windows ye people have there. But I see how things are easier and more convenient. Most importantly, I see why 'tis better for Bryanna to be there and why 'tis impossible for her to be with me here."

"So would you have stayed with her if not for Seoc? That's what everyone had assumed you'd do. Coming back for Seoc was very noble of you, of course."

Raghnall let his head hang between his shoulders. "Nae, I dinna think I would have stayed."

"What? Why?"

Truth was, he'd been terrified of Bryanna's sickness and of losing her. But days spent here, without her, were dark and joyless. If there was a hell, it was on this side of the rock.

"I do wish I'd stayed now, though. I understand Seoc's wish, and I know there wilna be better parents for him than Catrìona and James. But now that I have fulfilled my promise to his dying ma...there's nothing for me here."

David nodded and threw another pebble into the hand. It bounced slightly but stayed inside the print.

"A man needs a purpose. And I dinna have one, nae without Bryanna. I..." Raghnall wasn't usually someone to share his feelings, but that was what Bryanna had done to him. She'd healed him. He felt his heart patched back up, whole and full of love. And he liked David, always had. The fact that he also had been in the future united them. "I love her. If I had a chance to go back to her, I'd go. I'm ready. And even though the possibility of losing her still makes me want to cut my heart out, I want to risk it even for one more day with her."

David nodded thoughtfully and picked up another small stone. "I'm sorry to hear it, man. It sucks that you want to go but can't." He stretched his hands to the sides and gave a sarcastic chuckle. "Again, welcome to the club. Look at the two of us. We desperately want to travel in time, but we can't." Suddenly, he froze. "You know what we should do?"

"What?"

"I bet you someone out there knows something. We can't be the only ones who know about these rocks and about Sineag and about time travel. If you and I unite and go out there and search the whole of Scotland, we'll find some information. Maybe we'll find a way to travel in time. What do you say?"

Raghnall stood up. "Did I go mad, or does it sound like a good thought...?"

He liked the idea of a friend, another warrior with the same goal to travel the country and try to find a way back to the twenty-first century.

"It gives me a purpose," Raghnall whispered. "And hope."

David clapped his shoulder. "Yes! Me, too. Come on, when do we leave?"

"Today," Raghnall said. "I'll ask Angus to lend me a sword."

David pumped his fist in the air. "Yes! All right, I'm going to talk to Rogene. She won't like it, but she'll have to deal with it..." He left the room, chatting more to himself than to Raghnall. "Go ask Angus for your sword..." As the door swooshed closed behind David, Raghnall smelled something...lavender and freshly cut grass. He didn't know why he'd lingered and not gone after David right away.

But now he was glad that he had.

Because as the door closed, a woman in a green cloak appeared from behind it, and Sineag's bright, button-nosed face beamed at him.

"Hello, Raghnall," she said cheerfully. Raghnall opened his

mouth to call David, but she interrupted. "Nae, dinna call David, please. I came for ye."

An explosive combination of dread and joy washed through him. This meant something—but was it something very good or very bad?

"Did ye come to tell me to stop throwing stones into the hand?" he asked.

She approached him soundlessly. "Nae. I heard ye talk with David. I've seen yer heart. I ken ye want to be with her and ye're ready."

Raghnall swallowed a painful knot in his throat. His fingers and his feet were suddenly cold. "I am. But we've used our three passes, aye?"

Sìneag took a deep breath. "Aye."

Silence filled the space, hanging between them like a boulder about to fall.

"So why are ye here, faerie?"

Her eyes watered as he said that, but she gave him a sad smile. She walked slowly to the rock and sat on it, right by the carving. It started to glow, and Raghnall blinked, not sure if he was seeing it right.

"Ye remind me of someone," she said and gently stroked the curve of the river carved on the stone. "The human that created this rock called me that." A tear rolled down her cheek as she met Raghnall's eyes again. "I am an impossibility, Raghnall. A faerie that loves a human. I ken what 'tis to never have that happiness. I ken what ye're feeling."

Raghnall came a step closer. "Ye do?"

She stroked the carving with her hand again, as though she stroked a dear one's face. "So I'll break the rules for ye and give ye another pass."

Hope filled Raghnall's chest like hot air. "Dinna play with me, faerie..."

She stood up abruptly, and there was no gentleness in her face anymore. Her face was like polished ivory, her eyes expressionless, looking somewhere he couldn't see. "But everything has its price, and ye'll have to pay dearly for me breaking this rule for ye."

Raghnall swallowed. "Anything. Name yer price."

She came closer, and suddenly, she didn't look human. She looked transparent and glowed, just like the carving.

"Something that is dear to ye, Raghnall. Something ye least want to forget. Yer song."

He blinked. "Which one?"

"Ye ken which one. The one that still tears yer heart like an iron splinter set too deep. But I want that. Human emotions... they're still new to me. I understand love a wee bit, but the other side of love is darkness to me. Yer grief, yer sadness are strong in ye. They smell silvery, like the pure rays of a full moon. I want to taste them fully while I think of the man that made these rocks."

Raghnall did know exactly which song she was talking about. The song that was his connection to Mòrag. The song that had gotten him through the years. The song that still pained him the most, and yet it was the most beautiful one he'd ever written.

His fists clenched. "Nae that one."

"The price for breaking rules of magic is high. I paid a high price myself once. 'Tis why ye can see me. 'Tis why ye met Bryanna at all. Ye and I have much in common. Give me yer song and ye may be forever with the woman ye love. What do ye say?"

Raghnall felt his jaw working. Did he love Bryanna enough to let go of the ballad that had been his lifeline for the past four years?

"Would I remember Mòrag?"

"Aye. Of course. But nae that song. And that sadness and grief, ye'll forget them, too."

The carvings on the rock were glowing, calling him. The handprint was dark, shadows from the torch dancing in its depths. There, on the other side of it, was Bryanna. Was his new life. If he forever forgot that song, would he even be who he was?

And then he knew. The guilt, the self-loathing in that song were his armor, his protection against the pain of losing the one he loved. It was a reminder to him to protect his heart, to avoid love.

But he didn't need that protection anymore. Because he was ready. A single day with Bryanna would be worth it. If this would be all he'd get, he'd take it.

"Aye," Raghnall said. "My song is yers."

Sineag clapped her hands in delight. "Good. Please, sing it to me. For the last time."

Raghnall took a deep breath. He didn't have his lute with him, but he didn't need it. For the last time, he let the music and the words come to him and he sang. Music poured through him, sinking him into the despair and the guilt, taking his fear, taking his pain. With every word, with every note, something shifted within him, and when he finished, his last words echoed from the stone walls, and then complete silence pressed on his ears.

He was empty. Scraped clean from the inside. But it wasn't a devastating emptiness.

On the contrary, it was the emptiness of a beginning.

Sineag's eyes shone, her face serene, hands pressed to her chest. "Yer tunnel through the river of time is open."

Light-headed, Raghnall walked towards the rock, but before he sank to his knees in front of the carving, he turned his face to her. "Wait...what about David? Can he come with me?"

She winked. "'Tis nae David's time yet," she said. And disappeared.

Raghnall's head fell between his shoulders for a moment. He liked the idea of a wee club, as David had called it, and he hated that David had to stay behind.

But he could now go and find Bryanna and ask her to spend the rest of her life with him.

Two weeks later...

BRYANNA RAN HER FINGERS THROUGH THE STRINGS OF THE *clàrsach*, the beams cast by the concert lights of the Old Rowan pub illuminated them like sunlight lit the strings of a spiderweb. The *clàrsach* was the Celtic harp. One of the musicians who was supposed to play after her during the concert had let her try her instrument.

The sound came quiet and round, beautiful, and mysterious. She tried another combination. "I can't wait for you to play this properly," she said to Jessica, the musician. "I can just imagine how well this will go with your Gaelic ballad."

Jessica smiled back warmly. "Aye, of course. I can show you later how to play it if you like."

Bryanna nodded enthusiastically as she stood up from Jessica's stool. A harp wasn't exactly a pub instrument in Bryanna's understanding, but it was, apparently, in Scotland...at least in Inverness. Normally, Jessica had a small band—a man who played a Celtic drum and a guitarist—but their guitarist had moved to London.

"You know," Bryanna said, "if you like how I play...I'm looking for a band to join."

Jessica raised her eyebrows. "Oh! 'Tis good because we're still looking for a new guitarist."

"Well, then let me know if you like my style. No hard feelings if not, really, but I'm open to possibilities. Wide open, actually. I quit my job back in the States, and I really want to stay in Scotland."

"Oh! Do you like it here?"

Bryanna's heart made a lurch. "I love it here..." She felt close to the man she loved here, even if she would never see him again. "And I don't know, I just have a feeling I should stay here. You know, everything is finally falling into place."

Everything but Raghnall.

Soon, the pub began filling, and the two went into the back room. There were four musicians playing tonight, and Bryanna was the second. She'd landed this gig by chance, when someone she'd met in the youth hostel had told her they were auditioning for musicians playing Celtic music. Since she had been practicing Celtic ballads a lot after her crazy adventure in time, she'd decided to try, and was delighted when they accepted her.

Before she knew it, her turn came, and she went onto the stage with her heart drumming in her fingertips. She had played on the stage of her school before, to accompany the performances of her students, but this was first time that she'd been on a real stage, in front of an audience who didn't call her Miss Fitzpatrick.

The beams of light were shining right into her eyes, and she couldn't see the faces of her audience. Perhaps it was for the best, as it created a sort of a protective wall between them and made her less nervous. They were chatting, laughing, clinking their pints of ale against the tables, but when she leaned towards the microphone, they became quiet.

"My name's Bryanna," she said, not recognizing her microphone voice, "and I'm going to sing you a medieval ballad that I heard in the Highlands from a very dear person. Here we go..."

She held the chord and ran her fingers over the strings. The sound plunged her back into Tigh na Abhainn, into the bedroom that she and Raghnall had shared, where she'd first heard him sing. She forgot everything, letting her love and her heartache pour through her voice and through her fingertips.

"There lived a man in a Kintail house, a man with a hole in his chest..."

The song flowed freely, and she lost all sense of time until she struck the final chord and a tear rolled down her cheek. The audience was silent. Her heart beat once, twice, a million more times. She couldn't see their faces.

Then the audience exploded into applause. She stood up, the move shifting her face out of the direct beam of light. She could see—they were standing, clapping, whistling. She bowed, and as she straightened, a familiar face flashed in the crowd.

Short black beard; broad, arched eyebrows; long black hair; dark eyes.

Thinking the lights had clearly messed up her vision, she stepped to her side to move out of their glare... And froze.

Stopped hearing. Stopped existing. Lightness filled her to the tips of her hair.

Standing by one of the round tables, clapping, was a man who resembled Raghnall like a twin. He had a ponytail and wore a leather jacket and black jeans, and was staring straight at her, with the intensity of a bushfire.

Then he crossed the distance between them. When he stood at the bottom of the stage, staring up at her, the applause around them began to die out, and the MC announced Jessica would be next.

Slowly, Bryanna stepped down from the small stage, staring at the man who looked like Raghnall, her heart tearing open and bleeding. She put her guitar against the wall and moved into the shadows of a nook by the bar.

"Hello," she said.

He chuckled, his eyes smiling. "Hello, lass."

God, he sounded just like Raghnall.

"Sorry if I'm staring, you look just like—"

"Yer husband."

Her throat closed from emotion. How could she dare to hope? "Oh good God, is it you, Raghnall?"

He leaned over her and cupped her face. All doubt evaporated as the scents of leather, musk, and iron and his own musk filled her nostrils.

As the divine sounds of the *clàrsach* filled the room, Bryanna had the strangest sensation that she was in some sort of Celtic myth and her Highland prince—well, her medieval Highland rogue—had just found her.

And then a vision hit her. Him and her, giggling, gliding,

loving under her silky sheets, in a room filled with golden light, with the Highlands peeking from behind the window.

"'Tis me, lass," he whispered. "I finally found ye, my beloved bride. I heard a song that sounded familiar...and followed the music."

"Familiar? It's your ballad."

He chuckled. "It doesna belong to me anymore. I'll tell ye later. I found ye, lass. I found ye. It was all worth it."

He leaned down and kissed her, filling her with the clean taste of his mouth and smelling like the fresh air of the Highlands. Every fear and every doubt she had melted into that golden light. This had been an adventure that had changed her, that had made her stronger, and now that she was heading into the life she wanted, the only thing she wanted was to share it with the man she loved.

And now that he had found her here, had done something they'd both thought was impossible, she knew that whatever would come their way, they would sing the song of their life together.

Difficult and joyful, adventurous and challenging, it would be the song of a life truly lived.

EPILOGUE

ONE YEAR LATER...

THE IRON DRAGON, OTHERWISE KNOWN AS AN AIRPLANE, shook and rattled as it dashed forward gaining speed. Raghnall's stomach dropped as the engines whirred and roared louder and louder. When he didn't think it could get any worse, the dragon lifted into the sky, and the ground, the trees, and the airport buildings were disappearing off into the distance.

Sitting next to him, Bryanna squeezed his tight fist on his lap. "You're flying," she whispered, beaming.

Sweat streaming down his back, he nodded, still staring out the window, both terrified and unable to look away. Tiny houses, the threads of roads and trees that looked like green curls slowly moved beneath. "Aye, lass. See what I'm ready to do for ye. I still canna believe ye talked me into getting into this iron dragon," he grumbled as he opened his fingers and squeezed her hand and turned to her. "I'm a madman with a death wish."

Her green eyes sparkled as she smiled. "Well, you wouldn't let me go home alone, so..."

He leaned down and planted a gentle kiss on her lips. "Never.

Whether 'tis distance I must cross or time, there's nothing I wouldna do for ye."

They'd spent the last year in Scotland, adjusting to life in the twenty-first century. Bryanna had been working on making something that was absolutely essential in this century— personal identification documents.

God's bones, the number of unnecessary long words in this century was astounding...

But now that he was officially a citizen of the United Kingdom, he could leave the country and cross the ocean to go see Bryanna's mother and sister again. Now that they'd also been officially married in this century, Bryanna wanted to show him where she came from and he wanted to talk to his mother- and sister-in-law and reconcile with them. They hadn't had the best start last year, and he knew it was important to Bryanna that he and her family got along.

Time was carefully measured and managed in this century. Everyone knew exactly what time it was, and although it was odd to him, he had learned to do that as well. So after ten impossibly long hours later, Bryanna and he finally stepped on the firm ground.

"Welcome to the United States of America," she whispered as they walked through another glass-and-concrete building... O'Hare International Airport.

"Thanks, lass. I am walking on ground that no Scotsman of my time ever walked on."

She giggled.

They got their luggage and walked out into the arrivals area. Raghnall knew Bryanna was nervous as her palm became cold and a wee bit sweaty in his hand. He wrapped his arm around her shoulders and pulled her closer, kissing her temple. "'Tis all right, lass. Nae matter what happens, I'm yers and ye're mine, and 'tis everything I wanted."

Then they saw them among the crowd of people. Bryanna's mother had a different hair color...blond! And her sister held the hand of a short, handsome man. Kris waved to Bryanna enthusiastically. Her mother's creased forehead relaxed as she spotted Bryanna and him, and she beamed and waved as well.

Bryanna let go of Raghnall and hurried to her loved ones, falling into their group embrace. Raghnall slowly approached them, giving them time to reconcile. Tears of joy streamed from her mother's and her sister's eyes, and he knew Bryanna was crying, too. After spending every day of her life in her mother's company, she hadn't seen her for a whole year, and he knew how a family reunion would feel.

When he'd returned home to Eilean Donan, his own heart had squeezed and lurched. And now that he knew he'd never see his clan again, part of him missed it—the sense of community, knowing there were people who'd have his back no matter what.

Bryanna was his clan now. He hoped her mother and sister would become part of it, too.

When they broke the embrace and everyone turned to him, he gave a polite nod to Pamela and Kris.

"Hello, Raghnall," said Pam, giving him a small, careful smile. "It's nice to see you again. Congratulations on your success."

"'Tis nae my success. 'Tis Bryanna's. Without her, none of this would have been possible."

It was his ballad, aye, that became so popular, but it was Bryanna who had adapted the music to fit the modern style, Bryanna who had rewritten the lyrics into modern English and expanded them into a full song, and Bryanna who had made the connection with Jessica and her band...which had become their band. It was Bryanna who had started their social media channels, which went viral after several months. She'd been their spokesperson when a recording label had approached them after they'd heard them in an Edinburgh pub, and she'd negotiated and managed their rights and the money and all their appearances since.

They'd finished recording the album last week, and now that it was in production, Bryanna wanted to see her family before they would need to give more concerts. He enjoyed playing the lute for small audiences in pubs and local outdoor concerts, but he never wanted to be famous, and the same was true for Bryanna. They agreed they'd only give small performances and would be happy with less money, as riches were never anything either had aspired to.

And in the modern world, one was rich with so little. Running water and a flush toilet were luxuries that modern-day people didn't appreciate enough. Electricity was still magic to him, and as long as he had a warm house and Bryanna could get her medicine without worrying about money, that would be a happy life for him.

He wasn't a warrior here, and, surprisingly, he didn't miss his sword. He liked peace. He liked that he didn't need to worry about enemies, spies, and raids on his property.

But at the same time, he liked being independent and he liked being a provider. It hadn't been easy for him, the adjustment to the modern world. He didn't have many skills that modern people had, so the fact that he could provide with his music, that it was valuable and unique here and that he could play music with the woman he loved... He couldn't have asked for more.

"We did it together," Bryanna said, linking her hand with his.

Pamela smiled. "Well...shall we go home? You two must be exhausted. It was a long flight, wasn't it, Raghnall?"

"Aye."

An hour's drive later, they arrived at Bryanna's home. Well, it wasn't her home anymore. Her home was a small cottage on the shore of River Croe, a piece of heaven on the exact place where they had visited Odhran's farm back in his time. Seven hundred years before, she and Raghnall had sat and talked and she told him she'd felt she was where she was supposed to be.

There were no farm buildings anymore, and the cottage that stood in that place was only a hundred years old and in a bad condition. Bryanna and Raghnall had bought it and renovated it together.

When he and Bryanna had unpacked in her old bedroom, it was time for dinner. In the dining room, Pam had set up the table and reheated the roast, boiled potatoes, and green beans that already stood steaming on the table. The mouthwatering aromas made Raghnall's stomach gurgle hungrily.

"Well," Pam said. "Please, take your seats."

The family sat at the table, and Pam served the food to each plate, pouring the steaming roast juice over them. After a short prayer, everyone started eating. The atmosphere wasn't easy, and when neutral questions about the trip and the weather were out of the way, silence hung in the room, interrupted by the quick ring of forks and knives against the plates.

Raghnall had learned to eat with the fork, but he was still clumsy and preferred to eat with his fingers. But he didn't want to offend his mother-in-law, so he did his best.

He felt Pam's eyes watching him and looked up at her. There it was again, that gaze like she was looking at an animal she didn't see very often. Curious. Careful. Studying his every move.

"So, Raghnall... Ahem. Are you really from the Middle Ages?"

He swallowed whatever was in his mouth and straightened in his chair.

"Mom!" said Bryanna.

"What? You told us that crazy story about traveling in time, and that he...he's from another century. So I want to know who my daughter married. Is he a lunatic? Or is...is there more to the world than we understand?"

Raghnall held her gaze for a long time. "I was born in the thirteenth century."

He saw Pam's face go paler and her cheeks pinken at the same time. Kris gave a half chuckle, half whimper.

Bryanna's mother straightened her back, her chest rising and falling quickly. "Will you promise to treat my daughter with respect? Love her, protect her, care for her?"

There was an edge to her voice, like she was struggling to keep it even. She must be in more distress than he realized.

Raghnall took Bryanna's hand in his. "I swore to it the moment she was my bride."

Pam nodded sternly. "This is all a parent can hope for. Whether you're from the Middle Ages, or just imagine you are, as long as you're good for my child—and I can see that you are— I accept you as my son-in-law." She looked firmly at Bryanna. "Because I love my daughter, and everything I've ever done was to shield her from harm and keep her whole. I see that whatever your background is, you're on my team. And that's all that matters."

Raghnall nodded to her. Team was the modern version of clan, and he liked that. "Aye," he said, looking into his mother-in-law's eyes. "Team Bryanna."

Mom and Raghnall both looked at Kris, who rolled her eyes. "Gosh, you guys are so dramatic. All right. Team Bryanna, too."

Bryanna cackled and shook her head, taking another bite of the potato. "I'm team Kris on this. Way too dramatic."

That night, when Bryanna lay in his arms in their bed, after he'd thoroughly pleased her, he brushed his fingers through her hair, enjoying the silky softness.

"Thank ye for showing me yer home, Bryanna," he whispered and planted a soft kiss on the tip of her nose. "Thank ye for making your time home for me."

"Does it feel like your home?" She cupped the side of his face.

He smiled. "Ye are home. Ye always will be one."

"You, too."

They kissed, gently, tenderly, like they were time itself and could speed it up or slow it down or stop it.

When they finally pulled back a little, Bryanna's face lit up. "You know what, I forgot to tell you. I had a dream the other night... We should go to a sword-fighting championship. It's here in Chicago next week. There's someone important that we will meet. I only saw a silhouette of a female figure fighting with a sword, and one name...Marjorie."

He frowned. "Marjorie? I kent of a Marjorie of clan Cambel. But she disappeared...do ye think she may be here?"

Bryanna giggled. "I guess we'll find out!"

As Raghnall felt his stomach lighten up with a possibility of meeting someone else from his time, he took her into his arms again.

"There's something else I saw..." she whispered, hiding her face from him, her breath warm against his chest.

"What?"

"Us...three children...in our cottage on River Croe."

His throat clenched and worked as he fought an emotion. "Three bairns? Are ye...already?"

She looked up at him, a luminous smile on her face. "No. But I don't mind the idea. If you want."

"I want everything, lass. Everything."

She did that thing where she nuzzled his neck and inhaled his scent deeply. "I love you so much. I never thought I could be this happy."

"I love ye, Bryanna. Ye brought light back into the darkest parts of my soul. Ye brought me back to life."

Thank you for reading HIGHLANDER'S BRIDE. Find out what happens when David, Rogene's brother, meets Anna MacDonald in HIGHLANDER'S PROTECTOR.

He's trapped in the past. She's trapped in a dungeon. Can they escape their bounds to fight for a forbidden love?

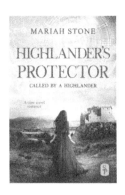

. . .

READ HIGHLANDER'S PROTECTOR NOW >

"Oh my goodness this book was so wonderful, and so very charming! Definitively my favorite out of all in the series"

SIGN-UP FOR MARIAH STONE'S NEWSLETTER:

http://mariahstone.com/signup

READY FOR YOUR PIRATE?

Other mysterious matchmakers help modern-day people find their soulmates; also during pirate times. If you haven't read James and Samantha's story yet, be sure to pick up PIRATE'S TREASURE.

A pirate desperate to lead an honest life. An executive who falls through time. One last chance to right the wrongs of the past.

ONE-CLICK PIRATES TREASURE NOW >

"A swash-bucking, adventurous, and heartwarmingly unique MUST-READ"

. . .

OR STAY IN THE HIGHLANDS AND KEEP READING FOR AN excerpt from HIGHLANDER'S PROTECTOR.

~

DUNADD FORT, ARGYLL AND BUTE, MAY 1313

"A FOOTPRINT." DAVID WAKELEY SHOOK HIS HEAD AND stabbed his index finger at a carving in the stone he was standing on. It was in the form of a foot, or an ancient axe head, depending on how you looked at it. "I can't believe this is what two years of searching has led to."

Dùghlas Ruaidhrí furrowed his blond eyebrows and crossed his huge arms over his chest, muscles bulging. A tall, broad Highlander with a claymore in the sheath at his back, he stood several steps away from David. They were on top of the Dunadd hill-fort, surrounded by the moss-covered remnants of the ancient stronghold and blown by strong winds from all sides. But despite the cold, Dùghlas wore a pale blue linen tunic with his braies, or medieval breeches, because it was May, and May was warm for Highlanders.

Cool gusts coming from the sea in the west made David shiver in his *leine croich*. He hadn't grown up in an icy medieval castle. He'd grown up in Chicago, and though the winters there were freezing, they'd had down jackets, scarves, and hats to keep them warm. And he'd never take central heating, hot water, and warm cars for granted again.

"Um," Dùghlas said, "are ye surprised, man? 'Tis where ye asked me to take ye."

David went into a pocket at the side of his tunic and retrieved a rolled piece of vellum with a hand-drawn map of Scotland showing ten crosses around it. It was soft and smooth, and it was the most precious possession he owned. His way to freedom.

"I did." He looked up at the horizon to the west, where the coast of Loch Crinan silvered between dark hills and mountains. A cloud hung above it, spreading rain like fog.

River Add snaked around Dunadd hill, cutting through green, rusty, and yellowish fields. The country spread all around them in brown, green, and gray valleys, hills, and mountains. The bogs of Moine Mhor extended in a rust and ochre carpet to the west. Black sheep, their fleece still short after the spring shearing, grazed peacefully on the slope. Seagulls squawked above them. Gusts coming from the sea brought the scent of rain and salt and trouble. The wind caught the birds and shut them up, and they soared, fighting against the invisible force, hanging in the air as though someone had put them on pause.

David bit his lower lip. He brought his pointy-shoed foot closer to the carved footprint, attentive to any feeling of strangeness in the air—a buzzing, sucking sensation, the scent of lavender and fresh grass that had accompanied Sineag, the faerie who had sent his sister, Rogene, through time. And because he had foolishly not believed Rogene and grabbed her arm to stop her, he had traveled in time, too.

And he'd been hunting for that scent for two years.

But the scent of moss, wet earth, and stone, accompanied by a whiff of sea and sheep dung, was undisturbed. Sineag was nowhere around.

David's stomach flipped, churning and twisting. He had been hoping one of the rocks he had visited over the past two years would glow and buzz and open for him, let him return to the twenty-first century.

Back to the life unlived.

Back to fulfilling his full potential.

Back to the football scholarship that would allow him to go to college and get a degree and make something of himself.

That would allow him to prove to himself—and to everyone —that he wasn't just a dumb fuck with a reading disability born into a family of geniuses. The scholarship was being held for up to three years and would expire in July.

He was only twenty-one; he had his whole life ahead of him. But he was wasting it among fourteenth-century warlords, medieval knights, and warriors.

He had his sister here, but nothing else that held him. He was stuck in this medieval prison the goddamn faerie had put him into without his consent.

Three years. Two of them spent searching. Nine stones he had slammed his hand onto.

Zero faeries found.

Zero tunnels through time open.

Zero chances to go back.

"I just didn't think it would be this, Dùghlas," he said. "This nothing. You told me this place is supposed to be swarming with faeries and spirits or whatever. You told me faeries leave glass beads here and carve things in stone, and people goddamn *disappear.*"

Dùghlas's silvery eyes were like a sharpshooter's rifle scope on him. "Aye, 'tis what folk *say*. Did ye really expect to see a faerie?"

Yes, he had. But he couldn't say it out loud. When Rogene had told him a faerie had sent her through time to 1310, he'd laughed at her. Dùghlas would think he'd lost it.

"This was my biggest hope," David murmured. "My sister told me something about this place, but I didn't listen very well. It's a place of power, apparently. The inauguration stone, right?"

Yes, Rogene, a historian in 2021, and wife to Laird Angus Mackenzie in 1310, had told him many things about Scottish history. Only, he'd been too drunk—or too tired of being lectured—to pay attention.

Now, it wasn't like he could pick up a phone to ask her. And Eilean Donan was about a week away on horseback in good weather.

The inauguration stone was different from the time-travel

stones, of course, but the principle was the same. Carved symbols in stone had power. There were some carvings next to the footprint that David couldn't quite decipher. They could be connected to the time traveling rocks for all he knew. Maybe they would even work when the time travel stones wouldn't.

Your time will come after you meet the woman you're destined for. That was what James—one of the other time travelers and the husband of Angus's sister, Catrìona Mackenzie—had told him the day David set off on his travels. Sìneag had apparently told James about this when he'd tried to take David back to the twenty-first century with him.

David didn't want to believe it. He was afraid of being stuck here forever if he fell in love like his sister had with Angus, like James had with Catrìona... Others, too.

He stubbornly believed he could find a way through the rocks without Sìneag's unwelcome condition.

But, proving James's words, none of the time travel stones worked for him—the ones with a handprint, with the river of time, and the tunnel carved on them. So, he'd considered Albert Einstein's quote "The definition of insanity is doing the same thing over and over again and expecting different results" and decided to try something new.

This rock.

Holding his breath, he stepped into the footprint.

Nothing happened. He didn't travel in time. He was just standing there, inhaling the wind, and trying to fit his large foot into the small footprint.

"Ye're now King of Dál Riata," Dùghlas proclaimed. "Congratulations."

David cursed under his breath and stepped back, disappointment dripping from him like sweat. Dùghlas went to a bowl carved in a stone five steps away from the inauguration stone, sank to his knees, and gathered rainwater from the bowl in both hands. Then, still on his knees, he stretched his arms to David.

"Would Yer Grace allow Taranis, the feared god of thunder and rain, to bless yer reign for years to come?"

David gritted his teeth. "Only if Taranis sends a lightning bolt up your ass."

The anger, the constant sense of helplessness, of being locked down against his will, was a sickening, corroding storm in his guts. He needed the only thing that helped him to forget.

Uisge.

With a sigh, he sat down on the rock, still warm from a few hours in the morning sun, and took out his flask—a horn with a cork—filled with uisge. He tucked his map under one foot so that the wind wouldn't carry his most precious possession away, pulled the cork, and took three long, satisfying gulps. The fiery liquid burned his mouth and his throat as it descended into his stomach. It was pretty much pure alcohol, bitter but oaky and smoky, and there was the beginning of real scotch somewhere in there. Though whisky wouldn't be invented until the fifteenth century, Rogene had told him. The familiar high hit his brain cells and he started to relax, his senses swimming.

Finally.

Wiping his wet hands off on his braies, Dùghlas came and sat by his side. "By God's teeth, friend, yer fascination with things sent up an arse hasn't stopped surprising me in the whole moon we have been traveling together." Rolling his eyes, David offered the uisge. Dùghlas drank, croaked, and handed it back to him. "The things I remember ye wishing up my arse were a tree branch when we slept in the woods and it was too wet to kindle. A wet cloth when I tried to wipe the vomit off yer face after ye got drunk. And...oh, 'tis the best one yet, one of the rocks ye've been chasing and slamming yer hand into. The whole seven-foot-long rock." Dùghlas shook his head and laughed.

David drank more, chasing that numbness he needed. "Well, you can now add 'go fuck yourself' to the list."

"Ah." Dùghlas pulled the map out from under David's foot.

"'Tis a good one. I prefer pleasuring myself to shoving things into my body that dinna belong there."

David chuckled and toasted to that. "You're not wrong there." He drank more.

"Where do ye want to go next?" Dùghlas asked, staring at the map. "Man, I'm glad ye understand this child's drawing and can orient yerself. 'Tis ogham to me."

"Well," David said, "I don't know. This is the last rock I know of."

"There are more," Dùghlas said. "The Picts were everywhere. They conquered Dál Riata, too, at some point. Perhaps yer rocks are somewhere in Galloway or even England. But I'll tell ye one thing. Be careful. Dinna ask folk about them. Dinna talk about them to someone ye dinna ken. And if ye can help it, dinna go near them longer than necessary."

David gulped more of the uisge, his head already spinning pleasantly. The wind from the sea gusted stronger now, throwing the long strands of his dark-blond hair, which he hadn't cut in three years, into his eyes. A few raindrops fell on his face and on the map, but he registered them only distantly. Scotland and rain. That had been his life for what felt like forever.

"Why? Would faeries make me disappear?" He drank more. He needed more of that warm burning in his stomach, to chase the cold of the wind and the rain away. He'd already stopped caring that the rain might ruin his precious map. A few more gulps of alcohol, and he'd stop caring that he was stuck in the Middle Ages. That was what he was going for.

"Nae." Dùghlas frowned. "But there's folk that dinna take people who believe in such things kindly. Especially priests."

David nodded. A sweet light-headedness tricked him into thinking he had no dark thoughts, that he was joyous and light and fun. Everything he wasn't when sober.

"We should go," Dùghlas said, then rolled up David's map and handed it to him. "The farmhouse down there"—he pointed at a croft—"mayhap they'll take us in."

David stood up, swaying, and pointed two fingers at his friend like Elvis. "Yeah, man. I'm glad you're traveling with me. You keep me out of trouble."

As they walked down the hill, David balancing over the worn-out, ancient rocks that indicated ancient ramparts, Dùghlas said, "Ye're glad? 'Tis a nice change from wishing things up my arse and telling me to go and pleasure myself."

Black clouds darkened the world. Rain intensified, and David was blinking water away. He was almost there, almost in that oblivious state where he could tolerate his miserable life and where the obnoxious, self-deprecating voice in his head was silent. But something bothered him. As he stepped over one wet, moss-covered step, his foot slipped a little, but he regained his balance.

"Careful," said Dùghlas.

"Thanks for the warning, man. I've been nothing but careful for three years."

Dùghlas frowned, a question born in his eyes at the mention of three years, but he withdrew, sighed, shook his head, and resumed walking.

They reached their horses, which were tethered to a bush at the bottom of the hill, and rode to the farm through what was now a true downpour. It was a typical Highland croft, with low stone walls and a thatched roof. They banged at the door, and a man opened it. He was in his fifties, short with a gray beard, a tired, weathered face, and a thin, pointy nose. The impression of a skull filled David's drunken mind.

"Maybe we should find another place," he whispered into Dùghlas's ear, but based on the man's deepening frown, he had probably said it too loudly.

Dùghlas waved his hand at David as if to shoo him. "Friend," he said to the old farmer, "we are looking for shelter for the night in this weather. We are happy to do work for ye in exchange."

The man's lips thinned, and his chin moved forward as he

looked at the ground and pushed the door to close it. But Dùghlas laid his hand on the door and stopped him. "Any work. Please."

The man's milky eyes were tired. "I can use two pairs of strong hands."

"Good," Dùghlas said.

"As long as ye dinna mind a leper in the house."

Dùghlas froze. "A leper?"

David shook his head. Leprosy was a common, incurable disease in the Middle Ages. David didn't know much about medicine, but he knew that it was a bacterial infection, treatable in the twenty-first century by antibiotics. But it was a slow and painful death sentence in the Middle Ages. If he and Dùghlas were careful about hygiene, they should be fine. And David always had a cake of soap with him. Plus, uisge would help to disinfect...if he had any left.

"We don't mind," said David. "We can sleep in your stables."

The man nodded. "If ye clean them, feed the horses, and cut the firewood, ye may."

Dùghlas looked at David with big, angry eyes. As a medieval man, he was terrified of leprosy. Maybe David should be, too.

"My friend here will," Dùghlas said.

"Good." The man stepped aside and let them come in. "My wife just made dinner."

As they entered, the scent of woodsmoke, unwashed bodies, and overcooked pottage hung in the room. There was a hearth in the middle of the house. The dirt-packed floor was covered with reeds, except for a healthy circle around the hearth so that any sparks wouldn't start a fire.

In the golden semidarkness, smoke hung under the thatched ceiling like a rainless cloud, and David's eyes started to burn. But even with the only light coming from the flames in the hearth, he could see the woman. She was bent over the cauldron, her back as round as a wheel. Her face was illuminated by fire, and there were the clear signs of long untreated leprosy.

As David stood by the door, blinking raindrops and smoke away, he drunkenly thought this must be where the old witches from fairy tales came from.

Her deep-set eyes were milky, the skin on her face dark and purple and hugging her skull like papier-mâché. She held the long, wooden ladle in her hand with three dark, rotting fingers. She watched David with a frown, her cloudy eyes menacing.

Dùghlas cleared his throat. "Good day."

David felt an urge to add *madam*, but stopped himself.

"Good day," she replied. "Supper isna ready yet."

"I'll show ye the stables," said the man. As they walked back into the torrential rain, the old man led the way through the yard of the farm. "My name is Padean, and my wife is Peigi. We are farmers. I lived in Carlisle before. I am a Scot, though," he added defensively.

He showed them the stables, gave them two shovels and two axes. David and Dùghlas worked for a couple of hours. The scent of manure and freshly cut wood were rich in David's nostrils. Physical work sobered him somewhat. When all was done, they went back into the hut.

"All done?" asked Peigi, still leaning over the cauldron.

"Aye," Dùghlas said, and put his sword against the wall by the door.

"Pottage?" she asked.

"Thanks." David unbuckled his own sheath with his sword that was held by his girdle and proceeded to sit at the table next to the hearth.

Padean took another ladle and poured the pottage into two clay bowls. He put the bowls in front of David and Dùghlas. The steam of something hot and freshly cooked tickled David's nostrils, and while Dùghlas introduced them, David shoved spoon after spoon into his mouth. The thick soup was mainly barley with a few root vegetables, but it was the best thing David had tasted in days. Padean poured two more bowls for himself and Peigi. He put them on the table, then came to help her stand up and led her to sit next to him, shielding her away. David glanced at Padean's hand as the man ate and noticed his fingers were dark, too. He hadn't escaped the disease.

For a while, the little house was filled with the crackling wood, the drum of rain against the thatch, the slurping of pottage, and the wind howling in the slits of the door. Halfway through the meal, Padean said, "Ye two are brave men. Nae everyone would come into a house with lepers. They say, 'tis God's punishment, a corruption of the very soul. Dunadd Fort helps to keep people away, and the Cambel tacksmen are kind enough not to bother us or put a too heavy of a strain for rent and produce. What brings ye two here?"

David relaxed, warm and full. He stood up and removed his wet *leine croich*. His long hair, gathered at the back in a tail, still dripped with water.

"Do you mind if I let it dry?" he asked as he stood up.

"Aye, lad," said Padean. "Do so."

"I look for faerie stones," David said as he stood by the fire with his *leine croich* hanging from his hands. "The ones that are up there—"

He stopped because the woman gasped, and the slurping stopped, and the only sounds were of rain and fire and wind.

"Leave," said the woman. Her voice was like a thunder strike. "Get out now."

Dùghlas chuckled. "Please, 'tis nothing. My friend is just curious—"

The woman turned to David, her face dark under her hood. "'Tis a curse. Those stones are a curse. The same curse that hit me. 'Tis the faeries' fault, all their fault that God is punishing me, and now my husband. Leave before ye bring death to us!"

"Peigi," said Padean placatingly, "the lads have nowhere to go. It rains and there're nae other farms nearby. Come now, calm down, they can just go to the stables—"

"Nae, ye fool. I already brought the curse on ye. This man is just another one sent by God." She looked straight at David. "Up there, Dunadd hill, is the stone with the foot. But 'tis nae what ye've been looking for, aye, lad? Or ye wouldna have asked. Ye've been searching for the stone with the hand, aye?"

Mumbling angry curses, something along the lines of *I told ye nae to tell folk the wrong things*, Dùghlas stood up from the table and came to the fire, quickly rubbing his hands. His tunic, his hair, and his shoes were still wet, and David knew his friend didn't want to go out into the rain any more than he did.

David slowly picked up his *leine croich*. "Yes. I was looking for a hand."

The woman laughed hysterically. "Ye fool. 'Tis nae in the open like that, facing the sky, looking over the country. 'Tis in a place darker than night, where nightmares are born."

Even drunk, David felt a chill go through him. He stood, holding the wet *leine croich* that weighed as much as a sheep. "You know where it is?" he asked.

"Shut up," murmured Dùghlas as he put the baldric back on.

"I ken," Peigi said, narrowing her eyes at him. "But I wilna tell ye. I follow God's path. Only when my soul is healed, will my body heal."

He looked helplessly at Dùghlas, who shrugged. David shook his head, attempting to make his drunken head work faster.

Padean took David by his elbow and led him to the door. "Ye must go. Ye are upsetting her."

David picked up his sword. "Where then?"

But she didn't reply. Disappointment weighed at David as Padean opened the door and gently pushed him and Dùghlas out into the gray, muddy rain. Water poured over them as Padean led them firmly to the farm gates.

"Where is the stone with the hand?" David asked.

Padean pushed them out of the low gate and closed it, creating a barrier between him and David and Dùghlas. Then he sighed and shook his head, looking down.

"'Tis in Carlisle Castle," he said. "I was born here, but as a lad, I was brought to my uncle, the mason who worked on the castle dungeon. I remember seeing that stone—the handprint, the odd carvings of waves and a tunnel or something similar. 'Tis odd and pagan and shouldna be talked about by God-fearing Christians," he added with anger.

Carlisle...David thought. English territory. His next destination.

Padean's eyes softened. "If ye think about going there, lad, be careful. The castle is probably still well guarded. But I remember a way in. See, as a young lad, I fell in love with Peigi. She lived in the town, but I wasna allowed to leave the keep after dark. So I sneaked out. On the northwestern side of the curtain wall, the stones form a sort of stairway. They stand out a wee bit. The enemy wilna notice that, only them who kens 'tis there. My uncle, a Cambel, told me about it, to help me see my love. So mayhap it will help ye in yer search. Ye helped us with the stables and the firewood. We didna give ye shelter. 'Tis the very least I can do."

Then he turned, and, slouching like a question mark, returned to the sick love of his life. The girl for whom he'd spent his youth climbing the castle walls. Look where love had gotten them. David shuddered.

Sighing, he took out his map. Rain still poured, but he hoped to make the mark quick enough for moisture not to destroy it. He laid the parchment on top of the stone wall surrounding the farm, then took out a quill and a small jar of ink Rogene had given him so that he would write to her.

His sister was a dictator. What did she expect from a dyslexic who could barely write with pen and paper, let alone with quill and ink? He hadn't written her in two years. He hadn't seen Paul, his nephew, for two years. David had left Eilean Donan Castle when Paul was about two months old.

He missed Rogene and Paul and thought of them often. Paul would already be a toddler, walking and babbling. He was a sweet baby, and his sister and Angus couldn't get enough of their son.

With a quill, he made a cross where Carlisle was, approximately. Rain poured on top of it, and it smudged. "How long till Carlisle?" he asked.

"About one week on horseback," Dùghlas said. "But I am nae coming with ye."

David put away the map so that it wouldn't be destroyed by the rain. "What?"

Dùghlas sighed heavily. "I canna set foot on English land, man. And I do need to get back to my own business, as much as I enjoyed this odd adventure with ye."

David frowned. He wished he could convince Dùghlas to keep traveling with him and helping him, but he knew the man had his own life, his own agenda, and his own mission. As with all relationships for David, this was only temporary. No woman, man, or child could keep him here.

With regret, he squeezed Dùghlas's shoulder. "I am sorry to hear that, buddy. As annoying as you are, I would rather make this insane journey with you than without you. You kept me safe. You taught me how to survive. You..." His throat caught. This was no use. Why was he being emotional when there was no way for him to make any connections in this age that he hated so much?

Dùghlas's rifle-scope eyes were sharp on him again as he squeezed David's shoulder.

"Dinna dismiss friendships so quickly, man," Dùghlas said. "Whatever ye look for in those stones...mayhap 'tis nae there at all. Mayhap, if ye accepted whatever life is throwing at ye, ye'd realize ye already have all ye need. They are just rocks, after all."

David shook his head. The man had no idea what he was talking about. They hugged, rain pouring over them as if from a bucket. Wind cut through David like a knife. Then they went their separate ways.

As Dùghlas's horse grew smaller in the distance to the north, swallowed in the Scottish landscape like another dark spot of moss, David huddled in his *leine croich*. Loneliness crept into him with the wet coldness of the Highlands. Wondering if he would ever get back to Chicago, he led his horse south to Carlisle.

There, in the dungeons of the castle, somewhere where nightmares were born, could be his way back through time.

His way home.

Keep reading Highlander's Protector.

ALSO BY MARIAH STONE

MARIAH'S TIME TRAVEL ROMANCE SERIES

- Called by a Highlander
- Called by a Viking
- Called by a Pirate
- Fated

~

MARIAH'S REGENCY ROMANCE SERIES

- Dukes and Secrets

~

VIEW ALL OF MARIAH'S BOOKS IN READING ORDER

Scan the QR code for the complete list of Mariah's ebooks, paperbacks, and audiobooks in reading order.

GET A FREE MARIAH STONE BOOK!

Join Mariah's mailing list to be the first to know of new releases, free books, special prices, and other author giveaways.

freehistoricalromancebooks.com

ENJOY THE BOOK? YOU CAN MAKE A DIFFERENCE!

Please, leave your honest review for the book.
As much as I'd love to, I don't have financial capacity like New York publishers to run ads in the newspaper or put posters in subway.

But I have something much, much more powerful!

Committed and loyal readers

If you enjoyed the book, I'd be so grateful if you could spend five minutes leaving a review on the book's Amazon page.

Thank you very much!

SCOTTISH SLANG

aye – yes
    bairn - baby
    bastart - bastard
    bonnie - pretty, beautiful.
    canna- can not
    couldna – couldn't
    didna- didn't ("Ah didna do that!")
    dinna- don't ("Dinna do that!")
    doesna – doesn't
    fash - fuss, worry ("Dinna fash yerself.")
    feck - fuck
    hasna – has not
    havna - have not
    hadna – had not
    innit? - Isn't it?
    isna- Is not
    ken - to know
    kent - knew
    lad - boy
    lass - girl
    marrit – married

nae – no or not
shite - faeces
the morn - tomorrow
the morn's morn - tomorrow morning
uisge-beatha (uisge for short) – Scottish Gaelic for water
or life / aquavitae, the distilled drink, predecessor of whiskey
verra – very
wasna - was not
wee - small
wilna - will not
wouldna - would not
ye - you
yer – your (also yerself)

ABOUT MARIAH STONE

Mariah Stone is a bestselling author of time travel romance novels, including her popular Called by a Highlander series and her hot Viking, Pirate, and Regency novels. With nearly one million books sold, Mariah writes about strong modern-day women falling in love with their soulmates across time. Her books are available worldwide in multiple languages in e-book, print, and audio.

Subscribe to Mariah's newsletter for a free time travel book today at mariahstone.com!

facebook.com/mariahstoneauthor

instagram.com/mariahstoneauthor

bookbub.com/authors/mariah-stone

pinterest.com/mariahstoneauthor

amazon.com/Mariah-Stone/e/B07JVW28PJ

Made in United States
North Haven, CT
10 July 2023

38805503R00168